THE GIRL IN THE MOTEL

This is a work of fiction. Names, characters, places, and incidents either are the product of the author's imagination or are used fictitiously. Any resemblance to actual persons, living or dead, events, or locales is entirely coincidental.

Copyright © 2018 by Chris Culver

All rights reserved. No part of this book may be reproduced or used in any manner without written permission of the copyright owner except for the use of quotations in a book review. For more information, address: chris@indiecrime.com

First hardback edition October 2018

www.indiecrime.com
Facebook.com/ChrisCulverBooks

THE GIRL IN THE MOTEL

A Joe Court Novel

BY

CHRIS CULVER

ST. LOUIS, MO

Other books by Chris Culver

<u>Ash Rashid novels:</u>
The Abbey
The Outsider
By Any Means
Measureless Night
Pocketful of God
No Room for Good Men
Sleeper Cell

<u>Gabe Ward Novels</u>
Counting Room

<u>Stand-alone novels:</u>
Just Run
Nine Years Gone

To my mother.

1

Megan's hands trembled as she unlocked her motel room's deadbolt. Clouds covered the sky all the way to the horizon while bright sodium lights hummed like giant bug zappers in the parking lot and illuminated the asphalt. As she pushed open her door, the smell of stale cigarettes, bleach, and some kind of lemon cleanser wafted over her. No one was around. Even the prostitutes had left to attend the fireworks.

Megan should have brought a gun. She knew half a dozen people who would have sold her a pistol without asking a question, but her sister had persuaded her not to buy one. If the people chasing her found her unarmed, they might simply take her hostage, but if they found her with a gun, they'd kill her without hesitation.

According to the calendar, it was early spring still, but winter had relinquished its grasp on St. Augustine months ago. The crocuses had long since bloomed and then returned to the earth. Soon, there'd be day lilies and honeysuckle growing alongside central Missouri's roadways and streams. Spring was usually Megan's favorite time of the year. It symbolized new beginnings and a renewal.

Now, she couldn't help but feel chilled despite the balmy weather.

She slipped her key into the front pocket of her purse and then looked over the parking lot one last time to make sure she was alone. There was a strip club across the street and a truck stop down the block. Aside from two scruffy-looking men walking beside one another along the side of the road, nobody was out. Neither of them looked toward the cheap motel across the street, and neither seemed to notice her at all.

She was alone still. Good.

The moment she stepped into the room, she shut the door behind her, drew the curtains over the window, and then locked the deadbolt. The suite she had rented only had one exit and one large window. She would have liked a second escape route, but she didn't plan to stay long enough for anyone to find her.

She sat on the bed and leaned forward, running her hands through her hair. She had made it. She was safe. She had left in time.

A tear slid down her nose and onto her jeans. Megan tried to hold it in, but a sob welled in her gut. Twelve years ago, Megan and her sister had framed a gangster for murder. It had worked perfectly. The police had arrested Christopher and sent him to prison for the rest of his life, and for twelve years, Megan and her sister had hidden from his crew.

Now, hiding wasn't enough.

A week ago, Christopher's men had found them, and Megan and Emily had been running ever since. It was the most exhausting thing she had ever done. She deserved a break.

Marijuana was illegal in Missouri, but that didn't stop people from buying and smoking it. Megan and her sister, Emily, specialized in selling high-end strains to doctors, lawyers, and business people. When working, she and her sister wore business clothing and carried briefcases. They took credit cards and gave invoices with fake product names. Anyone who saw them dropping off their illicit goods might think they were attorneys or realtors; instead, they were two of the most successful drug dealers in St. Louis.

Megan reached into her purse for a small glass pipe hand painted in psychedelic colors. Though she sold marijuana, Megan had never seen herself as a drug dealer. In her mind, she helped people who needed help, none more so than the cancer patients she was lucky enough to service. Where modern medicine gave them poison so powerful it robbed their lives of joy, she gave them relief. She was proud of that.

She sorted through her sample packages until she found an Indica strain her cancer patients loved.

Almost the moment she lit up, the knot in her belly unwound, the muscles of her shoulders loosened, and she felt better, more like herself. Everything would blow over. She'd be fine.

She took deep breaths before putting her pipe on the

dresser beside the television and then reaching into her purse for her cell phone. Megan hadn't told any of her clients when she left town. Some of them would feel betrayed, but they'd find new suppliers soon enough. Only Emily knew where she was. That was how it should have been. Her sister was the only person she could trust.

She took more deep breaths and then closed her eyes. Her suite had cost three hundred dollars a night, but she was lucky to even get that. It was Spring Fair week, something St. Augustine was famous for.

Megan had never been to St. Augustine's Spring Fair, but everybody in the state knew about it. For one week, St. Augustine—a tiny college town along the Mississippi River—turned into the biggest tourist attraction in the Midwest. There were free concerts every night, fireworks displays, art fairs, beer gardens, and then a hot air balloon race to close the festivities. It was perfect for her needs. The fair brought in tens of thousands of people, allowing Megan to disappear in the crowds.

She pressed the power button on her phone to wake it up. She had sent her sister a dozen text messages over the past few hours, but Emily had yet to respond. It made her gut twist. Once more, she called her sister's number, and just as before, Emily's phone didn't even ring before going to voicemail.

"Em, it's me. Where are you? I'm in St. Augustine. I went by Joe's house, but I couldn't find her. I'll try again later tonight. I know she'll help, but I'm getting worried. I need to talk to you. I've sent you a dozen messages.

Where the hell are you?"

She paused for a moment, feeling her throat tighten again.

"I'm scared. I don't know where you are. Please just tell me you're safe. Call me, okay?"

She pulled the phone from her ear and ended the call. For a moment, she stared at the screen, expecting it to light up with an incoming call or text message. Nothing happened, though, so she leaned back on the bed and rubbed her eyes. She wanted to smoke again, but that'd knock her out, and she needed every ounce of awareness she had.

As she lay there, the room's silence weighed on her chest, making her lungs tight. She'd have to get used to silence, though. Until she and Emily were safe, they'd each have a lot of silent nights far from home.

Their plan had been simple. Emily would prepare a cabin in Mark Twain State Park while Megan went to St. Augustine to get help from the only cop in the world who would help them. Cell reception near the state park could get spotty, but Megan needed to hear her sister's voice. She needed to know Emily was okay.

Megan took deep breaths, calming herself and allowing the cannabis she had just smoked to work its potent magic on her system. She had to think this through. It was almost nine at night. Joe was a police officer, but even police officers had to come home. Megan had already spent most of the day trying to track her down, but she hadn't been able to find her. She'd swing by her house again after the fireworks, but for the moment, she let herself sink into the soft bed. Slowly, she began to drift to sleep.

Then, somebody pounded on the door.

Megan's breath stopped, and she bolted upright, shooting her eyes around the room for a hiding spot. She thought about squeezing under the bed, but the people after her weren't stupid. She had nowhere to go, so she dug through her purse for a can of pepper spray. She had bought it years ago but never needed to use it. Hopefully it would still work.

The person at the door knocked again.

"Pizza."

It was a man's voice, one she didn't recognize. The men who had found her earlier both had the raspy voices of lifelong smokers. This voice was smooth and mellow. She held her breath, waiting and hoping he'd go away, but he knocked again.

"I've got your pizza," he called again. "Get it while it's hot."

Her fingers trembled, and her belly ached, but she palmed her pepper spray and walked to the door to look through the peephole. Her legs felt like rubber. The man outside wore a red shirt and matching red hat from a place called the Pizza Palace, and he carried an insulated pizza delivery box.

"You've got the wrong place," she called, only realizing once the words left her mouth that her voice trembled. She coughed and drew in a deep breath, forcing her voice to sound calm. "I didn't order a pizza."

The driver stepped back and looked at his order slip. Then he furrowed his brow and looked at the door again.

"You sure?" he asked. "I've got a medium, hand-tossed pepperoni with a small Greek salad and a side order of cheese bread for room 127 at this motel. It's already paid for and everything."

"That's my room, but I didn't order anything. Just take your pizza and go. Okay?"

"Okay. Sure," he said. "Sorry to bother you."

He took two steps but then stopped and turned toward the door.

"If you'd like, I can leave it at the front desk for you to pick up. Or I can even just put it on the ground. It's paid for. Tip and everything. If I take it back, we throw it out. I'd hate to waste good food."

Megan's stomach rumbled, reminding her that she hadn't eaten anything since breakfast almost twelve hours ago.

"Fine. Just put it on the ground. I'll pick it up."

"Great," he said, kneeling. "Have a good one."

The driver walked back toward his truck just as a firework burst over the distant tree line. It took a few seconds for the sound to hit. Somewhere close, thousands of people would be watching the display without a care in the world. It seemed unfair. As the pizza guy pulled out of the lot, she cracked open her door and then looked left and right before picking up the box.

More fireworks crested the hill, illuminating the night

sky in reds and purples. She leaned against the doorframe, allowing herself to enjoy the spectacle. To her surprise, the dazzling display calmed her. It seemed so normal. Everything would be okay. Joe was a cop. She'd help them survive. This wasn't the last fireworks display she'd see.

As Megan reached behind her for the door, another crack echoed in the distance. It was louder and higher-pitched than the boom of the fireworks. Megan barely registered the noise before the round tore into her chest and all the lights in the world went out one final time.

2

I hated fair week. It was just after seven in the morning, and the line at Rise and Grind, our local coffee shop, was already out the door. If I could believe the conversations people were having around me, the shop was out of blueberry scones and running low on pecan rolls. St. Augustine had a lot of wonderful things, but those pecan rolls were sometimes my only reason for rolling out of bed in the morning. If the tourists took that from me, I'd never forgive them.

I glanced at my watch. My boss had scheduled roll call to start at seven-thirty, but most of my colleagues would show up late. Last night had been long and rough. Tommy B's, a local dive bar, had given away free beer to celebrate the first night of fair week. It had not gone well. Our uniformed officers on foot patrols had spent half the night breaking up fights while the rest of us arrested drunk drivers. It was not fun.

I crossed my arms and glanced at a little girl standing near me. Her mother struggled to carry a tray laden with coffee cups and pecan rolls while steering her daughter to one of the outdoor tables beside the shop.

"Did you see the fireworks last night?" asked the girl.

I smiled at her and shook my head.

"I was fighting with drunk men at a bar. My partner said he liked the fireworks, though."

"They were awesome," she said.

"Glad to hear it."

The mom hurried her daughter away from me as the line crept forward. When I reached the counter, Sheryl, Rise and Grind's proprietor, smiled at me.

"Morning, Joe. I thought you'd be by, so I saved you a pecan roll. You want the usual latte to go?"

I smiled my first real smile since getting up that morning. "Yes, thank you. You're truly a saint."

"That's what I'm told," she said, smiling. "I'll bring it out as soon as I can."

I thanked her again and took a step back from the counter to wait. A man in his early twenties stood beside me. He was about six feet tall and looked as if he weighed around a hundred and ninety pounds, most of which was muscle. His black hair was unkempt, and his eyes were bloodshot. He looked and smelled as if he had slept the previous evening in a ditch, but I tried not to judge people. I nodded a polite hello to him and then ignored him.

"I heard you tell that girl outside you were fighting drunk guys at the bar last night," he said, taking a small step toward me. "Sorry I wasn't there. We could have been a team."

I narrowed my eyes at him. "You need something?"

His gaze traveled down my torso. I wore jeans, a white oxford shirt, and a black blazer. Beneath my blazer, I wore a vertical shoulder holster, which held a Glock 19 chambered for a nine-millimeter round. On my belt, I wore a silver badge from the St. Augustine County Sheriff's Department. Somehow, I didn't think he was checking out my sidearm.

"Are you local, or are you in town for the fair?"

"I'm a local," I said, putting my hands on my hips to push my blazer back and expose my badge. "What do you need?"

He looked at my chest and then my hips.

"So you're a cop?"

I raised my eyebrows. "That's what my paycheck says."

He didn't seem too interested in talking after that, which I appreciated. As I waited for my coffee, my phone buzzed. Even in bucolic St. Augustine, early-morning phone calls never portended good news. I sighed before answering.

"It's Joe. Yeah?"

"Morning, Joe. Hear you got into a fist fight last night. You doing okay?"

The voice belonged to Travis Kosen, my boss. I had met him twelve years ago when I was still a teenager and he was a detective in St. Louis. I must have done something right in those first few meetings because I became a cop seven years later once I finished college and got my first job in his department.

"I'm fine, and it wasn't a fist fight. A drunk guy took a swing at me, missed, and fell down. I put cuffs on him before he could stand up again."

"So you won."

My lips curled into a tight smile. "If that's your definition of winning, I guess I did. I'm on my way in. What do you need?"

The boss grunted. "We've got a murder at the Wayfair Motel."

I rubbed sleep out of my eyes and groaned.

"I haven't even had my coffee yet. It's too early for a body."

Two or three tourists looked at me askance, but I ignored them.

"Death pays little mind to our creature comforts," said Travis. "Nicky and Dave were the first on site. You're the lead. As soon as I can find him, Harrison will be your second on this one."

Sheryl whistled to get my attention as she placed my order on the counter. I picked my breakfast up, mouthed a thank you to her, and pinned my phone to my head with my shoulder as I stepped from the counter.

"Delgado and Martin won't appreciate this. It's their turn."

"They're already on a case," said Travis. "Theft from a motor vehicle out on Pinehurst."

I couldn't help but laugh. "Yeah, this'll go over real well. Our two most experienced investigators miss out on a homicide because some rich guy on Pinehurst thinks the kid next door broke into his BMW."

"I believe it's a Mercedes, and they'll get over it," said Travis. "You seen your partner this morning?"

"Nope," I said, sipping my drink. "You try the parking lot outside Club Serenity?"

"Are you implying your partner passed out in his car outside a cheap strip club?"

I smiled to myself.

"I hear they raise their prices for lap dances during fair week. It's actually a very expensive strip club."

"I think I'll try his house first," said Travis.

"Well, if you strike out, don't blame me, boss."

"Just get to the motel, smartass."

He hung up before I could say anything else. I balanced my pecan roll on top of my drink and then slipped my phone into my pocket. The man who had admired my chest earlier took a step closer.

"You have a nice smile. You should break it out more often."

I narrowed my gaze at him. "Why are we talking?"

"You're here. I'm here. It seems like fate brought us together."

I didn't even roll my eyes. I just walked away.

"You've got to tell me," he said, hurrying to walk beside me. "What happened on May 12th?"

The question made me stop. My back was straight as I adjusted the sleeve on my blazer to cover the date tattooed on my wrist.

"It's none of your business. Stop talking and stop following me."

"May 12, 2006. It can't be when you graduated from high school. You're not that old."

He probably thought I was playing hard to get. I wasn't, so I kept walking out of the shop. He must have taken that as a challenge because he followed me. I almost told him off, but I knew that wouldn't have deterred him.

"Is that the date you lost your virginity?" he asked, lowering his voice. "I bet it was in the back of your boyfriend's car."

"If you keep following me, I'll arrest you for harassing a police officer."

He held up his hands and stopped walking. "I was just trying to be nice."

"No, you weren't," I said. "You said something outrageous to persuade me to talk to you despite my request that you leave me alone. Now you've got two choices. You can either stop following me, or I'll call my station and let them know I need help. Half a dozen large men will come and drag you to a jail cell. They might Tase you on the way. They might even pepper spray you. It all depends on who answers the call. It's your choice. What do you want to do?"

He opened his mouth to say something, but then he thought better of it and walked back inside. I watched the door shut before turning and looking for my truck.

Rise and Grind occupied the bottom story of a hundred-year-old, three-story brick building in downtown

St. Augustine. There were restaurants, antique stores, and a candy shop up the street. Already, the sidewalks were growing crowded with tourists and vendors. Many of them would go to the art fair that afternoon when it opened, but for now, most of them looked content to wander the historic downtown area.

I slipped through the crowd and walked half a block to my car where I took my first bite of my pecan roll. It was worth getting out of bed for, but I couldn't focus on it too much. I had a body to see.

3

January 1998

It was so cold in the car I could see my breath. Mom had left a few hours ago, and already snow and ice had piled up against the window, blocking some of my view of the motel's parking lot. I huddled under a thick pile of threadbare sweaters in the back of our car.

My mom and I didn't know where we'd spend the night most days, so we kept our clothes in bags in the back of her old SUV. She'd be mad when she found out I had used her sweaters as a blanket, but she wouldn't hit me if I promised to put them away.

We didn't sleep in the car often, but it wasn't too bad when we did. In the summer, we'd open the windows and let the breeze in. In the winter, we'd snuggle together in the back. I liked those nights. We were like a real family then.

It hadn't always been like this. When I was little, Mom and I had an apartment. I had a room with a window and a bed. It was nice. Mom slept on the pullout sofa. She had made us dinner almost every night, but even when she forgot to come home, Mrs. Sanders, the old lady who lived next door, took care of me. I liked Mrs. Sanders. She gave good hugs. Unfortunately, the man who ran our building was stupid and made us leave. That's what my mom screamed as we were leaving, at least.

After that, we lived in a big building with a lot of other women and their kids. I liked it there, too, because there were always people to play with. We all went to church every day, but that wasn't too bad. We even got to eat dinner together at night. I had friends there, so I liked it. The nuns who ran that place were stupid, too, though, so we couldn't stay long. My mom, I guess, was too smart for them.

Tonight, though, we'd sleep in a real bed. Mom had a job. I didn't know what it was, but she visited men and made them happy. I guessed they talked or something. Afterwards, we'd have a hotel for the night, and we'd order a pizza or Chinese food. The next day, we'd sleep until ten or eleven in the morning. Sometimes, if my mom was in a good mood, we'd go to Walmart. She'd buy me socks. She always told me socks were important. If you wore socks, you wouldn't get sick.

Sometimes, people would get mad at Mom and tell her I should be in school, but they didn't know what they were talking about. I went to school some. When we lived in the apartment, I had gone every day. It was fun, and I had learned stuff, but not the stuff I learned with my mom. Mom taught me to wear socks to avoid getting sick and to go to restaurants right when they closed to get free food.

Restaurants always gave out free food at closing time. The managers were always nice, too. They smiled at me. Sometimes they even gave me ice cream. They didn't seem to like my mom, but as long as I was there, they were nice. I didn't know what Mom had done to them, but sometimes people were just stupid.

That was something else Mom taught me. The world had two kinds of people: smart and stupid. Most people were stupid, but there were smart ones, too. Sometimes I wondered whether some people Mom thought were stupid were actually smart, but I didn't know.

I wrapped my arms around my chest, clutching an itchy wool sweater. A tickle built in the back of my throat. My nose already felt a little stuffy. I had been sneezing a lot, but I didn't want my mom to know that. She always got mad when I got sick. She liked to work and said she got sick every time I got sick. Nobody, she said, wanted to be with her if she had a runny nose. Runny noses didn't bother me, but my opinion didn't count. I wished I had money to pay her to make her happy, but I didn't.

Something tickled my nose, so I covered my mouth to keep myself from sneezing all over Mom's sweaters.

And then the police car pulled into the lot.

Two men in uniforms got out. They had guns and a lot of other stuff on their belts. I slunk lower in the SUV so they wouldn't see me.

I didn't know much about police officers except that they were mean. Mom always said the police wanted to take me from her. They were motherfuckers. I didn't know what that word meant, but my mom's boyfriend told me it. He was weird, and he always smelled bad. And he was always smoking these cigarettes he made himself.

He and Mom broke up a long time ago, but he still came around some. When he was around, we'd drive to a park so I could get out and play. He and Mom would stay in the car for a while. They must have been working because Mom didn't want me around then. After they finished their work, he'd take us out to eat. Sometimes, we even stayed in his apartment. I slept on his couch while he and Mom slept in his room. Sometimes, we'd even stay there for a few days, but then he and Mom would fight, and we'd leave.

One of the police officers stopped outside my mom's room and knocked hard. The other one ran for the front office. I slunk even lower in the car so my back touched the floorboards. I pretended I was invisible. They couldn't see me if I didn't move, I thought.

Within seconds of the police officers arriving, an ambulance pulled into the lot. Curious, I sat up a little. The door to my mom's room was open. My stomach plunged into my feet. My nose had been itchy for a couple of days, but I hadn't told Mom because I didn't want her to get mad. She must have gotten sick, though. I was so stupid. I should have told her. She could have worn thicker socks.

I sat upright and put on my shoes so I could tell the paramedics that Mom just needed socks.

Then I saw a police officer walking from one car to another. He had a flashlight, and he was looking in the backseat of each vehicle. I slipped my shoes on but didn't get the laces tied before I had to slide down again and hide.

The cop was right beside our car, peering into the windows of a hatchback beside us. I held my breath as he panned his light across the gap between our vehicles.

Then I felt it in the back of my throat. A sneeze.

The light passed over the sweater covering my face. I shut my eyes tight, hoping he would go away. If he caught me, he'd take me away. I didn't know where I'd go, but that was what Mom always told me. Stay away from the police. They'd break up our family.

So I stayed there and felt the tickle grow in my throat. Then, the light left my car as the cop went to the vehicle beside ours. My shoulders relaxed, and I felt better. Then it happened. A great, loud sneeze—like something out of a cartoon. The light panned to my car again.

I didn't know what else to do, so I scrambled onto the middle seat and opened the door. The night air was freezing, and the wind bit through my sweater and jeans. The moment my feet hit the asphalt, I ran.

"She's running," said the cop.

To my seven-year-old ears, his voice was a wicked snarl, a battle cry from a monster who would catch me and eat me up. I sprinted. The tears froze on my cheeks. I didn't know where I was, only that I had to get away.

There was a grocery store beside the motel, so I ran toward that, unsure where else to go.

"Honey, stop!" he called. "It's okay."

I hardly heard him. My feet pounded across the pavement. The cold squeezed my chest and made my lungs hurt, but still I ran. My shoes were loose, so I kicked them off. When I reached the grocery store, the front doors slid open, and I went inside. A man in a red apron near the door saw me coming and pulled a cart out of my way.

"You okay, honey?"

Like the police officer, I ignored him, too. I had to run. I had to find somewhere safe. Mom had taken me into that grocery store before, so I knew the layout. I ran through the produce section, pulling apples onto the floor behind me. There were two police officers chasing me. One of them knocked into a display of bananas, making a mess on the floor. He stopped, but the second guy kept going.

Please, God, don't let him get me.

I said it over and over in my head, pleading and crying at the same time.

Finally, I reached the rear of the store. Between the deli and a bakery, there was a hallway that led toward the bathroom, and I darted right toward it. The cops were both men. They couldn't go into the girls' bathroom, so I was safe. Once I got in, I huddled under the sink with my back to the wall and my arms across my chest, breathing hard. No one was in the stalls.

For a moment, I was alone. Then the door cracked open.

"County police. Is anybody in here?"

I held my breath.

Please go away. Please go away. Don't eat me.

I pleaded with him in my mind, and I prayed to whatever God had ears to hear. Then the door swung open, and I saw him. He had a bushy brown beard, brown eyes, and a hateful black gun on his hip. When he saw me huddled beneath the sink, he knelt down near the door but stopped moving otherwise.

"Hey, hon," he said. "I'm Ross. Are you Mary?"

I pulled my legs tighter to my chest but said nothing.

"I saw you lost your shoes in the parking lot. Are you hurt?"

I eyed him but said nothing. He nodded as if I had said something profound anyway and then sat down with his knees bent in front of him. The door opened again, but he waved away whoever was behind it before I could see them.

"Your mom got sick. We're taking her to the hospital."

"She wasn't wearing socks," I said without thinking. "That makes you sick. And my name is Joe. Only my teachers call me Mary, and I hate them."

He looked down at his hands. "Your mom overdosed on something, but we're not sure what yet. She's going to the hospital. We think we got to her in time."

I didn't know what an overdose was, so I didn't

respond. Officer Ross stayed with me for two hours. He even turned off his radio. He did most of the talking and told me about his two daughters in middle school. One was a cheerleader, but the other played basketball. I told him about how important socks were, and then I told him which restaurants gave out the best food at closing time. That seemed to make him sad.

After I ran out of things to talk about, he asked whether I wanted a blanket. He didn't have one with him, so somebody outside the bathroom gave it to him. I got out from under the sink, and he draped it over my shoulders. It warmed me up, which was nice. I let him pick me up after that. He seemed sad, so it felt like the right thing to do.

As we walked out of the grocery store to another ambulance, he whispered that everything would be okay. Without realizing it, I cried and sobbed against him. I couldn't help it. He kept telling me I had nothing to be afraid of and that he'd keep me safe, which made me cry even harder.

My mom had told me a lot of things. She told me to shut up at least once a day; she told me that socks would keep me from having to go to the doctor; she told me to be quiet when the police came by; and she told me never to upset her boyfriend by crying when he was over. She never told me she'd keep me safe, though, and she never told me everything would be okay.

I didn't cry because that police officer scared me; I cried because he didn't. I felt like somebody cared about me. I felt safe.

    And even then I knew it would never last.

4

The Wayfair Motel was a two-story building wrapped in white aluminum siding. From a distance, it looked pleasant enough, but on closer inspection, it was hard to miss the cigarette butts and broken glass, the cracked asphalt, or the broken spindles on the second-story railing. The parking lot was full of minivans and other family cars. During fair week, the motel did a brisk business with tourists, but during the rest of the year, few of its guests stayed overnight.

I parked in an open spot near the front office, ate the last of my pecan roll, and grabbed a fresh notepad from my glove box before stepping out of my old truck. Three uniformed officers stood near a pair of police cruisers parked in the fire lane at the far end of the building. A fourth officer strung yellow crime scene tape from the support poles that held the second story aloft.

A local man named Vic Conway owned the Wayfair Motel and surrounding businesses. He had sat on the County Council for almost two decades and even ran for a seat in the Missouri House of Representatives once. That was before my time, though. I only knew him as a dirty old man who owned a strip club, truck stop, and a cheap motel by the interstate.

The Wayfair Motel was the crown jewel in Vic's portfolio. Whether by design or happenstance, his businesses formed a cozy triangle for the young and desperate. Young women—some fourteen or fifteen years old—came from St. Louis and the surrounding areas to work the parking lot of the truck stop as prostitutes. Those industrious enough could earn upwards of a thousand bucks a night, half of which Vic took for protection.

When those girls turned eighteen, they got boob jobs and worked in the strip club. After their dancing shifts were over, many took clients to the Wayfair for paid trysts. Girls could earn good livings well into their late twenties, but once his employees got too old to dance or turn tricks, Vic hired them as maids for his motel or clerks for his convenience store.

We had half a dozen active investigations into Vic's activities, but none of them ever went anywhere. He had enough money to buy off most witnesses, and those he couldn't buy disappeared. Sooner or later, he'd slip, and we'd put him in prison, but not today.

The uniformed officers perked up when they saw me. St. Augustine County had almost fifty sworn officers on staff, and we all knew each other well. Some of my colleagues had a gift for police work, but most didn't. Everyone tried their best, though, which was all I could ask for.

"What have we got?" I asked, reaching into the inside pocket of my blazer for a pair of polypropylene gloves. I snapped them on and then took out my notepad. Nicole Bryant stepped forward. She was in her mid-forties and had brown hair pulled back from her face. At five-seven, I wasn't tall, but I had at least three inches on her.

"Morning, Joe," she said, reaching to her utility belt for her own notepad. "Dispatch received the phone call from the front desk at 6:43 this morning. A guest had returned home and found what he thought was blood on the ground. He contacted the front office, and they contacted us. Dave and I arrived at 7:09 and found what appeared to be blood spatter on the ground outside room 127. No one inside the room answered our knock. Fearing that we might have had someone hurt inside, we contacted the front office. The clerk let us in with his master key. Inside the room, a young woman lay on the floor. I felt her neck for a pulse and found nothing. I then stepped out. Nobody else has been inside, and nobody's touched anything."

Most of the time, they would have needed a search warrant to enter someone's room, but the blood and lack of response gave them exigent circumstances. It sounded like a good search. It also sounded as if they had protected the scene well.

"That's good work. Nicky, call Harry. He's supposed to be my second on this case. Tell him everything you told me and then tell him to get to the station. I need him to fill out an affidavit for a search warrant for the motel room."

She wrote the request down and nodded but then looked at me with her eyes narrowed.

"We still need a search warrant with a body on the ground?"

I nodded. "Yeah. You had exigent circumstances, which allowed you to go into the room, but there's no murder scene exception to the Fourth Amendment."

She nodded. "Learn something new every day. Anything else?"

"Yeah. Once you get in touch with Harrison, call Dr. Sheridan and tell him we've got a body and need his expertise. Once you've got that done, I need you to start a log book so we can keep the scene secure."

I looked to the other officers. "Dave and Bill, I need you knocking on doors. We need to talk to as many guests as we can before they leave. If anybody heard or saw anything weird last night, tell me. I want to talk to them myself."

Dave nodded, but Bill looked a little uncertain.

"I'm supposed to be working the information booth at the fair this morning," he said.

"Now you're working a homicide," I said. "Is that a problem?"

He blinked a few times and then straightened. "Shouldn't we wait for the real detectives on this? Delgado and Martin will be taking over anyway, right?"

My cheeks grew warm, and I locked my eyes on his.

Bill had at least four inches and fifty pounds on me, but he took a step back beneath my glare. I pushed my jacket back to expose the badge on my hip.

"Do you see my badge, Officer Wharton?"

He straightened. "Yeah, I can see your badge."

"Does it look like the ones Detectives Martin and Delgado carry?"

He closed his eyes but said nothing. I repeated my question, so he crossed his arms and nodded.

"Yeah."

"Good. I am a real detective, and this is my case. Do you have a problem with that?"

He tilted his head to the side. "It's just that they handle the murder cases is all. I'm used to working with them. You're a good detective on burglaries and thefts, but this is a murder. Have you ever worked a murder?"

"Stop talking," I said. "I'm the detective assigned to this case. I earned it, and it's mine. Do as I asked or go home. Your choice."

He stood straighter. "Don't get your panties in a bunch. I'm just trying to clarify everybody's role on this."

I nodded toward his cruiser. "Get out of my crime scene. You're done for the day."

"I'm doing my job, lady."

"If you were doing your job, you'd be knocking on doors right now with Officer Skelton. You're not, which means you're wasting my time. Now get in your car, call Trisha, and ask her to send somebody who brought his big-boy pants to work today."

He muttered something, so I took a step closer to him.

"Something you want to share?" I asked.

"I'll talk to Travis about this," he said. "You can't just send me away like I'm some kind of naughty kid."

"As the primary detective on the case, I can, and I am," I said. "Now leave, or I'll write you up for insubordination."

He straightened to his full height and then looked down his nose at me. He was trying to be intimidating, but I didn't plan to back down. After a few seconds of posturing, he got in his car and left, and I took a deep, relieved breath.

My department had over a dozen female officers, but I was the only female detective, and they had made me claw and fight my way to the position. I'd earned my badge the same way every other detective on staff had: I busted my ass. This was my job. I wouldn't let some lazy asshole tell me how to do it.

Once Bill left, I looked to Officer Marcus Washington. He stood straight and nodded.

"Marcus, you're going across the street. There are security cameras outside the truck stop and strip club. Find out whether any were pointed this way last night. Once you've done that, talk to the manager and any dancers you can find at Club Serenity. Ask them whether anybody saw something weird. They're not going to talk to you, but we might get lucky. While you're over there, if you find any prostitutes working the truck stop this early, detain them, call for backup, and then interview them to see whether they saw anything."

He nodded and looked over his shoulder to the truck stop before looking at me again.

"Yes, ma'am."

I looked at each of my officers.

"Everybody clear on what to do?"

Nicky said yes. The men nodded again.

"Okay," I said. "Let's get to it."

I watched for a moment while my team shuffled off to do their tasks. Our officers weren't perfect, but they did good work on most cases. St. Augustine didn't get too many murders, and when we did, we had three experienced detectives on staff. I had assisted other detectives on four homicides, but this was my first murder as the primary officer.

A small part of me—the part I allowed everyone else to see—knew I had the experience and expertise to work the case. The other part of me—a far bigger part—was scared shitless.

I took a breath and did the same thing I did when I was a girl standing on the high-dive board for the first time: I jumped in.

I walked toward the room, taking pictures of the exterior door frame with my cell phone. Though we needed a search warrant to process the scene for fingerprints and other forensic information, I could still look around and take pictures now. Those things I found in plain sight, I could use in court. Anything else, I'd have to wait for a warrant.

I stepped over the blood in the doorway and walked inside. Aside from the blood, the room looked clean. Someone had rumpled the comforter near the foot of the bed, but it didn't look as if anyone had slept in it. The victim's body was near the bathroom, but I didn't pay her much attention yet. She wasn't going anywhere.

There was a brown leather purse stamped with gold rosettes on a table near the front window. A brass buckle on the side of the bag identified it as a Louis Vuitton. If it was real, it would have cost more than I made in a month.

I snapped pictures of the purse with my cell phone before crossing the room. There was a black Tumi suitcase on the dresser beside the television. Whoever the victim was, she had liked expensive things.

Since I was already deep into the room, I looked at the body next. She lay on her belly with long black hair covering her face. Her skin—at least so far as I could see it—was caramel colored, and she looked young. She wore gray yoga pants and a loose-fitting turquoise shirt. By her clothes, she could have just come from the gym, or maybe she was getting ready for a relaxing night inside.

There was a large exit wound on her back. About a year ago, the sheriff and I had worked a homicide in which a man shot his neighbor with a .45-caliber full metal jacket round at about four feet. The entrance wound on the victim's forehead was about the size of a dime, but the exit wound on the back of his skull was the size of a golf ball. Whatever hit my victim here was larger. This wasn't a handgun; it was a rifle, and a damn big one. Somebody should have heard it go off.

Aside from the blood, her shirt looked clean. A shot at point-blank range would have left powder marks, but I couldn't see any.

I left the body and focused on the table by the front window. I could think of two scenarios to explain what I had seen. In the first, the shooter hid outside in the parking lot with a rifle until the victim opened her door. The moment he saw her, he opened fire. He then crossed the parking lot while carrying his rifle, dragged the victim inside, and then shut the door to hide the body.

In the second scenario—the one I found more likely—we had two murderers. The first murderer knocked on the door and then ducked. When the victim opened the door, the second murderer opened fire. The first murderer then dragged the victim inside and shut the door behind him.

However it happened, we'd have ample forensic evidence. Unfortunately, I doubted we could use it. A motel room wasn't a public space, but even if we could find a usable fingerprint or hair that placed a suspect at the scene, he could claim he had been in that room weeks ago. It was a seedy motel, and I doubted the maids got on their hands and knees to scrub the place down between guests.

We'd collect as much evidence as we could, but this investigation wouldn't come down to forensics. We'd have to find our shooter the old-fashioned way: We'd comb through our victim's life to find out who wanted her dead, we'd talk to everyone within a two-block radius to see whether they saw anything, and then we'd use forensic evidence to bolster our case in court.

And it all started with our victim.

I unzipped her purse and caught a whiff of marijuana. Inside, she had a glass pipe and several vacuum-sealed bags full of dope. It was more weed than a recreational user would have. Her wallet was near the bottom, so I pulled it out and put the purse down.

Then I saw the victim's picture on her driver's license, and I brought my hand to my mouth. I couldn't look away from her picture, but the longer I looked, the weaker my legs felt. It was her. I hadn't seen her in twelve years, but she was never far from my mind. I palmed her license and backed out of the room, my heart thudding in my chest and my legs threatening to buckle with every step. Once I reached the parking lot, I called my boss.

"Hey, Travis, it's Joe Court. I'm at the Wayfair Motel with the body. I need you to come out here. The victim's dead."

Travis paused for a moment but then spoke slowly. "I know the victim is dead. That's why I sent you out there."

"No, Travis, you're not hearing me. The victim is dead. I'm looking at her ID right now. It's a fake. It says her name is Kiera Williams, but this is Megan Young."

Again, Travis paused. "That can't be right. Megan

Young died twelve years ago."

"Yeah, but no one found her body. I think we now know why."

For a third time, Travis paused before speaking. "I'm on my way. I hope you're wrong."

"Me, too."

I hung up and stepped outside the crime scene tape. Several motel guests had already woken up and left, but most were still in their rooms. It seemed like a peaceful morning, but that would change. If I was right, news vans from every TV station, radio station, and newspaper in St. Louis and the surrounding area would descend on that parking lot like locusts.

Because if that was Megan Young in that room, and if she had died last night, my boss and his former partner had sent a man to prison twelve years ago for a murder that never happened.

This would be bad.

5

March 2000

A hush fell over the classroom as the principal's voice came over the speaker. It was my third week in the school, so I didn't know many people yet. Half the class didn't even recognize my name when the principal called for me, but the kids who knew me gave me knowing glances. Several kids tittered, thinking I was in trouble.

As a long-term ward of the foster care system, I had bounced through a lot of homes and schools over the years. This was the third school I had attended in the past year alone, but it had been my favorite so far. I hadn't bothered to make friends, but the other kids were nice. They didn't even try to fight me on my first day like kids at other schools had. I left people alone, and they left me alone, so it surprised me when the principal called my name over the loudspeaker. She wanted to see me in her office, so I looked at my teacher.

"Go ahead, Mary," she said, smiling.

"It's Joe," I said. "That's my name."

"Okay," she said. "Go ahead, Joe. You don't want to keep Mrs. Hall waiting."

I slipped off my seat and walked out of the room. In other schools, I had gotten called to the principal's office every other week for getting into fights, but I had behaved well here. I liked it here. My foster family was nice. The first day I met them, they took me out to buy new school clothes, and then we went to a bookstore, where they let me pick out a story. I chose *Harry Potter and the Sorcerer's Stone*. Heather, my foster mother, had read a little with me every night. None of my other foster parents had ever bought me a present before. Holding that book had made me cry.

My footsteps were slow. Every part of me trembled. I knew they were kicking me out, but I didn't want to go. I didn't want to leave Heather and Todd. They weren't my real parents, but I liked them. She barely knew me, but Heather still hugged me at night. It felt nice to hug somebody and not have them want something in return.

Once I reached an intersection in the hallway, I stopped. There were a pair of glass doors to my left. Outside, two squirrels were chasing each other up a tree. They looked so happy, just running around and doing squirrel things. I wished I were a squirrel. Squirrels didn't have social workers. They could go wherever they wanted. They weren't screw ups, like me.

I thought about pushing that door open and running. It wouldn't have been the first time I ran from a foster family, so I knew the routine. I'd run, they'd chase me, and then I'd come back. They'd put me in a new home, but that wasn't always such a bad thing. Now, I wished everybody would just leave me alone with Heather and

Todd.

By the time I reached the office, my cheeks hurt from holding back tears. Mrs. Hall, the principal, was waiting for me, but so was Mrs. Shapiro, my social worker. The moment I saw Mrs. Shapiro, everything inside me broke. I couldn't hold back the tears, but I didn't want to let them see me crying. I looked at the ground and swallowed hard as my vision blurred.

"Please don't send me away, Mrs. Shapiro," I whispered. "I don't know what I did, but I'll be better. I promise. Tell Heather I'll be better. Whatever I did, I won't do it again. Please tell her not to send me away."

"Oh, honey," said Mrs. Hall, crossing the small reception area to put a hand on my shoulder. She knelt in front of me and looked in my eyes. "You're not going away. Mrs. Shapiro brought someone here to see you."

"Heather and Todd aren't making me leave?" I asked, looking to Mrs. Shapiro. She shook her head and smiled.

"No, Mary. Heather and Todd care about you a great deal. I talked to them this morning. They're thrilled to have you."

"Who's here, then?"

"You'll see," said Mrs. Hall, leading me out of the office. "She's in the conference room."

I followed my principal and social worker down the hall to a room I had never noticed before. There was a big table and a lot of chairs. Motivational posters covered the walls. My mom waited for me inside.

"Hey, baby," she said, standing from a chair at the far

end of the room. "You've gotten big."

"Mom," I said, walking toward her. She hugged me, and I was so surprised I didn't hug her back. We talked on the phone three or four times a year, but I hadn't seen her in person since she overdosed three years ago.

"I'll give you guys privacy," said Mrs. Shapiro. "Mary's class just went to recess, so you've got about twenty minutes before she needs to go back."

"Thank you," said my mom, smiling as the social worker and principal left. When she looked at me, she shook her head. "They can't even get your name right, Joe. I'm sorry about that. Did you miss me?"

"Yeah," I said, lying. "I've missed you."

She smiled and cupped my cheek.

"How have you been, baby? Tell me everything."

"Everything's good," I said, unsure what she wanted me to say. When Mom and I talked on the phone, she had always dominated the conversation. I didn't know how to talk to her in person. "We're playing the recorder in music. I'm thinking about joining the band next year. Heather—she's my foster mom—said she'd take me to and from practice."

She reached over and touched my hand. "You don't have to worry about what Heather says anymore. You'll be coming home soon. It'll be like old times. My lawyer is helping me put together a good case. She's got me in these parenting classes. They're a waste of time—I mean, how stupid do you have to be if you can't even raise your kid, right?—but my lawyer thinks the judge will like it.

And do you remember Tony? We're married, now. We've got a place to ourselves. The lawyer says having a stable home looks real good."

I nodded, feeling my heart skip a beat.

"Great," I said, trying to smile. For a moment, Mom narrowed her eyes at me, and then she grabbed my forearm.

"Don't you look at me like that, girl," she said, her voice sharp and low. "I'm working my ass off for you. At least look happy to see me."

"I am happy, Mom," I said, letting the tears streak down my cheek. "I miss you. I didn't know if I'd see you again."

Gradually, Mom let go of my wrist, and then she brought a hand to my face to wipe away a tear.

"Oh, baby, they've got you so messed up, you don't even know up from down. I'll take you home soon. Things will be okay again."

"Okay."

She didn't notice I had started crying again. For the next ten minutes, she told me all about her life with Tony. We had stayed at his apartment years ago, so she thought I'd remember him. And of course I did. I couldn't forget him. I remembered that he yelled at me, and that he drank all the time, and that he used to hit her. She mentioned none of that, though.

Then she told me stories about work. According to her, she worked as a research assistant for an attorney who specialized in international business. She said she traveled the world and saw exciting places. What was more, she went to church and had good friends. It sounded nice, but I knew my mom. It was a fantasy. Mom may have had a job at a law firm, but she wasn't a research assistant. She could barely read.

Still, I smiled and pretended to feel excited, all the while my insides twisted. After we talked for a while, Mrs. Shapiro came back in and told my mom we had just another minute. Then she went in the hall again. Mom looked in my eyes and smiled.

"I'll put things right, okay, baby?" she said. "Nobody'll break us up again."

"Great," I said. Mom smiled.

"This family you're with," she said, "are they good to you?"

I didn't mean to, but I thought of Heather, and I felt a warmth spread all over me. My lips curled to a smile.

"They're nice."

"Do they have a nice house?"

I nodded again, smiling now. "Yeah. I even have my own room. We have a dog. His name is Chance, and he's so funny—"

"Your foster father's a doctor or something, right?" asked Mom, interrupting me. I nodded and forced the smile off my face.

"He's a dentist," I said. "He said I had good teeth, but I might need braces soon."

"That's real good," she said. Her eyelids fluttered, and then she looked at me in the eye. "You think you

The Girl in the Motel

could get some money for me? My job's going well, but these lawyers are killing me. I want to get you back, baby girl, but it's expensive."

I didn't know what she wanted, so I reached into my pocket and put my lunch money on the table.

"It's all I have," I said. Mom picked it up and rubbed it between her fingers.

"This is two dollars. I can't buy anything with two dollars."

"It's all I have," I said, a tear falling down my cheek. "I was trying to help."

She stood and put my lunch money in her pocket. "Do better next time. I'll see you later."

She left without looking at me again. I stayed there and cried until Mrs. Shapiro came into the room. She rubbed my back and whispered into my ear.

"Don't worry. You'll see her soon," she said. "Your mom's not going anywhere."

That was the problem. I had gone to school that morning content with my place in the world. I almost felt like I had a family with Heather and Todd, but they weren't my real parents. I was cursed. My life wasn't my own. I didn't have a choice in what happened. The sooner I learned that, the better.

If I stayed with Heather and Todd much longer, I'd love them. I had to leave while I still could. It would hurt too much to lose them otherwise. I looked at Mrs. Shapiro.

"Can I go back to the girls' home?"

Mrs. Shapiro startled and then furrowed her brow. "I thought you liked living with the Cohens."

I wanted to nod and tell her they were the sweetest, kindest couple I had ever met and that I wanted to spend the rest of my life with them. I wanted to tell her that Heather read to me at night, that Todd and I played video games together after school, and that Chance slept at my feet and made me feel safer and more loved than I had ever felt in my entire life. I didn't, though.

"They're okay, but I liked the girls' home better."

Mrs. Shapiro hesitated but then nodded. "I'll see what I can do."

I went back to the classroom feeling an emptiness build in me. I didn't cry. I didn't want anyone to see me cry. I got in a fight on my way home and punched a girl on the bus. I didn't even know her. I didn't know why I hit her, but it felt right. I gave her a bloody lip, and the school called my foster family. Heather and Todd tried talking to me. I wanted to tell them everything I was feeling and that I didn't want to leave, but I held back. It was easier that way.

Mrs. Shapiro came through two days later, and I returned to the facility for girls. That was the right place for me. No one loved me there. More important than that, nobody could take anything from me there because I didn't have anything worth taking. The world hurt too much when I had something to lose.

6

After leaving the motel room, I got status updates from my team. Officer Skelton was still knocking on doors and talking to potential witnesses, but he wasn't getting very far. If I could believe the witness reports, someone had shot Megan—or whatever my victim's name was—with a powerful but silent rifle and then escaped completely unseen. That didn't make sense.

Across the street, Officer Washington was running into problems of his own. The prostitutes wouldn't talk to him, and the managers at the strip club and truck stop refused to let him look at their video surveillance without a warrant. When Marcus tried to push them, they pushed back and told him to leave or they'd file harassment complaints against him. So we struck out there, too.

While my team worked, I walked through the parking lot in a grid pattern, taking pictures of anything that appeared out of place. In half an hour, I found almost two dozen cigarette butts, three used condoms, thirty-eight cents in change, and a receipt from an ATM. None of that would help my case.

When I reached the edge of the asphalt, I stopped and looked around.

Vic Conroy had built his motel, strip club, and truck stop at the bottom of a bowl-shaped depression. Wooded hills surrounded the buildings on all sides. The shooter could have stood anywhere on those hills in a thirty-degree arc and still made the shot. This would not be an easy case.

My boss arrived as I was walking the perimeter of the parking lot. Sheriff Travis Kosen was in his early sixties and had been the elected sheriff of St. Augustine County for about ten years now. Before becoming sheriff in St. Augustine, he had been a detective in St. Louis. He managed the department well, but he was an even better cop. I had learned a lot from working with him.

He parked his SUV near the motel's front office and met me by the room in which our victim had died. I filled him in on what we had done so far. He nodded and looked around.

"I'll put a team together to search the woods. I think we've still got a pair of metal detectors in storage."

"How's our search warrant coming?" I asked.

"Last I heard, Harry was trying to track down a judge. Meantime, Dr. Sheridan is wrapping it up in Bollinger County and will be here within the hour. If we don't have a warrant by then, I'll drive up to St. Louis and find a district court judge who owes me a favor."

"If that's how you want to do it," I said.

"It is, so let's talk about your victim," he said. "You think this is Megan Young."

"Yeah," I said, turning toward the room. "I only saw

her ID, but she's got the same dimple in her chin, she's the right age, and she has the same type of hair and skintone. It's her."

"Except that your victim was alive in the very recent past," said Travis. "Megan died twelve years ago."

"We thought Megan Young died twelve years ago," I said. "Nobody found her body."

"Who's Megan Young?" said a small voice behind me. I turned to see Office Nicole Bryant with a sheepish smile on her face. "Sorry. I didn't mean to interrupt. I was just standing there with the log book. It was kind of boring."

I looked to Travis. He sighed.

"Joe thinks the victim in room 127 is really a young woman named Megan Young. Megan and Joe lived together in a foster home when they were teenagers. Twelve years agos, Megan went missing. We never found her body, but my partner and I investigated, determined that she was murdered, and arrested Joe's foster father. Christopher confessed, by the way."

"He wouldn't be the first person to confess to a crime he didn't commit," I said, quickly. "The case against him was strong. If he had gone to trial, he would have lost, and he would have gotten the death penalty. Confessing saved his life."

Travis crossed his arms and stood straighter. "Tread carefully with that line of inquiry, Joe."

I took a step back and held up my hands. I got where he was coming from. Travis and his partner, Julia Green, had worked the case hard twelve years ago. Without their work, Christopher would still be walking the streets.

"I didn't mean to imply anything about you. You guys did good work, and I know you wouldn't knowingly put an innocent person in jail."

He held my gaze for a moment and then lowered his chin.

"You think Hughes's lawyer would have allowed him to confess if he hadn't done it?"

"I don't know," I said, shrugging. "Given the evidence against him, maybe his lawyer thought confessing was the only way to keep him out of the gas chamber. Or maybe his lawyer thought he had done it. Or maybe he didn't take his own lawyer's advice."

Travis scratched his temple and then looked down. "Case is closed, Joe. Megan Young died a long time ago. I don't know who your victim is, but it's not her."

"You think I'm nuts, but this is Megan Young. She lived with me. I know her, and this is her."

Travis looked at the ground and nodded. "Okay. I'll bite. Devil's advocate, if this is Megan Young, do you understand what that means?"

I nodded and drew in a slow breath.

"Yes. If this is Megan, it means Christopher Hughes didn't murder her. He'll get out of prison."

"Are you prepared for that?"

At first, I didn't have an answer. Christopher had been my foster father when I was fifteen, and for the first few months, he treated me well. Then he changed and ruined my life. Even if he hadn't killed Megan, he deserved to rot in prison for the rest of his life, but that wasn't my call.

"If he didn't kill Megan, he shouldn't be in jail for her murder." I paused before speaking. "You're right. This probably isn't Megan. We need to consider every possibility, though. It won't take Dr. Sheridan long to compare the victim's dental X-rays to Megan's."

Travis nodded, his face serious. "It wouldn't take long if we could find Megan's dental records. She's been dead for twelve years."

"They're at Todd Cohen's office. He's a dentist in Kirkwood. He took care of the teeth of a lot of kids in foster care."

"Fine," said Travis, nodding. "This is your investigation, and you seem to know the dentist. You call him."

I shook my head. "Dr. Sheridan should call him. Todd might remember me."

"And that's a problem?"

"Yeah. Todd and his wife tried to adopt me when I was in elementary school. I screwed it up."

Travis knew more about my past than anyone in St. Augustine County. He nodded.

"Okay, Detective. I'll ask Dr. Sheridan to make that call. For now, I'll keep you on this case. If this turns out to be Megan Young, though, Jasper and George will take over. That clear?"

"We'll see," I said.

"No," said Travis, shaking his head. "If this is Megan Young, you're too close to this case. No arguments."

I blinked and drew in a breath. "This may not be her."

"I'm glad you see that. What's your next move?"

I put my hands on my hips. "I've got my team set up here. As soon as Harry gets the warrant, I'll have him supervise the search of the victim's room. I'll go to St. Louis."

"Sounds nice," said Travis, tilting his head to the side. "Do a little shopping, get lunch, maybe see the Arch. Sounds like a nice day."

"Hilarious," I said. Neither of us smiled. Travis blinked.

"Why are you going to St. Louis?" he asked.

"My victim's ID says she lives in St. Louis. I'll check out the address on her license and talk to her neighbors."

Travis looked into the motel room and then to me.

"Sounds like you've got this. I'll get back to work. When you get the city, make sure you call Julia. She'd like to hear from you, and you need to let the locals know you're working a case in town."

I took a step closer and then wiped away some powdered sugar on his collar. "Will do, boss. And next time you get attacked by a funnel cake, be careful. They're vicious."

"You're funny," he said. "Now get out of here, Joe. I've got work to do."

I smiled as I left, but I understood the task I had

ahead of me. I had no illusions about this case. If I was right and that was Megan Young in the motel, I would spend the next few days gathering evidence that would exonerate one of the most vile men held in Missouri's prisons. The thought made me sick.

7

It was ten in the morning, and the line for the visitor center at the Potosi Correctional Center already stretched outside the building. James "Sherlock" Holmes went to the prison dozens of times a year, and every time, he found it strange to see kids playing on the lawn while their moms visited inmates. It didn't seem right. If he had kids and was in prison, he'd call them, but they'd never see him. No kid should see his father in chains.

Sherlock wore a pair of jeans and a blue shirt with the logo of a fruit delivery service stitched across the breast. Beside him in the pickup sat a man he had just met that morning, having been introduced by one of Sherlock's long-term clients. Though he would enter the prison as a worker from the Franciscan Fruit and Vegetable Company, Sherlock carried a defense attorney's burnished leather briefcase at his side.

On a routine visit, Sherlock would have walked through the main gate, signed the visitor log, and waited for a corrections officer to show him to his client. He couldn't afford to have his name on a ledger or his face on a security camera's feed this time, though. Sherlock had come to talk about a murder.

When the pickup reached the gate, a pair of guards sauntered toward the truck, laughing amongst themselves. For the convenience of a clandestine visit to the facility, Sherlock had paid three thousand dollars to a guard who worked for the Missouri Department of Corrections. With luck, that would become money well spent.

While one guard passed a sign-in sheet through the truck's window, another reached beneath a pile of romaine lettuce in the back to remove a backpack. Sherlock wasn't the only thing being smuggled in that morning. Not that he begrudged the Franciscan Fruit and Vegetable Company a little extra profit; he doubted there was much money in produce that most grocery stores would have discarded.

When a guard handed Sherlock the clipboard, he slid an envelope stuffed with hundred-dollar bills under the clip and handed it back without signing a thing. The guard smiled to himself and pretended to study the clipboard and Sherlock's face before taking a step away from the truck and waving them through.

When they arrived at a loading dock, another guard opened the rear door and motioned them forward. Sherlock and the fruit delivery person stepped out.

"You've got fifteen minutes, buddy," said the delivery man, already picking up a box of lettuce and carrying it to the dock. "Make them count."

Sherlock hadn't done this before, but his driver had

briefed him on the procedure. There was only one rule: He could talk to one inmate unsupervised and bring in whatever drugs, food, cell phones, or cash he wanted, but if he brought a weapon, the guards would ban him permanently from the property.

If he followed that rule and paid the price, he'd have fifteen minutes of complete privacy with his client. Three grand was a lot of money for fifteen minutes, but Sherlock considered this an investment. If he could figure out how, he might even deduct it from his taxes.

As Sherlock approached the loading dock, a guard stepped to the edge and held out his hand to pull Sherlock up. Without saying a word, he led him inside to an office in the kitchen. Someone had taped shopping lists, inventories, and work schedules to the walls. The desk was a mess of papers. Inmate #453312, Christopher Hughes, sat in the only chair.

He stood when Sherlock entered. He had the clean and straight teeth of a man who had grown up with money, something few of his fellow inmates could boast. His eyes darted around the room—probably looking for threats—before settling on Sherlock. They looked cool at first, but then they warmed.

"It's been a long time," said Hughes.

"Sit down," said Sherlock. "We've got a lot to talk about and little time."

Christopher sat but didn't take his eyes from Sherlock.

"When Catfish came to my cell and said I had a

visitor, I expected to see somebody in the visitor center."

"That is where most visitors go," said Sherlock. "This visit is special."

"I see," said Christopher, nodding. "You're not my lawyer. Why are you here?"

Sherlock pulled a pen and file folder from his briefcase. Inside the folder was a simple representation agreement that listed Sherlock's hourly fees, his duties, and a brief summation of the attorney-client privilege.

"Knowing what I do, you'll want me as your attorney of record," he said. "Sign the paper, and then we'll talk."

Hughes scanned the document and then glanced up. "You think you're worth five hundred an hour?"

"Oh, I'm worth far more than that to you," he said. "I can get you out of here."

"My last attorney said the same thing."

"I guarantee it," said Sherlock, holding out his pen. "Sign this paper, and I'll have you out of here within a week."

Hughes took the pen and signed his name. "All right. You're my attorney now. Not that I can pay you."

"I know your monetary situation better than you realize," he said, countersigning the agreement and then closing the folder. "That's why I'm here. How much is your freedom worth to you?"

Hughes crossed his arms. "A man who could get me out of here could name his figure."

"Half a million cash," said Sherlock. "I know you've got it because I know what you did for a living. This is above the hourly fee you pay me. I will also ask for a third of any fees I can recover from the city and county on your behalf. That five hundred grand isn't in the contract, so we'll call it a gentleman's agreement."

"A half-mil is a lot of money," said Hughes, cocking his head to the side. "If you think you can get me out, though, you're welcome to it."

Hughes reached into his bag for a second folder. It held a single picture he had printed at his office computer that morning.

"That is a picture of Ms. Kiera Williams, but you know her as Megan Young. An associate of mine shot her last night in St. Augustine."

Hughes picked up the picture. His hands trembled, and his breath was shallow.

"No shit?"

"No shit," said Sherlock. "Even in St. Augustine, it won't take the police long to see through the Kiera Williams identity. Once they find out the victim is Megan Young, I'll file the paperwork to get you out of here. I'll also work with the media—they love stories like this. You pled guilty to murdering Megan, but you didn't do it. I think we'll have a lot of support."

"You did this for me," he said, his voice low and incredulous. "You found her and took care of her for me."

"Yeah," said Sherlock. "That's what friends do. I know you didn't kill her, so I've had a private detective on my staff looking for her for twelve years."

Hughes put the picture down. "How'd he find her?"

"We tracked down her sister and paid her a visit. Emily gave us everything we needed."

Hughes nodded and then reached across the table to shake Sherlock's hand.

"You're a friend. I won't forget this. My wife persuaded me to hire that schmuck lawyer, but I should have gone with you."

Sherlock squeezed the convict's hand before dropping it. Then he looked around.

"If you had, I sure as hell wouldn't have advised you to confess."

"They had my balls in a vise," he said. "I told my lawyer it was all bullshit, but he didn't care. He told me a plea deal was the only way to save my life. I didn't know what I was doing. I trusted him, but once I signed the papers, he disappeared."

"It will cheer you to know he's dead now."

Hughes raised his eyebrows. "You do that, too?"

Sherlock chuckled and shook his head. "That was all God and grease. He had a massive heart attack while giving the closing arguments in a negligent homicide case."

"Son of a bitch deserved it," said Hughes, sitting straighter. He shook his head and looked at the picture in front of him. "I've sat in chains for twelve years because of this bitch."

"It won't be too much longer."

"If you're right, it won't," he said, leaning forward

again. He exhaled a slow breath. "Megan's not the only one who screwed me. I've got a list of names if you're willing to work. I'll make it worth your while."

Sherlock crossed his arms. "How worth my while?"

Hughes thought for a moment. "Fifty each, starting with my wife. The money's in my house. A quarter-million cash. It's inside the wall in my master closet."

"That's a big thing to ask of your attorney."

"You're not just a lawyer," said Hughes, grinning. "If it's not enough money, you can sleep with my wife before you kill her. That was about the only thing she did right. Either way, I want her to die screaming. She's the reason I'm here."

Sherlock snorted as he gathered his files and put them in his briefcase.

"For fifty a head, I'd take out my mom. Consider it done. Get your bags together and make your goodbyes, Mr. Hughes, because you're going home. Nobody in the world can stop that now."

8

On a normal day, I drove a red 1982 Dodge Ram pickup truck I had purchased at a used-car lot after college for eight hundred dollars cash. At the time I bought it, the engine had over four hundred thousand miles, the transmission didn't work, and the headlights dimmed whenever somebody pushed on the brake pedal. The car dealer thought he was getting something over on me when I bought it, but I had done my research. I liked the truck, and I knew I could fix it.

Back then, I was a cadet in the police academy, and I lived with my adoptive parents in Glendale, Missouri. My adoptive father—Doug Green—found my choice of vehicle amusing. My adoptive mom—Captain Julia Green of the St. Louis County Police Department—understood.

I spent every moment of free time I had for an entire summer on that truck. When I had questions or came across something I didn't know how to fix, I watched videos on the internet, read books at the library, and once even visited a retired mechanic who had worked on my truck back when it was new. There were days I felt as if I were wasting my time, and sometimes I felt like an idiot, but I rebuilt the engine, patched the electrical system, cleaned up the transmission, replaced the brakes, installed a new exhaust, and reupholstered the interior.

For the money I put into that truck, I could have bought a reliable used one, but I didn't care. I had an affinity for broken things. The world would be a better place if more people recognized that a lot of broken things could be fixed again.

Since I was driving to St. Louis on a case, though, I needed something more official than my pickup truck, so I went by my station and signed out one of our marked SUVs. It was big and comfortable, but even more important than that, it had a laptop with an unlimited 4G data connection similar to the one on my cell phone. That would come in handy today.

My victim's driver's license told me her name was Kiera Williams and that she lived on Manchester Road in Rock Hill, a suburb west of St. Louis. Even at a glance, though, I knew that was bullshit. Manchester was a major commercial thoroughfare. I doubted my vic lived in a grocery store's parking lot. Still, I had to check it out.

I headed northwest and drove for about an hour before I hit the suburbs south of the city. Within another half hour, I pulled to a stop in the parking lot of a small strip mall in Rock Hill. If I could believe Kiera Williams's license, she lived in the lobby of Postal HQ. That was a problem.

I parked in the fire lane out front and pulled the SUV's laptop toward me. Time to earn my paycheck. I called up the license bureau's database and searched for other women named Kiera Williams in the area. That gave me nine results, none of whom looked at all like my victim.

Kiera—or Megan—was young enough that she had grown up with social media, which meant she should have had a presence somewhere. I looked her up on Facebook and then Twitter. Both websites had hundreds of users named Kiera Williams, but none matched my victim.

Then, I Googled her name, hoping she would have shown up somewhere in the paper in the past twenty-six years. Again, though, I found nothing that matched my victim. After striking out once more, I searched the Missouri court system for cases involving women named Kiera Williams. I got fourteen results there, most of which involved a woman who loved speeding and driving while intoxicated.

The world had all kinds of people. Some liked to live under the radar while others loved the spotlight. Everyone, though, left footprints in his or her wake. Even a hermit who refused to grace civilized society with his presence would have left a record somewhere. My victim hadn't, though. Travis might have been right—the woman killed in St. Augustine might not have been Megan Young —but she sure as hell wasn't Kiera Williams.

Unlike me, Megan Young wasn't an only child. She had an older sister and a half brother. Emily Young, Megan's older sister, didn't have a license in her own name, so I looked up names Emily had used on fake IDs when we were in high school.

For most of us who grew up in the foster care system, it was hard to escape our pasts. I considered changing my name and joining the Navy. Others ran to a new city. Some killed themselves. Emily became Jessica Martin, a twenty-nine-year-old woman who lived half a block from Lafayette Park in south St. Louis. I recognized her picture in the license bureau's database. Though her hair had changed, and she no longer had the angry, haughty smirk she wore when we were teenagers, it was Emily. Some people were hard to forget.

I put her address into the GPS on my phone and headed out. St. Louis had changed since I had left. With a high crime rate and poor schools, the north side of town was still an unpleasant place to live, but the south side of town was gentrifying.

When I reached Emily's neighborhood, I found dumpsters in front of at least one house on each block. There were vans for plumbers and trucks for carpenters and handymen on each corner. Based on the upscale housing and the well-dressed people walking the sidewalks, this neighborhood wasn't just up and coming; it had arrived, and Emily owned a very nice French Tudor row house facing Lafayette Park.

I parked about a block away and walked to the home. It was three stories tall and had a wrought-iron fence and a well-landscaped garden out front. Her neighbors had well-maintained gardens and neat front doors. I didn't know much about the local real estate market, but the cars that lined the street were pricey. This was a neighborhood for doctors and lawyers and accountants—professionals with money to spend.

Of course, even as a kid in foster care, Emily had money to spend. Intelligent, ambitious drug dealers did well for themselves.

I unlatched the wrought-iron gate, walked up a brick pathway to her front door, and knocked hard. Immediately, the heavy oak door swung open. It looked as if someone had shut it tight, but the lock must not have engaged. Oak parquet floors led down a long hallway to the rear of the house while a doorway opened to a dining room on the right. A carved staircase led to the second floor. The house's woodwork was gorgeous and looked original.

"Hello?" I called.

No one answered, so I knocked hard and then called out again. Still, nobody answered. As much as I wanted to walk in there and search for signs that Emily knew her sister had been alive, I had no cause to search the house. I took a pen from the inner pocket of my jacket and a business card from my back pocket and wrote a quick note.

Emily—call me.

I'd come by later, but I slipped the card into her mailbox and reached into the house to shut the front door. I stopped when I saw the dining room. There were two chairs overturned and papers on the ground.

Someone had fought in there.

I slipped my firearm from its holster and crept inside, staying close to the walls so I wouldn't cause the hardwood floor to creak. The front hallway led to the kitchen and backyard. The kitchen was immaculate save a broken white coffee mug and a puddle of coffee on the ground. The butler's pantry had glass panels in the cabinetry. Someone had broken one, so glass littered the ground.

The second floor had five bedrooms and three bathrooms. All were clean. Someone had even made the beds. I checked out the basement next. It was an open space with a bar, a giant TV, and a pool table. Emily must have been a baseball fan because there were St. Louis Cardinals decorations on the walls.

Blood spatter stained the carpet.

My heart beat faster as I crossed the room to one of two closed doors on the far wall. The first led to a bedroom with an attached bathroom, but the second led to an unfinished room that held the furnace and water heater. Someone had tied Emily to a chair in the center of that room. She was nude, and there were burns up and down her arms and legs. The room smelled like excrement and blood.

My chest felt tight, and bile crept up in my throat. I didn't need to check Emily's neck for a pulse. The moment I saw her, I had known she was dead; anyone still alive who had been hurt that badly would have been screaming.

9

October 2005

The house was one of the biggest I had ever seen. Thick columns held the front portico aloft while the red brick facade stretched all the way to the tree line. Leaves littered the yard and skittered in the afternoon breeze while the squeal of a school bus's brakes carried through a thin copse of trees near the road. Two kids got off and walked across the street to an equally impressive home.

I looked at Mr. Ballard, my social worker.

"Is this the right place?"

He smiled and nodded. "This is it. You'll be living with Christopher and Diana Hughes. They don't have kids of their own, but they've been foster parents for years. They understand how things work. We've got one girl here at the moment. Her name is Emily, and she's seventeen, so she's a little older than you, but you've got a lot in common. Her younger sister, Megan, will join the house soon from what I'm told. A lot of young women have thrived here."

I hoped he hadn't lied to me. At fifteen, I couldn't move out on my own for three more years. Foster care had been hard, but I had dealt with it for years as a child. Then, I hit puberty and grew boobs. My foster fathers watched me as I tied my shoes or bent down to pick things up. A few times they "accidentally" walked in on me while I was in the shower. One guy even kept trying to persuade me to go bathing suit shopping with him. He thought it'd be fun. Even the thought creeped me out.

My foster mothers were even worse. Most of them wanted a baby to hold and then give back when the baby got too old. Other foster moms, though, wanted a servant who let them sit on their asses. I didn't have a problem doing the dishes or folding laundry, but I wasn't Cinderella, which they learned quickly.

Mr. Ballard and I walked to the front door. Mrs. Shapiro, my previous social worker, had retired two years ago. I didn't know her well, but she gave me a hug when she left. Mr. Ballard was okay. I called him every couple of weeks to tell him how things were going, and he listened when I spoke. When I had problems, he took care of them. Most of the time, he didn't bother me. That was nice.

He knocked on the door, and I turned around to look at the yard. The grass looked like a golf course, and the shrubs were all trimmed and neat. I had lived in some nice foster houses, but none were like this. The governor should have lived here, and if not him, then somebody else important.

The door opened, and I turned around. A girl stood in the entryway. She had light brown skin, brown eyes, and brown hair down to her shoulders. A big dimple dominated the center of her chin. It looked like a butt. Her lips were thick and red, and she wore an angry smirk on her face. She looked at me up and down.

"What the hell are you smiling at, Cinderella?"

So that was how we'd start. Fine by me.

"Your face looks like a gym teacher's ass," I said. "It made me laugh."

"Whoa, ladies," said Mr. Ballard, holding up his hands and stepping between us. "You will live together, so you need to be polite."

"So you're the new girl," she said, looking at me again. "Christopher said we were getting somebody new. You better watch yourself around here."

"Is this where you tell me that snitches get stitches?" I asked. "Because if you are, don't waste your time. I've heard it all. My last foster home had cable, and I've seen every episode of *Scared Straight*."

"You think you're funny," said the girl, standing straighter and glaring down at me. "We'll see how funny you are tonight."

"That's enough, Emily," said a voice from deeper within the house. Mr. Ballard turned his attention to the new arrival. Emily drew in a sharp breath, and her shoulders slumped. She seemed to shrink, making her look like a dog fearful that its master would strike. Good. She deserved it.

The man joined us at the front door. He was a little under six feet tall, and he had a thin build and pockmarked face. He was ugly, but ugly in a way a lot of women might find attractive. My mom had taken a lot of men like him home.

"I'm Christopher Hughes," he said, looking at me and holding out his hand. I took it and squeezed hard, just as one of my foster fathers had taught me years ago. He looked down and tilted our hands to the side. My fingers were tiny compared to his. "That's a good grip. You must be Mary Joe."

"Just Joe," I said. "After Joe Montana."

"Ahh," he said, nodding. "I read your file. You were born in 1990, the same year he won his second MVP title. Was your dad a 49ers fan?"

"My mom was," I said. "She told me Joe Montana was my father, but I'm pretty sure that was bullshit. She probably just fucked a guy who looked like him."

Mr. Ballard gasped, while Emily laughed. Christopher looked at me appraisingly.

"Young ladies don't use language like that, Joe," said Mr. Ballard, looking down his nose at me. "It's inappropriate."

"Mr. Ballard's right," said Christopher, a crooked smile forming on his lips. "But that's okay. I like this one. I think she'll fit in here pretty well. You have a bag?"

"It's in my car," said Mr. Ballard.

"I'll get that and fill out the paperwork," said Christopher, looking to Emily. "How about you show Joe around and tell her the rules?"

"Okay, Christopher," said Emily, her voice almost

meek now. It was a sharp contrast to the young woman who had greeted me earlier. She knew how to play to a crowd. She looked at me and smiled. "Since you'll be staying with us, I'll show you the house."

"I'll see you before I leave," said Mr. Ballard, patting me on the shoulder. He and Christopher turned to walk outside while Emily shut the front door. Her nostrils flared as she glared at me. The meek young woman had disappeared.

"Seems like you're making friends," she said.

I drew in a breath. "Sorry. Sometimes my mouth goes off before I give it permission. Can we start over? I'm Joe. I'll be living with you for a while."

Emily crossed her arms. "There ain't no starting over."

"Okay," I said, taking a step back. "Can you show me the house?"

She gestured around the entryway. "This is the house. See it?"

I looked around for a moment. The entryway was oval shaped with a curved staircase that led to the second floor. There was a big dining room to the left and a living room to the right. Someone had painted the walls beige and the trim white. I couldn't see far, but even the rooms I saw were bigger than the apartment my mom and I used to live in.

"I like the hardwood floors," I said, looking down. "Are they original?"

"How should I know, Susie Homemaker?"

I ignored her and then walked into the dining room. The table had eight white chairs around it. A hutch along the far wall held silver-rimmed plates and crystal glasses. It looked like something from a magazine. I couldn't believe a family who could afford that would house strays like me and Emily.

"So what's the story with this place?" I asked, walking through the dining room to the kitchen. There was a breakfast room with a small table to the south and a big, two-story living room to the west. Everything seemed to have its own neat place. Someone had pushed a stainless-steel coffee maker against the wall beside the refrigerator while an immaculate red KitchenAid mixer sat beside the stove.

"What do you want to know?"

I held out my hands and raised my eyebrows. "Why do the people who own this house have us? Are we maids, or are we guests?"

Emily smirked. "Depends on how much Christopher and Diana like you."

"They'll like me," I said, tilting my head to the side. "I'm lovable."

"Could have fooled me."

"I'm not sure fooling you is the difficult task you think it is," I said. Before she said anything, I walked to the breakfast table. There was no dust anywhere. "Christopher said something about rules."

"Yeah, go to school. Curfew is midnight. If you're out later than that, Diana locks the door, and you sleep in the garage. Dinner is at seven. You clean up after yourself, and you do your own laundry. Diana likes a clean house. Quiet hours are eight at night to eight in the morning. During quiet hours, you study or you sleep."

"Okay," I said, nodding. "Any other rules?"

"Stay out of my way. I've got another year here, and then I'm getting out. I don't want you screwing anything up."

I nodded to myself and looked around the breakfast room, evaluating the place. This would work out just fine. It seemed as if I had hit the foster kid lottery.

Of course, little in my life was ever as it seemed.

10

My hands trembled as I holstered my weapon. My legs felt weak, and my stomach roiled. I needed to get out of that basement before I vomited, so I ran upstairs and then to the front porch where I sucked in deep breaths of warm spring air. Years had passed since I last saw Emily, and we had never been friends, but seeing here there with those burns all over her body…it was just wrong.

A cold chill ran down my back, and I sat down on the brick steps of the front stoop. A pickup truck drove by on the road. Its exhaust hit me a second after it passed, seeming to cleanse the odor of blood and burned hair from my nose. I took a few more deep breaths, feeling my heart slow. My hands still shook, so I balled my fingers into fists and squeezed them tight enough that my knuckles turned white.

When I closed my eyes, I saw Emily's dead body. Megan's body had bothered me, but the gunshot would have killed her before she even felt it. She died without pain or fear. Someone had tied Emily to a chair and hurt her, though. Her murderer took his time.

I had seen bodies before but never one like this.

Emily wasn't just killed; they had tortured her.

I forced my hands to relax. As the initial shock wore off, I pulled out my phone and called 911. The dispatcher answered before the first ring finished.

"911. What's your emergency?"

"This is Detective Joe Court of the St. Augustine County Sheriff's Department. I'm in St. Louis on Mississippi Avenue overlooking Lafayette Park. I'd like to report a homicide."

My voice didn't feel like my own, so I cleared my throat hard. The dispatcher typed something for a moment.

"Okay, Detective. Tell me what's going on."

"I found a dead woman in the basement of a house on Mississippi Avenue," I said. The more I spoke, the more I felt like myself. I forced myself to picture the scene in my head and think through it. "The blood on the ground has dried, and there are signs of a struggle inside the home. The front door was open on my arrival. Believing someone inside might have been in trouble, I cleared the house. I found the victim in the basement tied to a chair."

The dispatcher paused. "So she's dead?"

"Yeah," I said. "I need help here. Please inform the first responders that the woman sitting on the front steps is an armed police officer."

The dispatcher typed for another moment. "All right. I have officers en route. They'll arrive within five minutes."

"Thank you."

I hung up and rubbed my eyes, hoping I could stop seeing my foster sister's broken body. Somehow, I didn't think that would happen soon.

By the time the first police cruiser arrived, I felt a little better. I introduced myself and told them what I had found. One officer then went inside while the second stayed out with me and asked me questions to verify my identity. It was standard procedure. I forced myself to stay as detached as I could.

When the first officer left the house a few minutes later, his skin looked almost green. He bent over, rested his hands on his knees, and drew in great big breaths. He nodded to his partner.

"She's telling the truth," he said between breaths. "We need a supervisor and an ambulance. This is ugly."

The St. Louis police could handle a homicide, so I stayed in the back of the first responders' cruiser while they worked. Since I had a moment, I called Harry, my partner.

"Harry, it's Joe. Where are you?"

"Searching Kiera Williams's room at the Wayfair Motel. We've got a lot of prints and a lot of body fluids. I'll be honest; it's kind of disgusting here."

"Sorry it offends your delicate nature. Get a pen and paper because I've got multiple things to tell you. First, your victim is not Kiera Williams. Best I can tell, Kiera Williams doesn't exist. The address on her license is a postal shop in Rock Hill, Missouri. Second, I think she's a young woman named Megan Young. Travis already knows my theory, but he's not on board with it yet. Third, I looked up Emily Young in St. Louis. She's Megan's older sister. She's also dead. By all appearances, someone tortured her. It's bad."

Harry whistled. "This just got interesting. Any idea why these two sisters are living under fake names, or why someone would want them dead?"

"I haven't talked to her in years, but Emily used to deal weed. According to the government, Christopher Hughes murdered Megan twelve years ago. Hughes is in prison. If you want details on that, talk to the boss. He worked Megan Young's case when he was still a detective in St. Louis."

Harry paused for a few moments.

"So our records say Megan died twelve years ago. Your victim, her sister, was a drug dealer. This sounds like a terrible soap opera."

"I'm sorry it doesn't live up to your expectations of what a homicide should look like."

"Me, too," said Harry. "Are you still in St. Louis?"

"Yeah," I said, turning and looking over my shoulder while an unmarked police cruiser parked behind me. A man and a woman sat inside. I nodded to them although they didn't seem to see me. "I'll talk to you when I get back, but I think I'll be here for a while. Keep working the case, and call Travis to let him know what's going on. And make sure Dr. Sheridan IDs Megan as soon as possible."

He grunted. "I'm on it. Good luck, and I'll keep you updated."

I thanked him, hung up, and tried opening my door. Nothing happened, which shouldn't have surprised me in the rear seat of a police cruiser. I had to knock on the glass for a uniformed officer's attention before I could get out. He smiled.

"Sorry about that," he said. "I should have warned you to sit in the front."

"It's my fault," I said, looking to the unmarked cruiser. "Are they homicide detectives?"

"Yeah. That's Jeff Driscoll on the left and Amy Ledgerman on the right."

"Thanks," I said, already walking toward the cruiser. The male detective, Driscoll, stepped out first, while his partner, Ledgerman, made a phone call. I shook his hand. "Joe Court, St. Augustine County Sheriff's Department. Nice to meet you."

"Jeff Driscoll. My partner's Amy Ledgerman. My dispatcher says you found the body."

I nodded and looked toward the house. Most days, I would have waited until his partner was with us to go through everything, but Detective Driscoll had questions, and I had answers. I took him through my entire day from the moment I got the call about the body in St. Augustine to the moment I found Emily's corpse in St. Louis. I also went through my suspicions that the body in St. Augustine belonged to a woman who records said died in St. Louis County twelve years ago. He took notes throughout and asked clarifying questions where appropriate. His partner joined us about halfway through.

"Take me back to your victim in St. Augustine," said Ledgerman. "How sure are you that she's Megan Young?"

"It's been twelve years since I've seen her, but she has the same facial features, and she's the right age," I said. "I requested that our coroner examine her teeth and compare them to Megan Young's dental records."

Detective Ledgerman wrote that down but then glanced at her partner.

"We need to call somebody from the county. Should we bring in the prosecutors on this, too?"

Driscoll nodded. "Not a bad idea if Detective Court is right. We'll need a supervisor here, too, to deal with the media."

"If you plan to call a county detective, ask for Julia Green," I said. "She knows the victim."

Driscoll nodded, but Ledgerman furrowed her brow. "I know Captain Green. She works sex crimes, not homicide."

"Yeah, but she worked part of the Megan Young case twelve years ago." I paused and then cleared my throat. "And she's sort of my mom. She'll be mad if I don't call her."

Driscoll smiled, while his partner snickered.

"We'll let you make that call," he said.

I nodded, and the two detectives went inside to check out the scene. While they worked, I leaned against the trunk of the nearest police cruiser and called Julia's cell phone. Her phone went to voicemail before it even rang.

"Captain Green…Julia, it's Joe. Sorry I haven't called for a while, but I've been a little busy. I'm at a murder scene near Lafayette Park in the city. You should come. The victim is Emily Young. Somebody tortured her," I said. I paused for a moment and sighed, unsure how to approach this conversation. Blunt was best. "I think Megan Young is dead in St. Augustine. You know what that means. So get down here. It's on Mississippi. It's the house with all the police cars out front. You can't miss it. I'll talk to you later, okay?"

I hung up and waited a few minutes for her to call back. She didn't, which meant she was probably in a meeting. As a member of her department's command staff, she had a lot of those. Or maybe she didn't want to hear from me.

I loved Julia, but it had been a while since she and I had last spoken. Our last conversation hadn't been a fight, but she did question every life decision I had made in the past decade. The conversation shouldn't have bothered me. Julia only wanted what was best for me, but even a decade after she had adopted me, I hadn't gotten used to having someone who cared about me in my life.

I waited for about half an hour and watched while the police officers worked the crime scene. Then, I heard a familiar voice to my right. My adoptive mother and I looked almost nothing alike. Where I was five seven and blonde, she was just a little over five feet tall and brunette.

She was slight of build with high cheekbones and bright green eyes. She laughed and smiled more often in a day than I did in a year, and it showed in the laugh lines around her eyes and mouth. Looking at her, I realized how much I had missed her.

"Hey, Joe," she said. "It's been a while."

"Hey, Jules," I said. "Sorry I haven't called earlier. I've been busy."

"That's okay," she said, looking toward the crime scene. "We'll get coffee later. For now, let's talk shop. What have you got?"

I led her through everything I had seen and done so far, and she nodded just as Detectives Driscoll and Ledgerman had.

"Any confirmation on your St. Augustine victim's identity?"

"Not yet, but my partner's working on that."

"Well, damn," said Julia. "We tried Christopher Hughes in St. Louis County, so he'll be our problem. You'll focus on Megan and Emily. Even after everything he's done, I don't know whether I'll be able to keep him in prison."

"I know," I said. Julia put a hand on my elbow and squeezed.

"You're strong," she said, her voice low. "Your father and I will be here for you."

"I know."

We stayed still for a few minutes. Detective Ledgerman must have seen us because she came out of the house. She shook Julia's hand and then looked at me.

"Did you see the pictures upstairs in the hallway?"

I shook my head. "I cleared the house and secured the scene, but I didn't look at the decorations."

"You should now," said Ledgerman. "Since you knew the victim, I want to see whether you can ID anybody."

I agreed, so Julia and I walked into the house and up the stairs to the second floor. As Detective Ledgerman had said, there were about a dozen pictures on the wall in the hallway, including a very old one of Emily. She wore her hair in pigtails and had pink lipstick on her lips. It looked like a school picture from fifth or sixth grade.

Ledgerman directed my attention to a much more recent picture taken from what looked like Times Square in New York. It was night, and hundreds of people milled about in the background. Front and center, though, were two young women, and they both wore heavy coats and purple sunglasses with 2016 drawn on the lenses. It was New Year's Eve, and they were out on the town.

"The girl on the left is in the basement," said Ledgerman. "You recognize the girl on the right?"

I nodded. "Yeah, that's Megan Young. She's our victim in St. Augustine."

Detective Ledgerman looked to Julia.

"Now sounds like a good time to call the lawyers, Captain."

Julia nodded and pulled out her phone. I looked at the other photos and swore aloud. Detective Ledgerman looked at me.

"Yeah?"

I pointed to one picture. Megan and Emily stood on either side of a minister outside a church.

"We have two dead siblings," I said. "What do you think the chances are we've got a third?"

Ledgerman looked at the picture I pointed to.

"They've got a brother?" she asked.

"Half brother. I haven't seen him in a long time, but I think his name was Cameron. Looks like he became a minister."

Ledgerman looked closer at the picture and then tapped something into her cell phone.

"That's New Pilgrim Baptist," she said. "It's on the north side of town."

I nodded and hurried toward the stairs. "It's your town, so you're driving. Let's go."

11

I considered following Detective Ledgerman in my car, but I didn't know the city well and didn't want to get lost. So I climbed into her cruiser, and we headed out. Where Emily Young lived in a gentrified, stable neighborhood full of young professionals, her brother worked in one of the most dangerous neighborhoods in town.

His church had a red brick exterior with an exposed limestone foundation. Plexiglass panels and thick bars protected hundred-year-old stained-glass windows in the sanctuary hall while the church's exterior grounds sprawled across two city blocks. It had a basketball court, a tennis court, and even a small playground—all of which looked well used.

This church served its community well. Cameron ought to have been proud of that.

Detective Ledgerman parked on the street near a two-story brick home with elaborate dentil molding on the roofline. Had someone restored it, it would have fit into Emily Young's neighborhood well. Here, the entire west side had crumbled, leaving the building open to the elements.

It wasn't the only derelict building on the street, either. Across from it sat a three-story home in similar disrepair, and there was an overgrown, vacant lot beside it. Even here, though, there were a few homes that looked better than others. They had neat front lawns and flowers in window boxes. Cars parked up and down the street.

"I'm surprised there are so many vacant lots," I said, walking around Ledgerman's cruiser to join her on the sidewalk. She tilted her head to the side and shrugged.

"Didn't used to be this many," she said. "The city owns a lot of this property, and the mayor's office would rather have a vacant lot than a crumbling house that could hurt a kid who goes exploring. Hurricane Katrina hurt, too."

I smiled. "I didn't realize the hurricane reached this far north."

She glanced at me and walked across the street to the church. "St. Louis brick built New Orleans a hundred and fifty years ago. When Katrina hit, it damaged a lot of brick buildings. Contractors needed old St. Louis brick, and the best place to get that was in St. Louis. They drove into neighborhoods like this with semis and offered a hundred bucks per ton of bricks—no questions asked. People all over the city came in with sledgehammers and tore this place apart."

"That's awful," I said.

She shrugged. "Especially for the people who lived here."

We reached the other side of the street. Some boys

up the street saw us and scattered, leaving a bright orange couch and a washing machine on the sidewalk. Ledgerman nodded in their direction.

"You think they're helping their grandmother move?"

I stopped and looked for a moment. "Why would anyone steal a couch and an old washing machine?"

Detective Ledgerman stopped in front of me and shrugged again. "Probably found the washing machine and thought they could sell it for scrap metal. The couch, well…maybe they wanted somewhere to sit."

The boys looked as if they were twelve or thirteen years old. Had I seen them dragging a washing machine down the street in St. Augustine, I would have stopped them and taken them home to their parents—or to school. Ledgerman didn't seem too concerned about them, though. We had other worries than truancy.

Someone had locked the church's side doors, so we walked around to the front, where we found an elderly woman pushing a small cart laden with canned goods out a door. I held the door for her, and we slipped inside. The church's interior smelled like dust, coffee, and old paper. It reminded me of a library. Tile the color of faded red brick covered the floor while fluorescent lights buzzed on the ceiling.

Neither of us knew the church's layout, so we followed the sound of voices to a large storage room in the basement. Crude wooden shelves made from plywood and two-by-fours filled the space like aisles in a grocery store. Refrigerators and freezers lined the back wall. Volunteers had stacked boxes of canned goods on every inch of open floor space. Three elderly shoppers walked the aisles and occasionally put cans of creamed corn or green beans in their trolleys.

Cameron Brody, Emily and Megan Young's older half brother, stood near the freezers with an older woman. She had a hand on his tricep, and he nodded along to everything she had to say. When he saw us, he sighed and stopped speaking. The elderly woman pulled her hand away from him and looked from him to us before excusing herself and returning to the aisles.

The minister walked toward us a second later, a concerned look on his face.

"Cameron?" I asked, once he drew near. He looked at me up and down before his gaze turned into a glare.

"Do I know you?" he asked. "Because the only people who call me Cameron are my congregants and friends. You may call me Mr. Brody or Pastor Brody. It's a sign of respect, something lacking from the police these days."

"I apologize, Pastor Brody," I said, clasping my arms behind my back. "We met a long time ago. I thought you'd remember me."

"Sorry, Detective."

"In that case, I'm Detective Joe Court," I said, looking to Ledgerman. "This is Detective Amy Ledgerman."

He blinked a few times, and then his expression

softened.

"Joe Court," he said, almost under his breath. "I never expected to hear that name again."

"Glad to hear I made an impression," I said.

"Hard to forget a girl named Joe," he said. He looked at me up and down again. It wasn't a leer; it was more of an inspection. "You've grown up. I don't suppose this is a social call."

"No, it's not," said Ledgerman. "Do you have an office we can talk in?"

He turned and looked over his shoulder and then back to us.

"I do, but I need to make sure my friends receive the help they need first. Meet me upstairs. I'll speak with you in the sanctuary in a few minutes."

Ledgerman and I agreed and then followed signs to the sanctuary. None of the overhead lights were on, but plenty of sunlight filtered through the stained glass windows. Detective Ledgerman and I sat in a pew near the back. Growing up in as many foster families as I had, I had attended dozens of churches. Baptist, Catholic, Lutheran, Methodist, Episcopal, Presbyterian, the pews were all uncomfortable. That wasn't the reason I had stayed away from church all these years later, but it didn't help, either.

Cameron entered a few minutes later. He sat in the pew in front of us and turned around.

"Okay, Detectives," he said. "My last client has left, and I've closed the food pantry for the next hour. I hope this is important."

"We're here to talk about your sisters," said Ledgerman.

"I can't help you much there," he said. "I haven't spoken to Emily in almost a decade. Joe can tell you why I haven't spoken to Megan."

Even as a small-town cop, I interviewed a good number of people, and I had learned a few things over the years. If the first sentence out of a witness's mouth was a lie, everything that followed would be, too. I didn't like being lied to.

"I give people one lie before I get pissed off," I said, speaking before Detective Ledgerman could. "You used yours. Start over, Pastor Brody."

He looked at me and smiled, but I couldn't see much mirth in his eyes.

"Funny how time changes people," he said. "You used to be polite."

"And you didn't used to be a liar. It's not a trait I associate with a man of the cloth."

He crossed his arms. "And what did I lie about, young lady?"

"Your relationship with your sisters, for starters," I said. "How would your congregation react if they found out their pastor had let an innocent man go to prison for Megan's death?"

He drew in a breath and looked at me. "You know what Christopher Hughes did to the girls in his house. He wasn't innocent."

Ledgerman looked at me askance, but I didn't take

my eyes from Cameron.

"You're right. Hughes is a vile human being, but he didn't kill your sister."

He stood and shook his head.

"I don't have to listen to this," he said. "If you two want to talk to me again, you can call my attorney."

"Please have a seat," said Ledgerman, her voice soft. "We're not here to interrogate you. We came because we have news you need to hear."

He glared at me before sitting. "So this isn't an interrogation. You could have surprised me."

"When was the last time you talked to your sisters?" asked Ledgerman.

He cocked his head to the side and snorted. "I believe I've given you my answer. If this is all you have, you're welcome to leave."

"I found Emily's body this morning in her house," I said. "Megan died in St. Augustine yesterday. I'm sorry. I know you cared about them."

For a second, his glare fell on me hard, but then his expression changed. He swallowed and then leaned back without saying a word.

"Emily kept a picture of the three of you in her house," I said. "She was proud of you, I think."

He blinked. It was like watching a dam fail in slow motion. First one tear came, and then another and then another. Ledgerman and I gave him a few minutes to compose himself. Then he reached into his pocket for a handkerchief and wiped his cheeks.

"I'm sorry," I said again. "And I'm sorry for the way I delivered the news. I wish there were easier ways."

He held up a hand and closed his eyes. "Just tell me how they died."

I looked at Ledgerman. She leaned forward. "Somebody killed them. We're trying to find out why. Detective Court is working the case in St. Augustine, while I'm working in St. Louis."

He nodded. "I can tell you why they were murdered right now. Joe can, too, I bet. I tried to get them to change. I told them they should go to college. They were smart girls. They could have done anything in the world."

"Emily still sold drugs?" I asked. Cameron looked at me and nodded.

"Megan, too. They were a team. They tried to tell me it wasn't dangerous because their clients were rich, but rich people do stupid things just as often as poor people do. Maybe more often because they can get away with it. They didn't listen."

"Can you think of anyone who would want to hurt them?" asked Ledgerman.

He shook his head. "They sold weed. They weren't out there shooting up neighborhoods. Emily and Megan were businesswomen. They owned real estate together. They bought and sold houses together. Weed was just part of what they did. They had this idea of opening marijuana dispensaries as soon as Missouri made it legal. They wanted to go legit."

"Their clients ever threaten them?" asked

Ledgerman.

Cameron chuckled. "Their clients were college professors and stock brokers who liked to get high after work. They weren't working with Pablo Escobar."

"How about problems with suppliers?" I asked.

"They never talked about that end of their business," he said. "I loved my sisters, but I'm a man of God. I tried to stay out of their business."

It wasn't the most helpful interview I had ever sat through, but at least we had viable leads. I doubted there were many distributors of high-quality weed in the city. Cameron may not have known who they were, but the drug enforcement officers in Detective Ledgerman's department would.

"Is there anything else you want to tell us?" I asked. "Anything you think could help our investigation?"

Cameron hesitated but then nodded. "A guy came by about a week ago. He said he was a writer, and he was looking into Megan's death for a potential book."

"Oh?" asked Ledgerman, leaning forward.

"Yeah," said Cameron, nodding. "He wasn't a writer, though. He didn't remember me, but he was a cop. He picked me up when I was in high school for trespassing at the Galleria Mall. I was there to buy Christmas presents for my foster mom."

"Did he tell you his name?" I asked.

"Scott Gibson."

"That's helpful," said Detective Ledgerman, standing. "I'm sorry about your sisters. If you'd like to make funeral arrangements, I'll have someone from the Medical

Examiner's Office call you here."

"I'd appreciate that," said Cameron. He stood. He seemed to wobble for a moment. In other circumstances, I might have questioned whether he'd had a little too much to drink. Today, though, he had the unsteady legs of the bereaved. "I'm going to take the rest of the day off. If you need me, call the church office. My assistant will put you in touch with me."

Detective Ledgerman nodded, and the minister walked out of the sanctuary. Once we were alone, I looked at her.

"Scott Gibson," I said. "The name familiar?"

"Yeah. Brody was wrong, though. Gibson's not a cop, at least not anymore," she said, already heading toward the exit. "He's a private investigator with one of the slimiest defense attorneys in town."

"Think he'd torture and murder a woman in her basement?" I asked, hurrying to keep up with her.

"If there was enough money involved, oh yeah."

"Are you up for paying him a visit?" I asked.

"I'm up for kicking his teeth in," she said. "But I'll settle for a visit."

If he had been the one to torture Emily and murder Megan, I would have preferred the former, too.

"Let's go," I said. "Maybe if we're lucky, he'll resist arrest and we'll get to pepper spray him."

"We can always hope."

12

January 2006
Every dollar counted, and I had just made thirty-seven of them pulling a five-hour shift at the movie theater. Thirty-seven bucks didn't seem like much money, but if I kept working fifteen hours a week for the next two years, I'd graduate from the foster care system with almost nine thousand dollars in the bank. With that much money, I could go to college part-time and work as a waitress to make ends meet. I had a plan that didn't depend on anyone else. That was the key to everything. I controlled my fate.

Melted snow seeped through my canvas shoes, soaking my socks. When I got home, I'd have to put my shoes over the vent so they'd dry by morning, but I could deal with that.

Christopher and Diana Hughes were decent foster parents, if by negligence more than practice. Diana worked all the time, and Christopher stayed out of my way. Sometimes, I caught him watching me, but it was nothing compared to the way some men at the movie theater undressed me with their eyes. I was fifteen, and even I recognized them undressing me with their eyes. Christopher at least kept his tongue in his mouth.

Things had worked out well since moving into Christopher and Diana's house. Emily was still a bitch, but she cleaned up after herself, and we ignored each other. Plus, she sold weed to kids at school, so she always had some with her, which was nice for a roommate. I didn't smoke much, but I had fun when I did. Life had turned out well, but some days I wished Christopher and Diana lived closer to the bus stop.

I trudged through the neighborhood. It was a little after eleven, so I had plenty of time to reach the house before curfew. The neighborhood had lights on every corner, so the only dark spots were those between houses, and I hadn't seen a single person since leaving the bus. I always kept a can of pepper spray on my key chain in case I ran into somebody creepy, but I had only used it once on a customer in the movie theater who tried to corner me in the bathroom. My boss had him arrested, and I got the rest of that night off.

As I walked, I imagined myself stepping into a hot shower and then falling into a soft bed. Both would feel amazing. I almost smiled despite the freezing temperature. As I turned down the driveway, I took out my cell phone and used its built-in flashlight to light my way. The living room looked dark, but the lights from the kitchen shone through the front windows. Somebody was still up. Emily almost never came home on Friday nights, which left Christopher.

Since getting the job at the movie theater, he always wanted to talk movies. I appreciated that he took an interest in his foster kids, but every muscle in my body ached. I just wanted to go in, walk upstairs, and get ready for bed. Hopefully he wouldn't be too talkative.

I walked through the side door in the garage, hoping I could sneak in unseen.

"That you, Joe?"

I groaned under my breath as I kicked off my shoes in the mudroom.

"Yep," I said, forcing a smile to my lips and hoping I sounded happy to see him. "Just got off work."

"If I had known your schedule, I would have picked you up. I planned to see *King Kong* before it left theaters."

I hung up my coat. "*King Kong* was okay, but you should see *Harry Potter and the Goblet of Fire* first. Most people liked it, and I'm not sure how much longer we'll have it."

As I turned, I found Christopher standing in the mudroom doorway. He wore flannel pajama pants and a thick robe, and he carried a glass of green liquid.

"What are you drinking?" I asked, walking past him.

"Something Diana told me to drink," he said. "It's full of antioxidants, and it's supposed to lower my risk of colon cancer. It tastes like death. You want to try it?"

I laughed, walked into the kitchen, and then sighed at the mess.

"You're not selling it," I said, glancing at him as he followed me into the room. "Diana'll kill you if you don't clean this up."

He waved my concern away as he put his drink on the counter beside the microwave. "She's gone until Sunday night. Drove to her mom's house."

"Well, enjoy your death-flavored drink," I said. "I need to go to bed."

"See you tomorrow."

I started toward the front staircase to go up when Christopher called out again.

"Do you like living here?"

I turned before I reached the front entryway. "Yeah. You and Diana are great."

"Good," he said. "You and I don't talk. That's okay, but I like to know the girls who live here. Sometimes it seems like you avoid me."

"We talk about movies," I said, hating that I sounded defensive.

"I guess we do," he said. He almost sounded crestfallen. "Okay. If you need anything, I'll be around. You can talk to Diana, too. My parents weren't around when I was growing up, and I remember what it's like. Anyway, good night. If my drink kills me, I've enjoyed knowing you."

"Is your drink that bad?"

"It's awful," he said. "I can't lie. If I didn't think it would save my life one day, I wouldn't even consider touching it."

I hesitated and then joined him in the kitchen.

"It can't be that bad," I said, holding out my hand. "Your wife gave you the recipe, and she still likes you."

"So she says," he said, sliding the drink across the granite countertop to my outstretched hand. "She sells this stuff in her health store in Ladue. Try it and tell me whether you think it could be healthy."

I didn't know Diana had a store, but I laughed and then picked it up. It smelled fruity, but I detected something strong beneath that. I furrowed my brow.

"Is there alcohol in here?"

"A little rum," he said. "I improved her recipe."

"I am your fifteen-year-old foster child. You shouldn't be giving me rum, you know."

"Don't most dads let their kids have a first sip of beer at fifteen or sixteen?"

I shrugged. "My mother said my father was Joe Montana. I never got to meet him."

Christopher leaned against the counter behind him and got a distant look in his eye. "I never met either of my parents. I used to tell people my dad was Neil Armstrong and my mom was Elizabeth Taylor."

"If you lie to somebody, you might as well lie big," I said, lifting the glass and raising my eyebrows before taking a sip. It was fantastic. It tasted sweet and fruity and tropical all at once with a subtle kick of rum. I didn't drink a lot, but this was the best drink I'd ever had. I almost smacked my lips.

"You seem to like that," he said.

"It's wonderful," I said, putting the glass on the counter. "It's like a kiwi smoothie, but better."

"I hate kiwi," he said.

"That explains it," I said. "You've got terrible taste."

He leaned over and picked up the glass. "I'll toss this unless you want it."

I hesitated for a moment. As I walked home, I had planned to take a shower and head to bed, but a refreshing tropical drink sounded nice.

"If you don't want it, I'll take it."

"It's all yours, sweetheart," he said, chuckling as he left and walked toward the family room. I took the drink and followed him.

"You want to watch a movie?"

"Sure," I said.

We started a comedy about a guy who tried to win back his girlfriend during a zombie uprising. I had seen it before, but it was even funnier with a little rum in me. About halfway through my drink, my head began to feel light. He had put more rum in there than I expected.

As I finished the drink, he looked at me. My vision was a little blurry.

"I'm glad we could hang out, but I think I need to get to bed," I said. My body felt heavy.

"Okay," said Christopher. "Good night."

I tried standing, but my legs didn't feel right. I couldn't move. Christopher paused the movie and looked at me.

"Hope you don't mind, but I figured we could watch it later," he said. I tried to say something, but my tongue and mouth wouldn't work. He smiled and then looked up and down my body. It wasn't the look any forty-year-old man should have ever given a fifteen-year-old girl. Even drunk I recognized that. "You're beautiful. I'm glad you liked my drink."

I wanted to run away, but I couldn't move. All I could do was fall asleep. As my eyes closed, I felt his breath on my neck and his hands unbuttoning my pants. In my dreams, I cried.

13

Scott Gibson, the private investigator who had questioned Pastor Brody, worked for a defense attorney named James "Sherlock" Holmes. We drove to his office in Clayton and parked in the garage next door. Many of the buildings around us stretched fifteen or twenty stories to the sky while expensive cars filled the streets. The homes we had passed on our way there likely cost well into the seven figures. Clayton wasn't the wealthiest suburb in St. Louis County, but it was close. I had never felt comfortable there.

Sherlock's office suite occupied the second floor of a low-rise building across from the county courthouse. The interior was modern with a slate-tile floor and a receptionist's desk made from a dark-stained wood. The receptionist looked at us and smiled.

"Can I help you, Detectives?"

If she recognized us as detectives right away, she must have known Ledgerman.

"We're here to see Scott Gibson," said Ledgerman. "He around?"

The receptionist's hands flew over her keyboard

almost faster than I could see. Then she glanced up at us.

"Business or pleasure?"

"Business," said Ledgerman. She paused and tilted her head to the side. "Maybe some pleasure depending on what he's got to tell us."

She typed again before glancing at us and smiling. "Mr. Gibson is unavailable at the moment. If you'd like, I can leave a message."

"If he's unavailable, what's with all the typing?" I asked.

She glanced at me and gave me a chipper but fake smile.

"I was checking his schedule."

We both knew that was a lie. She could have checked a schedule with a couple clicks of a mouse.

"Is Sherlock around?" asked Ledgerman.

The receptionist turned her vapid smile to her.

"He's on his way now."

"So that's what the typing was about," I said. "You have an interoffice messaging system, and you were exchanging notes with the boss."

The receptionist's unwavering smile grated on me.

"One more minute, miss."

I glanced at Ledgerman. She nodded and sat on one of the padded chairs in the waiting room. I sat next to her without saying a word. Sherlock arrived soon after that. He was in his late forties and had black hair with a few wisps of gray, and he wore a navy suit that hugged an athletic torso. He didn't look armed, but he had enough muscle on his upper body to be a threat if he wanted. Since I had a firearm, I wasn't too concerned.

"Afternoon, Detectives," he said, looking at the two of us. For a split second, his eyes traveled down my body before meeting my gaze. I smiled as if I hadn't noticed, but he winked anyway, knowing full well I had caught him checking me out. What a douche. "How about we talk in my conference room?"

We nodded, so Sherlock led us into the office suite itself. There were four cubicles, two private offices, a lavatory, and a conference room inside. We were the only people on the floor as far as I could tell.

"You sure you don't want anything?" asked Sherlock, holding the conference room door open for us as we walked inside. The afternoon sun glinted off a television mounted to the wall and the glossy wooden coffee table in the center of the floor. Ledgerman and I pulled out black leather office chairs from around the table and sat without saying a word.

"We're here to talk to Scott Gibson," said Ledgerman. "His name has come up in a homicide investigation we're working."

"I see," said Sherlock, nodding as he walked to the side of the table opposite from us. He sat and looked at me. "Before we discuss Mr. Gibson, who are you?"

I reached to my belt and unclipped my badge.

"Detective Joe Court. St. Augustine County Sheriff's Department."

He looked at my badge before looking at

Ledgerman.

"Based on the mutual trust we've developed over the years, I'll accept that Detective Court is who she says she is."

Ledgerman didn't blink. Her expression was as emotionless as a corpse's.

"Your trust fills my heart with joy."

"I'm glad," he said, crossing his arms and leaning back. "Tell me about your interest in my investigator. I will help as much as I can."

Ledgerman gave him a basic outline of our investigation so far. The lawyer nodded along but didn't ask questions—not that we would have answered anything. When Ledgerman finished, Sherlock laced his fingers together and leaned forward.

"So your concern is that my investigator asked Pastor Brody about the whereabouts of his sisters."

"Emily and Megan were in hiding," I said, leaning forward to match the attorney's posture. "Your investigator looked for them. A week later, someone murdered them. That seems suspicious."

"So your question comes down to timing," said Sherlock. "Had Scott asked about them last year, you wouldn't be here."

"Sure, let's say that," said Detective Ledgerman. "Why was your investigator looking for our victims?"

Sherlock cocked his head to the side. "Attorney-client privilege prevents me from answering that question."

"If this involves attorney-client privilege, he must

The Girl in the Motel

have sought them on your orders," said Ledgerman.

Sherlock drew in a breath and seemed to think for a moment before nodding.

"Yes. That's right. I requested that he find Emily and Megan."

"Why?" I asked.

He hesitated and narrowed his gaze at me. "I believe I've already told you I can't answer that. What part of that didn't you understand?"

Detective Ledgerman spoke before I could snap at him.

"Let's talk in hypotheticals. Hypothetically, why would a defense attorney ask his private investigators to find two young women like Megan and Emily?"

Sherlock opened his eyes wide and shrugged.

"I could think of many reasons. Do you know what they did for a living?"

"Independent pharmaceutical sales," I said.

He smiled at me. "You're a detective. Why would a defense attorney seek two young women who sold drugs for a living?"

"So you can kill them?" I asked, lowering my chin and smiling.

He shook his head and sighed as he looked at me. "I had hope for you. At least you've still got your looks."

"Excuse me?" I asked.

Ledgerman tried to say something, but Sherlock spoke over her.

"I'm sorry if that was a little fast for you, Detective.

You're pretty, and I'm glad for that, because you're not intelligent. It's nice to have at least one natural advantage over your colleagues. Detective Ledgerman doesn't even have her looks going for her anymore. In future conversations, I'll remember your mental limitations."

People had insulted me in interviews before, so it didn't bother me, but most lawyers were polite enough to hold their tongues.

"Why did you ask Mr. Gibson to find Emily and Megan Young?" asked Detective Ledgerman.

"It's possible that someone accused one of my clients of a crime committed by Emily Young." He looked at me and smiled. "Or perhaps I have a client in prison for Megan's murder. That'd be interesting, wouldn't it? Can you imagine the shit storm that would rain down on this city if it turned out St. Louis County detectives had sent a man to prison for a murder that didn't even happen?"

My stomach twisted.

"So Christopher Hughes is your client," I said.

"Would that be a problem, Mary?" he asked, looking at me.

"Please call me Detective Court," I said.

Detective Ledgerman glanced at me but said nothing. Sherlock lowered his chin and leaned forward a hair.

"But you are Mary Joe Court, right?"

I drew in a breath before nodding. "I am."

He gave me a curt smile and then looked to Ledgerman. "Did your partner tell you about her relationship with your victim?"

"They lived with each other in foster care," said Ledgerman. "It was a long time ago."

"Good," said Sherlock, nodding. He gave me that same curt smile before focusing on Ledgerman again. "As Detective Court guessed, Christopher Hughes is my client. Two weeks ago, I received a tip that Megan Young, the young woman whose death resulted in Christopher's incarceration, was alive and well. My investigator followed up but couldn't find her. I'm saddened to hear of Megan and Emily's deaths, but neither I nor anyone in my office played any role in their murders."

Ledgerman looked at me and then to Sherlock before standing.

"Thank you for your time, Mr. Holmes. If I need to talk to you further, I'll be in touch."

He stood and smiled. "I've enjoyed seeing you both."

I had questions to ask, but Ledgerman wouldn't have ended the interview without reason. I followed her out of the office and to the stairwell. There she appraised me and crossed her arms.

"Before we go any further, I need to know everything," she said. "You found a body in a motel in St. Augustine this morning. You then went to St. Louis to track down your victim's next of kin. There, you discovered another body. You were in foster care with both victims in the house of Christopher Hughes. Do I have that right so far?"

I nodded.

"Christopher Hughes allegedly murdered your victim twelve years ago. He didn't, though. Correct?"

Again, I nodded. "You're two for two."

She blinked a few times and then cocked her head to the side. "Why would Megan and Emily set him up for murder?"

"Because he raped them and a lot of other girls in his care. He raped me, too."

Ledgerman blew out a long breath and then turned around. For a moment, she said nothing. Then she faced me once more and nodded.

"Okay, Detective," she said, nodding. "I appreciate all the help you've given me on this case, but I can't work with you anymore. There's a reasonable shot Christopher Hughes ordered these murders from prison. If he raped you, you cannot investigate him. You can't be objective. It's as clear cut a conflict of interest as I've ever seen."

I wanted to argue with her, but she was right.

"I get it."

"For what it's worth, I'm sorry for what happened to you."

"Me, too," I said.

We walked to her car and then drove back to my borrowed SUV without saying a word. As I stepped out of the cruiser, Ledgerman cleared her throat.

"Do you have a number I can reach you at?"

I took a business card from the inside pocket of my jacket. "That has my office number."

"Good," she said, taking the card from my

outstretched hand. As I closed the door, she called out again, her voice low. "Hey, Joe, make sure you stay in Missouri for the next few days. I will need to talk to you again. This may get ugly for you. Sherlock is sleazy, but he's a good lawyer. If we charge Hughes with ordering Megan and Emily's murders, he'll drag you through the mud."

I swallowed and nodded. "I guess I'll just buy waders, then."

"Good luck, Detective," she said.

I thanked her and shut the door. For a few moments, I sat there, breathing. For years, I had thought I was done with Christopher Hughes and Megan and Emily. I wasn't, though. The monsters of your past never die. They just go dormant, waiting for you to turn your back on them so they can strike unseen.

14

March 2006

Almost three months had passed since Christopher assaulted me, and I had yet to sleep through the night. I had lost fifteen pounds and quit my job at the movie theater. No one else knew what Christopher had done. He was rich and charismatic. Everybody liked him. Even if I wanted to tell somebody, it would be my word against his. I tried to pretend it hadn't happened, but I couldn't ignore my nightmares.

Some of my teachers must have recognized that something was wrong because they contacted my high school's guidance counselor. The guidance counselor thought I was depressed, so he talked to my social worker and Christopher and Diana Hughes to make sure I was okay. We even had meetings where I sat and listened as they talked about my mental health. I wanted to run and never stop, but I had nowhere to go.

Then, one Friday night, Christopher came into my bedroom after everyone else went to bed.

"I saw your light on, so I wanted to make sure you were okay."

"I'm fine," I said, pulling the covers of my bed to my chin. "Please leave."

He crossed the room and sat down on my comforter. "I don't know what's going on with you, but I'm worried. You should talk to me. I'm your dad."

"You're not my dad."

A wicked, knowing grin spread across his face.

"Are you scared of me?"

I tried to tell him no, but my throat had tightened so much I couldn't say anything. He brushed the back of his hand across my cheek, wiping away a tear.

"You have no reason to fear me," he said, whispering. "I could be a friend. I could give you anything you want. Money, alcohol, clothes. You name it, and it's yours. Just give me what I want."

"Please get out," I said, scooting across the bed so I was as far from him as I could get. "I won't tell anybody what happened. Just leave me alone."

He sighed and then nodded before standing. Part of me thought he would leave. My shoulders relaxed, and the tremble left my knees. But as he crossed the room, he didn't leave. Instead he locked the door. My heart thudded against my chest, and my breath became ragged.

He walked toward me again. I wished I had a gun.

"Please just leave me alone," I said, pleading with him. My entire body trembled. "If you touch me, I'll scream."

He knelt beside the bed and looked in my eyes. His shape was blurry through my tears.

"You'll do what?" he whispered.

I tried to tell him I'd scream for Diana or Emily, but my voice caught in my throat. He shushed me and then reached forward to stroke my hair.

"Sweetheart, this is a big house, and I built it for privacy. Even the interior walls have six inches of insulation. You can scream all you want, but nobody will hear you. We need to talk about your future. I was very proud of you in your guidance counselor's office. You didn't make up any lies about me."

"You mean I didn't tell him you raped me," I said.

His smile broadened. He liked seeing me cower.

"You remember things one way, and I remember them another. I've been thinking about that night we spent together. I could contribute to your college fund if you wanted. Would you like that? If you cooperate, everybody gets what they need. If you don't, I will make you scream every day of your life, and I will take what I want anyway."

He put a hand on my upper thigh and then scowled as he looked down.

"Oh, you are disgusting," he said, standing up quickly. "You're cleaning this up right now."

He left the room and slammed the door shut behind him. I didn't know what set him off until I looked down and saw that I had peed the bed. I cried until I didn't have tears anymore, but then I changed the sheets and did the laundry.

Christopher didn't return that night or the next or

even the one after that. Life went on. I didn't sleep well at night, but I slept some.

Then, four weeks later, I got home from school and found Emily grinning from ear to ear. I had taken the bus home while she had gotten a ride from a friend with a car. She smelled like weed—which she always did when coming home from school. She had three or four ounces of it hidden in the storage shed behind the house. I suspected she had money, too, although I had never seen that.

"Why are you so happy?" I asked.

"You'll find out any minute now."

I didn't know what that meant, but I didn't care. I sat with my back to the wall at the table in the sunroom so I could do my homework. At ten to four, the doorbell rang, and Emily sprang to get it. I heard happy voices, so I walked to the foyer to see what was going on. Emily was hugging a young pretty girl in the entryway while Christopher and Mr. Ballard, my social worker, stood off to the side, beaming. Mr. Ballard and Christopher both smiled at me and beckoned me over.

"It's nice to see you, Mary," said Mr. Ballard. "I'm just dropping off your new foster sister."

Emily pulled away from the girl. Both had happy tears on their cheeks.

"This is my sister," said Emily.

"I'm Megan," she said, smiling at me. She had skin like caramel and bright brown eyes. She had the face of a young teenager but the body of a much older girl. I felt sick to my stomach knowing what would happen to her in this house.

I looked to Mr. Ballard.

"Isn't there a rule about housing siblings together?"

"Shut up," said Emily, stepping close.

"It's okay," said Mr. Ballard, holding a hand to her to keep her from coming any closer. He focused on me and gave me a patronizing smile. "We prefer to keep siblings together where possible. I think this is a great house. You guys will be very happy here."

Emily stepped behind me and squeezed my arm hard. "We are happy. We'll be fine. We're sisters."

"That's what I like to hear," said Mr. Ballard. He turned to Christopher. "I've got paperwork for you to sign, and then Megan is all yours."

I wanted to shout that Christopher had raped me and that he'd do it to Megan, too, but then I felt a sharp pinch at my back. Emily leaned forward so that I could feel her breath on my neck.

"Not another word, or I will gut you right here."

So I kept my mouth shut until Christopher and Mr. Ballard left. Emily shoved me away and then showed me the knife she had pressed to my back. The blade was small, but it had an edge that glinted in the afternoon light.

"What the hell is wrong with you?" she asked. "This is my sister. You want to break up my family?"

"She's not safe here," I said. "Christopher raped me."

Megan blinked and opened her eyes wide, but Emily

barely reacted.

"He raped you?" she asked.

"Yeah. He gave me a drink, and it must have had something in it because I passed out."

"Then what's the big deal? If you don't even remember it, it's like it didn't happen."

"But it did happen," I said. As soon as the words left my lips, I realized I was admitting it for the first time. It had happened. He had hurt me, and he'd do it again if given the chance. I didn't know how to deal with it, and I needed a friend. I barely knew Emily, and I didn't like her, but she was the closest thing I had to someone who cared about me. "I don't know what to do. I don't know who to tell. I'm so scared all the time that I hardly sleep at night, and I can barely keep food down. Some boy tried to talk to me at school, and I ran away and locked myself in the bathroom. I used to like him, but he looked at me like Christopher did."

Emily slipped her knife into her pocket. "What do you expect me to do about it?"

My lips moved, but no sound came out.

"What?" she asked again.

"I don't know."

"I don't care what you do, but deal with it," she said. "It's your problem. I've got my sister. I've got my family. I've got my own shit to deal with."

Emily led her sister away. Megan looked at me and mouthed that she was sorry.

"He'll hurt her," I said.

Emily turned around and shook her head. "No, he

won't because I won't let that happen. If you're smart, you won't let him hurt you, either. Now stay out of my way. I've got a good thing here. I've got a business, I've got my family. You screw this up for me, I will make you regret it."

The two of them left, and I felt a weight press down on me. I had been alone for most of my life, but it took that moment for me to realize what that meant: No one would help me. It was stupid to pretend otherwise.

I went into the kitchen. Emily was showing her sister around. I ignored them both and took a steak knife from the block on the counter. Both girls saw me do it, but neither said a word. They were lifers in the foster care system, too. They knew what it meant to be alone.

I had to solve my problems on my own.

15

It was after sunset when I reached St. Augustine, and people swarmed the streets. I parked two blocks from my station in the first open spot I found and walked. At over twenty thousand square feet, my station—an old Masonic temple the county had purchased and renovated years ago—had far more space than we needed, but we made it work.

I walked through the front door and smiled at Trisha, our dispatcher. She was in her mid-fifties and had curly brunette hair she kept secured behind her head with a clip. Technically, she was a sworn officer with the same training I had, but she didn't go on calls herself anymore. She liked being behind the desk. Four computer monitors surrounded her.

"The boss in?" I asked. She shook her head.

"No, but he wants you to call him," she said. "Also, Captain Julia Green from the St. Louis County police called. She wants you to call her, too."

"If Julia calls again, tell her you haven't seen me," I said. "And give me some warning if you see Travis."

She smiled. "Can do."

"Thanks, Trish," I said, walking deeper into the station. Almost the moment I took a step, I smelled the rank odor of vomit. There was a college-aged kid handcuffed to a bench in the reception area. He was asleep, but he had puked on the ground in front of him, somehow missing both his pants and shirt. Good for him. His future friends in the drunk tank would appreciate not having to smell vomit-soaked clothing all night. I stopped walking and looked at Trisha.

"Have you seen Sasquatch?"

She typed for a moment. "He and Officer Reynolds are on foot patrol at the fairgrounds."

At twenty-two, Officer Preston Cain—Sasquatch—was the youngest guy in our department. He was developing good instincts and would become a good cop one day, but he wasn't there yet. I liked working with him, though.

"When he gets back, tell him he's got puke to clean up," I said.

Trisha raised her eyebrows. "It wasn't long ago that you were the youngest officer in this building and had to clean up the puke."

"I know," I said, nodding. "Back then, I hated the system. Now, I see its utility."

She smiled and turned as a phone rang.

"I'll tell him."

I smiled and walked to my desk in the bullpen. On a normal evening, there'd be half a dozen officers at desks inside, filling out paperwork before they finished their shifts. With everyone busy with the Spring Fair, though, I had the room to myself.

For the next hour, I transcribed my interview notes and wrote reports about what I had done and whom I had talked to. It was the boring part of police work, but it was just as important as anything else we did. One day, those reports might put somebody in prison. Or in this case, they might help Christopher Hughes get out. I still didn't know how I felt about that.

At half after six, I drove far past the edge of town to my two-story American foursquare home. It wasn't pretty yet, but it was mine. The original homeowner had constructed it over a hundred years ago with parts and plans ordered from a Sears catalog. The materials had cost twenty-two hundred dollars plus the price of the land. I had purchased it and the surrounding five acres for forty thousand dollars.

Some days, I still thought I got ripped off.

When my realtor brought me by the place for the first time, she called it a teardown. The moment I researched the property, though, I fell in love. The home had fallen into disrepair—along with St. Augustine County—but for almost a hundred years, three generations of a single family had called it home. It deserved a second life, not a bulldozer.

So I bought the place and fixed it up. I took out a loan and replaced all the windows, the clapboard siding, and the roof my first year. A contractor did most of that work, but I provided manual labor. Once the contractor finished the exterior, I did everything inside myself. It was a work in progress, but it was dry and comfortable now. And it was mine.

I didn't go in right away. Instead, I parked in the driveway and walked about a quarter mile to my neighbor's house. Susanne Pennington sat on her front porch, drinking a cup of iced tea. Roger, my one hundred-forty-pound bullmastiff, sat at her feet. When the dog saw me, he raised his head, stood, and came running. His entire body trembled with excitement, but he stopped at my feet and sat down, looking up at me and licking his lips. I smiled, knelt, and held out my hands.

He jumped to greet me and licked my cheek before turning his head for me to scratch his ears.

"How's my sweet boy?" I asked. As if understanding me, he bowed before me, telling me he wanted to play. "We'll go for a walk soon."

I stood and started for the porch. "You doing okay today, Susanne?"

My elderly neighbor smiled and gestured toward the rocking chair beside hers. Roger joined us on the porch and sat beside me. I scratched his head and neck. Susanne, Roger, and I had ended a lot of days together like that. It was a good life.

"I feel good today," she said, looking over her front lawn. "The sun was out, a warm breeze blew, and Roger kept me company all day."

She smiled at my dog. Roger walked over to Susanne's house most days when I headed to work. He was about ten, an elderly age for a dog his size, and he had arthritis in his hips. I got him from an animal shelter when I bought the house. Back then, he was still young, and he used to chase every single squirrel, raccoon, or opossum that came into the yard. Now, he was content to sit on the porch and have someone stroke the fur of his back.

I patted him and talked to my friend, and with each passing moment, the weight of the day lifted a little more. At about seven, I stood up and walked Roger home. It wasn't much of a walk, but at Roger's age, it was enough. He stopped and sniffed things alongside the road, and then he barked at a truck that drove by. When we reached the house, he walked to his bed beside the fireplace and fell asleep.

I grabbed a container of macaroni and cheese from the fridge and then stepped to the bar in the living room. When people were around, I drank red wine. When I was alone, I skipped the pretenses and drank vodka on the rocks. It made things easier. I put on the TV for some background noise, but mostly, I sat and processed the day.

About half an hour after I got home, Harry called. He had read my reports at work and wanted to check in. We talked for a few minutes, but neither of us had much to say.

After hanging up with him, I poured myself another drink and then walked outside to the front porch. Roger continued to snore in the living room. It was a beautiful night, so I sat and looked at the stars, allowing their lonely stillness to calm me.

I was out there on my third drink when my cell rang again. I answered, expecting my boss. Instead, it was Detective Ledgerman.

"Hey. It's Joe Court. What can I do for you?"

"Just wanted to call and thank you for screwing me over."

It wasn't the first time a rude phone call had interrupted my evening, and it wouldn't be the last. Still, it surprised me. Ledgerman and I had ended things well.

"Okay. Message received," I said. "Any reason you're upset?"

She sputtered something, but I didn't understand her.

"You want to repeat that?" I asked.

"You have a lot of nerve," she said.

I didn't know whether she wanted an answer, so I didn't respond.

"You have nothing to say?" she asked.

I sipped my vodka and shrugged. My old chair creaked beneath me as I rocked.

"As angry as you seem to be, nothing I can say will lead to a productive conversation. Not only that, you've said enough for both of us," I said. "We can talk tomorrow when you've cooled off some."

"Did you call Angela Pritchard right after I dropped you off, or did you wait for a while and think things through?"

Angela Pritchard's name was familiar, but I took a moment to place it.

"The weather girl on channel three?"

"For fuck's sake," said Ledgerman. "You're slurring your words. Are you drunk?"

I looked down at my glass. "No, but I'm getting there."

"Angela Pritchard is an investigative journalist for channel three. She ran a story about Megan and Emily Young."

I put my drink glass on the ground, crossed my arms, and leaned back so my feet could reach the porch rail in front of me.

"You had to know the story would come out."

"I did, but my department planned to call a press conference so we could do it responsibly."

And by responsibly, she meant they wanted to release the information in a way most favorable to themselves.

"If you want to accuse me of leaking the story, go ahead, but I didn't do it."

"She knew their names, Detective. Even in my reports, the victims are Jane Doe 1 and Jane Doe 2. The leak didn't come from me or my department. Hence, it came from you."

I considered for a moment. "I think you're kind of missing the obvious third choice: Sherlock Holmes."

She paused for a moment, but when she spoke again, her voice had a measure of control it had lacked before. "James Holmes is cooperating with my department and the county prosecutor's office. He wants his client out of jail. They're already in discussions about a monetary settlement for Christopher Hughes's pain and suffering.

This leak didn't come from my office or his. Using the process of elimination, that leaves you."

"Okay," I said, nodding. "I see why you called me. What'd you hope to get out of this conversation?"

She started to call me a bitch, but then she caught herself and drew in a slow breath.

"You are a real piece of work."

"So you've told me."

"Stay away from my investigation," she said. "I don't care what you do down there in Hillbilly County, but if I see you at a crime scene in St. Louis again, I'll arrest you. And if I find out you had anything to do with the deaths of Emily or Megan Young, I will charge you with murder with special circumstances."

"That's out of line," I said. "You can accuse me of leaking a story to the press all you want, but accusing me of murdering two people is a step too far. I don't appreciate that."

"I don't care what you think," she said. "Here's what I think, though. Christopher Hughes raped you, Emily Young, and Megan Young when you were in high school. That's awful, and I'm sorry that happened to you. Instead of going to the police, though, you three got even. You faked Megan's death and framed Christopher Hughes for her murder. Then you laughed your ass off as the state dragged him to prison. When Sherlock's private investigator came asking around about Megan, you killed your co-conspirators before they could turn on you."

I shook my head and closed my eyes. "That's

ridiculous."

"It's plausible," said Ledgerman, her voice dripping with malice.

"Good luck proving that plausible theory," I said. "Anything else you want to tell me?"

She hung up without saying another word. Roger poked his head out the front door and came to sit beside me. I scratched him behind the ears.

"She doesn't seem to like me," I said, picking up my glass again and taking the final swallow. I didn't know who leaked the story or why, but I recognized one thing: This case had just gotten a lot harder. I was almost glad I wouldn't be part of it too much longer.

16

Breakfast was Sherlock's favorite meal of the day. He could order lox and cream cheese, or he could order gooey pancakes covered in syrup. He could start and finish in ten minutes, or he could stretch the meal to an hour. It all depended on what he wanted. Lunch was almost always a quick affair full of unhealthy food, while dinner came with too many expectations once it was over —sex, business, witty conversation. He had to become an entertainer after dinner. Breakfast, though, came with a freedom no other meal possessed.

Today, he had brought bagels, cream cheese, pastries, and coffee from a local bakery. It wasn't fancy or pretentious; it was food that tasted good. He liked that.

He had two employees with him in the car that morning: Scott Gibson and Alonzo Morrison. Both were former police officers who had become private investigators. They did as he asked, and he paid them well for their time. More than that, he protected them. Everyone had skeletons in his or her closet. In Scott's and Alonzo's cases, those bodies were real, and they had buried them in the woods or dumped them in the

The Girl in the Motel

Mississippi River or left them to rot in abandoned buildings in north St. Louis.

Behind him was a white Ford Focus. Its driver—a man Sherlock knew only as Mr. Mendoza—had picked it up from a rental car facility near the airport very early that morning. Most of the time, Sherlock preferred knowing everything he could about the men and women with whom he worked, but knowing too much about Mr. Mendoza or his business partners would earn him an unmarked grave. Ignorance in this case was bliss.

They pulled to a stop in front of McFarlane Motors in north St. Louis. A chain-link fence topped with barbed wire surrounded the lot, giving the business a menacing look and feel. The property had started as a gas station, and it still had the overhead metal canopy that had, at one time, shielded the pumps from the elements, but now the shop's owner had removed those pumps and expanded the main building from two garage bays to six. There was a warehouse next door with an additional five garage bays and ample room for storage.

Alonzo and Scott waited outside while Sherlock and Mr. Mendoza went in. Though it had been several years since he had last stepped foot in that building, Sherlock remembered the shop's layout. He and Mendoza walked to a smoke-filled employee lounge at the rear of the station. Linoleum tile covered the ground while kitchen cabinets lined two of the walls. In the center of the room was a sturdy formica-topped table with six chairs, four of which had men sitting in them.

Sherlock put the bagels on a clear section of counter and opened cabinet doors until he found a stack of paper plates. Those, too, he put on the counter.

"You want to tell us why you called a meeting, counselor?" asked Warren Nichols, the garage owner. "I've got a business to run and shit to do."

"I'll make it worth your while to listen," said Sherlock, pulling a chair from the table to sit down. "First, though, I brought cinnamon crunch bagels. They're delicious, and breakfast is the most important meal of the day."

Two guys laughed before standing and digging into the food. The others followed suit shortly. Sherlock waited at the end of the line and slathered a thick layer of apple cinnamon infused cream cheese on his own bagel before sitting down and enjoying the quick, unhealthy breakfast at the table. After a few minutes of relative silence, he took a drink of coffee and cleared his throat. The men focused on him.

"Don't stop eating on my account. It's breakfast. Let's keep it casual," said Sherlock, looking to the men around the table. "First, I'm here because you were all in business with Christopher Hughes. He's a friend of mine, just as he's a friend of yours. I'm here with a business proposal that can make all of us rich."

Randy Shepard, a hotel owner from East St. Louis, crossed his arms. "Who are you, and why should we trust you with any kind of business deal?"

Sherlock nodded to him.

"I'm James Holmes, but most people call me Sherlock. And you shouldn't trust me. You shouldn't trust anyone. Our business relationship will be transactional."

Randy raised an eyebrow, but Sherlock ignored him and reached into the briefcase at his side. He pulled out four manila folders and handed them to the men around the table.

"Open them," said Sherlock. "Each folder is custom made for you."

One by one, the men looked in their folders, and one by one, expressions around the table darkened.

"The hell is this?" asked Neil Wilcox, owner of several nutrition and supplement stores across the county. He tossed the folder to the table in front of him and leveled a malevolent glare at Sherlock. "You've got pictures of my kids. I don't appreciate that."

"I understand, but this is an important component of how I do business," said Sherlock. "This envelope ensures that you remain accountable. Each of you has something you love. If you lie, cheat, or steal from me, you'll lose it. It's as simple as that."

Steven Zimmerman, the owner of several office supply and copy centers in the county, stood up. Sherlock had figured he'd leave, so he hadn't included Zimmerman in any of his plans.

"I don't appreciate being threatened. That's not how I do business."

"Then you're free to go, Steven," said Sherlock, nodding. "Good luck with your future endeavors. Take your accountability folder with you. No hard feelings, but you'll miss out on a terrific opportunity."

Steven grabbed the folder and shook his head as he left the room. Mr. Mendoza followed. Warren stood and opened his mouth to say something, but Sherlock coughed and shook his head while holding up his index finger.

"Just a moment," said Sherlock. He held his breath, knowing what was coming next. The gunshot was loud and close. The other guys around the table jumped, but Sherlock sat straighter. "Does anyone else want to leave?"

Warren sat down.

"It's unfortunate how dangerous this neighborhood has become," said Sherlock. "Mr. Zimmerman's kids will miss their dad, but at least they'll sleep in their little beds in Glendale tonight, safe and sound."

"Who the hell are you?" asked Randy, his face pale.

"I'm the guy who'll make you rich," said Sherlock. "I'm also Christopher Hughes's attorney. Before his incarceration, I know you all worked for him. Warren, you allowed him to process and break down stolen vehicles in your shop here. It's a wonderful facility. Randy, you pimped his girls in your cheap motels in East St. Louis. You also provided drivers to take those girls across town. Neil, you helped him launder money through your stores. Steven—God rest his soul—did the same. Christopher was a gangster. You were his crew, or at least the closest thing he had to one. Now you're mine."

Nobody said anything for a moment. Then Randy

crossed his arms.

"Steven was a prick," he said. "I don't care if he's dead, but I'm not a fan of empty promises. Tell me about this money you'll make me."

"I had hoped to get the chance to talk to you," said Sherlock. "Using the foster care system to meet and recruit young vulnerable girls—and getting paid for housing them while you pimped them out—was one of the shrewdest business moves I've heard of. If I were a father, I'd tear your balls off, but since I'm not, I can be honest. It took guts, but you pulled it off."

"Thank you," he said. "But I'm not here for flattery. I've got a business to run. I'm not interested in having smoke blown up my ass."

Sherlock glanced toward the door, having spotted movement. Mr. Mendoza stepped inside. He had a pistol tucked into the front of his belt.

"We'll move into a new market," said Sherlock. "Pharmaceutical sales. Each of you has a business network chosen for this endeavor. Randy, you'll handle distribution. Your girls already deal some. Now, they'll increase that. They will also recruit and supervise our new dealers. Warren, you've got cars moving into this place twenty-four hours a day. You'll be our logistics man. Neil, you'll be our money man. We will funnel cash to you, and you will use your stores and our other businesses you will acquire to clean it."

Warren rolled his eyes and shook his head. Neil said nothing. Randy leaned forward and held up two fingers.

"Two problems. We've talked about moving into

narcotics, but the competition is intense, and it's hard to find a reliable supplier. If this is your plan, we might as well declare bankruptcy now."

"I like the way your mind works, Randy," said Sherlock. "I can see why Christopher relied on you so much."

"Like I said, I'm not here for flattery."

Sherlock looked to Mendoza and nodded. Mendoza took Steven's now empty seat. Warren shifted away from the diminutive Hispanic man.

"This is Mr. Mendoza," said Sherlock. "He represents a business conglomerate in Juarez, Mexico. They'd like us to set up a franchise in the city for them. Securing products to sell will not be a problem."

The men around the table looked to Mendoza. He had the cold, black eyes of a reptile. They took in the men around them but gave nothing away. Sherlock almost felt a cold shudder pass through him.

"As Mr. Holmes says, finding an adequate supply of cocaine will not be an issue," said Mendoza. "My organization would like to expand its regional distribution network to include a hub in St. Louis. Agents in my organization wholesale products in Chicago, Houston, and Miami, but our analytics data shows we are the primary supplier of cocaine, marijuana, and methamphetamines in your city.

"Because of our existing market saturation in our target markets, we'd like to increase our presence in smaller cities across the Midwest. St. Louis is our first trial. If we're successful, we'll expand to Indianapolis, Kansas City, Cincinnati, and other cities in the region."

He stood up and walked around the table.

"Our analytics data estimates that the St. Louis region consumes four tons of cocaine per year. Your organization will purchase five tons from us at a cost of fifty-two million dollars. As our regional distributor, you will be free to set prices as you see fit, but we suggest a retail price of twenty-six thousand per kilo. Assuming the pricing structure holds, your organization will net seventy-two million per year in profit. As you increase the size of the market, your profit will increase."

Somebody whistled. Randy, though, shook his head.

"What about the competition? What about security? What about capital?" he asked. "You may think you'll make us rich, but it sounds more like you'll make us dead."

"My organization will handle product security," said Mr. Mendoza. "We can also make our security personnel available should problems arise. As for competition, consider it eliminated. If you agree to our terms, you will become the sole distributors of our products in the region. Wholesalers in other cities will no longer sell to St. Louis-based distributors for fear of losing their own franchises. My agents will give your contact information to anyone who can no longer purchase in Chicago or Miami."

Warren looked at Sherlock.

"If he's providing the drugs, what do we need you

for?"

"Everyone needs a manager," said Sherlock, smiling. "I'll act as the liaison between our organization and Mr. Mendoza's organization. Not only that, I'm a criminal defense attorney who has been in private practice for the past twenty years. I have pre-existing relationships with an awful lot of people involved in the narcotics trade in this city. I can get you the dealers who will push our products. We'll split the proceeds equally among us. Given the size of the market and the generous terms Mr. Mendoza has offered, that will leave us each with eighteen million dollars a year."

"So how would this work?" asked Neil, looking to Mr. Mendoza. "Do you give us product on consignment and we reimburse you?"

Mendoza gave him a tight smile and shook his head.

"No," he said.

Neil looked to Sherlock and raised his eyebrows. "What do we do, then? I don't have fifty million dollars sitting around."

"Mr. Mendoza is not asking for fifty million dollars upfront," said Sherlock. "He's asking for ten."

Warren scoffed and stood but didn't leave the room. Randy stayed put, thinking. Neil leaned forward, ran his fingers through his hair, and sighed as if he were giving up.

"If you give me a week, I can put together a million—maybe even two if I'm lucky—but ten is a stretch," said Randy, looking at Sherlock. "You seem like a smart man. You wouldn't have come here and presented this unless you thought it was possible. So what's the plan?"

When he planned that meeting, Sherlock had assumed Randy was just a pimp who specialized in young women. He was smarter than that, though. Sherlock would have to watch him. If necessary, he'd have to eliminate him. He'd worry about that if the time came, though.

"Each of you has significant resources at your disposal," said Sherlock. "Ten million is a stretch, but one million isn't. That's all I ask from you. One million cash. I'll provide the same. When we need more product, we'll use the proceeds of our sales. After this seed capital, we shouldn't need any further cash infusions."

Warren leaned forward and rested his elbows on the table. "Counting you, there are four of us in on this deal. Math wasn't ever my strong suit, but my math says we'll be six million short."

"Christopher Hughes will provide the rest," said Sherlock.

Warren laughed and shook his head. "Good luck with that. I love Chris, but that guy's done. You know what life without parole means? He's never getting out, and he will never give you money. You got any other plans?"

Sherlock smiled at him. "You don't watch the news, do you?"

Warren narrowed his gaze and then looked to the other men still at the table. "What's he talking about?"

"Looks like Chris is getting out," said Neil. "Megan Young, the girl he confessed to murdering, was just found. She's been alive for the past twelve years."

Warren said nothing for a moment. Already, though, Sherlock could see the gears in the mechanic's head turning. He would be a problem sooner rather than later. He had a plan for that, though.

"And you're sure Christopher has that kind of money?" asked Neil.

Sherlock nodded. "He does, and he'll give it up. That's why I had Megan killed. Christopher's getting out. I'm already in negotiations with the St. Louis County Prosecutor's Office regarding a monetary settlement for his wrongful conviction. It will be substantial."

Randy blinked and drew in a breath. "Why did you have the girl killed? If she were alive, you could get him out quicker."

Sherlock smiled at him but didn't allow it to reach his eyes. "If she were alive, she'd say Christopher raped her, and that he had raped multiple other girls in his care. It was a lot easier just to shut her up early. You have a problem with that?"

"No," he said. "The police do, though."

"I'll worry about the police," said Sherlock. He looked to his three potential partners. "You've heard the proposal, and you've heard the cost. I need to know whether you're in or out."

"If we say no, you'll kill us, right?" asked Neil.

Sherlock looked at him and shrugged. "It's a tough

world we live in. This arrangement can make it easier for you and your families. If you cooperate, we all win. If you refuse…"

He let his voice trail to nothing. The men didn't even pause before agreeing, not that he expected them to. Randy and Neil even shook his hand as if this were a normal business deal. They all had dangerous work ahead of them, but the rewards outweighed the risk. They would be rich and powerful, none more so than Sherlock.

But first, he had to take care of Christopher Hughes, and that was easier said than done.

17

I got to my station at a little before eight with my head throbbing, my mouth dry, and my legs still shaking. Nobody was immune to hangovers, and I should have stopped drinking after Detective Ledgerman called, but she had pissed me off so much that I took two more shots just to calm down. That brought me up to five for the night, three above my self-imposed limit. Even those drinks, though, hadn't stopped the nightmares. Nothing ever did.

I rubbed my eyes as they adjusted to the comparative gloom of my station. Seth Eberly, a uniformed patrol officer with over twenty years on the job, sat behind the front desk, drinking coffee and monitoring the phone lines. He nodded when he saw me.

"Morning, Joe," he said. "The boss is looking for you. He's not happy."

I considered turning around and going home. Instead, I sipped the latte I had picked up at Rise and Grind on my way in and considered my options.

"Is he still around?" I asked. My voice sounded scratchy, so I coughed to clear my throat.

"Haven't seen him leave. Good luck."

I nodded my thanks and walked. On most mornings at this time of day, the scent of crappy coffee and vomit wafted through the building, but today, bleach overpowered everything. That was one perk of showing up after the morning shift cleared out the drunk tank: They had already cleaned up the puke. The other perk was that I missed the morning roll-call meeting. The downside was that if I enjoyed those perks too often by showing up half an hour late, I'd get fired.

When I reached my desk, I put the paper bag with my pecan roll on top and then bent to turn on my computer, which rested on the floor. As I logged on, Detective George Delgado left the conference room on the other side of the building and walked toward me. Even this early in the morning, he looked smug and proud of himself.

Delgado was about fifty. Acne had left his sand-colored skin pitted, while time had turned his once black hair gray. He wore dark jeans, a white oxford shirt, and a tan linen blazer. In other circumstances, he would have been handsome. Knowing him as I did, though, I saw only an asshole.

"Morning, Detective," he said, sitting on the edge of my desk and crossing his arms. My paper bag crinkled beneath him. Until my recent promotion to detective, Delgado and I had enjoyed a cordial, professional relationship, but after my promotion, he had become a dick.

"You're sitting on my pecan roll," I said, rubbing my eyes as pain exploded in my brain. Delgado stood and handed me the bag. "What can I help you with, George?"

He crossed his arms and leaned against the desk nearest mine.

"You can start by filling me in on your Jane Doe murder investigation."

I raised my eyebrows. "I'm not working a Jane Doe. My victim is named Megan Young."

"You shouldn't assume the victim is Megan Young without corroborating evidence. For now, she's Jane Doe."

I smiled but didn't feel any merriment. "Why are you interested in my investigation? I've already got a partner on the case, and I don't need another."

Delgado raised his eyebrows. "Travis didn't talk to you this morning, did he?" I grimaced, and Delgado smiled before becoming serious again. "From what I've heard, you impressed Detective Amy Ledgerman in St. Louis. She called Travis at home last night and shared her observations."

I groaned.

"I talked to her last night, too," I said. "She doesn't understand the case."

"I understand, but whether she's right or wrong, you've got a conflict of interest," said Delgado, brushing his hands together as if he were washing them. "Jasper and I are taking over the case, so I thought it'd be helpful to hear what you've done so far. If you're stuck on your victim being Megan Young, I might be wasting my time."

I didn't blink as I looked at him. "My victim is Megan Young. Her sister's dead in St. Louis. That's where you should focus your investigation."

He drew in a breath through clenched teeth and shook his head. "See, I'm not so sure. Her ID says she's Kiera Williams, she registered at the motel under the name Kiera Williams, and there's a car in the lot registered to Kiera Williams. Call me crazy, but I think your victim's Kiera Williams."

He smiled as if he were talking to a child. I kept the smile on my face so I wouldn't snap at him.

"So it's just a coincidence she looks like Megan Young and that her picture was in the home of Emily Young in St. Louis? And remember somebody else also murdered Emily Young."

"And that's where we disagree again," said Delgado. "You found the body of Jessica Martin in St. Louis. That's the name on her ID, that's the name on her mail, and that's the name of the homeowner. See, I'm not a magical detective like you. I don't enjoy your intuition. I've just got the facts, and the facts tell me you made so many assumptions you've led the entire investigation astray. Did you know our murder victim had pizza delivered to her room last night? I didn't see it in the reports you filed."

My throat grew hot, and my hands trembled, so I held them under my desk.

"I didn't find a pizza box in her room when we

searched it. If I had seen one, I would have followed up."

"Did you talk to anybody else at the motel? If you had done that, you wouldn't have wasted an entire day chasing your intuition across the state. Just food for thought."

I gritted my teeth. Of course I had asked our officers to talk to potential witnesses at the motel. We had canvassed every neighboring business, too, but we hadn't found anything. Even if I told Delgado that, he'd just tell me I should have gone back later—as he had. Given time, I would have done that, but my schedule hadn't given me the opportunity.

I closed my eyes.

"I'm not here to argue with you or justify my decisions," I said. "If you're only interested in second-guessing me, you can leave."

"I will, but first, I need to say something," he said. "As your union rep, it's my duty to warn you that habitual truancy is a fireable offense under our latest contract. And you smell like you just walked home from a bar."

My nails bit into my palms as I balled my hands. "I don't smell like a bar. It's none of your business, but I had a long day yesterday, so I had a few drinks last night at home."

"Are you hung over?"

"Again, that's none of your business," I said, catching his gaze. He grinned.

"As your union rep, it's not. As your friend, though, maybe you should cut back."

"Maybe it's time you minded your own business."

He held his hands up again and stood. "I didn't mean to offend you, Detective. Enjoy your day."

He walked away, but I cleared my throat before he got far.

"Hey, Delgado," I called. "Since you're working the Megan Young case, what am I supposed to be doing?"

"Speed trap, sweetheart. Like I said, enjoy your day."

As soon as he left, I swore under my breath. The speed trap was a punishment. About a quarter mile from town, the speed limit on the highway dropped from fifty-five to thirty-five miles an hour. About half the people who drove by slowed down, but the other half blew past the sign at sixty or seventy miles an hour. I wouldn't have minded ticketing those guys but for one simple fact. Two years ago, some asshole from the County Council planted a big bush in front of the sign. You could hardly even see it anymore.

The speed trap wasn't about protecting pedestrians or other drivers. It was about revenue. Each ticket averaged two hundred and thirty-eight dollars, about half of which went to St. Augustine County. On a good day, someone working the speed trap might write ten or fifteen tickets. With the fair going on, I'd write that many in an hour. I'd also piss off half the drivers in the state. Bitching about it wouldn't help anything, though.

I changed into a uniform in the women's locker room, signed out a squad car, and drove out for my shift. Over the next eight hours, people cursed at me in at least four languages, two different men asked me out, three nuns scolded me on their way to the art fair, and at least two dozen men and women gave me the finger as they drove past. It wasn't how I wanted to spend my day.

By the time I finished my shift and drove back to my station, I wanted nothing more than to walk my dog, grab a drink, and take a long, hot bath. Instead, I sat at my desk and called Harry, my partner in the murder investigation of Megan Young. His cell rang a few times before he picked up.

"Harry, it's Joe. How you doing?"

"Hey, kid. I'm tired. I'm working a murder, and my partner got kicked off the case because she can't keep her temper under control."

If any of my other colleagues had called me kid or chastised me for losing my temper, they would have pissed me off. Harry had earned that right, though. He had almost forty years on the job and could retire with a full pension, but he stayed on because he liked the work. Not only that, he solved a lot of tough cases. I had learned more in my first week working with him than I had in two years of supervised training when I first joined the department.

"To be clear, I didn't lose my temper. Travis removed me from the case because a detective in St. Louis thought I had a conflict of interest. I don't. You guys made any progress?"

"Sort of," said Harry. "Delgado and Martin spent the entire day at the Pizza Palace. I've been interviewing the staff from Club Serenity again to see whether they saw anything."

I smiled to myself. "And by interviewing Club Serenity's staff, you mean you've been talking to strippers all day."

"It's a sacrifice I make for justice," said Harry.

"You find anything?" I asked, my smile waning.

"Not a damn thing. The girls were busy dancing or watching the fireworks when the victim died, and the bouncers and manager were busy watching the crowd to make sure nobody got too handsy with the girls without paying."

"I assume Delgado and Martin fared well at the Pizza Palace."

Harry laughed under his breath. "They haven't got shit, and they're both pissed. By the end of the day, they had yelled at the owner so much that he offered to pay the legal bills of his employees if they wanted a lawyer."

It shouldn't have, but hearing that made me happy.

"Did Dr. Sheridan finish his autopsy?"

"Yeah, but he didn't find a lot. Somebody shot the victim with a .300 Winchester Magnum round. She died instantly. Beyond that, he doesn't have much."

"Did he check her teeth?"

Harry paused and then drew in a slow breath. "Detective Delgado cancelled your request to check the victim's teeth against Megan Young's dental records. He didn't think it was necessary."

I sat straighter and shook my head. "He may not

agree with me, but that's just stupid. He took prints, right?"

"No matches in the system," said Harry. "Your victim was never arrested, she never joined the Army, and she never registered her prints with any government agency as far as we can tell."

Which didn't surprise me if she were Megan Young. Few drug dealers would have given up their prints to the government if they could help it. The foster care system might have had her prints, but the courts routinely sealed those files when kids turned eighteen. We wouldn't get access to those without a court order.

"This is ridiculous," I said. "The victim is Megan Young. Delgado isn't going to find her killer by harassing pizza delivery drivers."

"It is what it is," said Harry. "For what it's worth, the St. Louis County Prosecutor's Office agrees with you. They want Sheridan to give them access to the body so they can confirm her ID themselves."

"But Delgado's still sticking to his theory that she's Kiera Williams."

"Oh, yeah," said Harry. "God blessed Detective Delgado with a mind resistant to both common sense and facts."

I rubbed my eyes and nodded. "All right, then. I know you're busy, so I won't keep you all day. If you need anything, let me know."

I almost hung up, but then Harry told me to wait. He drew in a breath and then sighed.

"I talked to Amy Ledgerman in St. Louis," he said. "She told me about your relationship with Christopher Hughes."

I wasn't ashamed of my past, but I didn't tell people about it, either. My life was my own, and I decided who shared in it.

"I don't know what she told you, but I didn't have a relationship with Christopher Hughes."

He sighed. "I didn't say that well. She told me he assaulted you. I'm sorry, hon."

The line went quiet. I drew in a breath.

"Harry," I said, after a pause, "I like you a lot, and I like your family a lot. I don't need your pity, though. It happened. He hurt me, but I'm over it now. And if he didn't kill Megan, he shouldn't be in prison for her murder. That's it. End of story."

"You okay with him being released?"

I leaned back in my chair. "No, but I don't have a lot of choice in the matter, either."

"I guess you don't," he said. His voice brightened a moment later. "I'll be busy tonight, but Irene and Carrie are home. Carrie brought her boyfriend home from college. He seems like a nice kid. They're making a lot of food tonight for dinner, so if you want company, head over."

I forced myself to smile even though I didn't want to smile.

"I appreciate the offer, but Roger needs me at home. He gets lonely without me."

"Sure. If you need anything, let me know."

I wished him luck with his case and then hung up. My chest and arms felt heavy. That phone call had sucked out every ounce of energy I had. On a normal night, I would have grabbed dinner and a few shots at a bar nearby, but during fair week, the bars would be full to the rafters. I didn't want to see anybody. I wanted to be alone.

After checking my email one last time, I turned my computer off and got in my old truck to go home. Christopher Hughes was the lead story on St. Louis Public Radio. They didn't mention me, but they discussed Megan and Emily and said they had lived with Christopher for a time and that Christopher and his wife had been well-respected foster parents. They threw around the word *innocent* a lot. I wondered what numbskull had done their fact-checking.

The story was going national. Even Delgado would have to recognize that we had Megan Young in our morgue soon. The whole thing made me want to scream at the top of my lungs. These people had never met Christopher Hughes, but they were championing his cause as if he were some kind of hero who could do no wrong.

I didn't want to believe the man who raped me would get out of prison soon, but I couldn't stop it. Not only would they let him go, though, they'd expunge his record, clear his name, and give him a few million bucks for his time. I couldn't stop that or even slow it down, so I'd deal with it in the only way I knew how: I'd keep my head down, I'd keep my ass in gear, and I'd do my job. Until somebody invented a time machine, I couldn't change what had happened, but I sure as hell could prevent Christopher from hurting anyone else. That was why I had become a cop. He didn't know it, but Christopher had made me into the person I was.

One day, he'd regret that.

18

May 2006

The cop took me out of my English class and drove me straight to the county police headquarters in Clayton. Megan Young had been missing for a week, but everybody knew she was dead. Christopher had gone from rape to murder, which didn't surprise me in the least. After the things he had done, I hoped Christopher would die in prison, and I hoped he died screaming.

When we got to the station, the cop dropped me off out front and directed me to Lieutenant Julia Green on the front steps. She was in her forties and wore jeans and a navy blazer. She would have done well in the foster care system. With one glance, I knew not to mess with her. Maybe it was the way she kept her chin up, maybe it was the way she held the gaze of everyone who walked by, maybe it was the gun and badge at her hip. I couldn't say what it was about her, but I liked her before she said a word.

"Hey, Joe," she said. "Sorry to interrupt your class, but we've got some things to talk about."

"That's okay," I said. "I'm not into school."

She furrowed her brow and turned toward the building. She didn't tell me to follow her, but she didn't have to. My legs followed of their own accord.

"I've heard a little about you, and I thought you liked school," she said, glancing at me as we passed into the building. From the exterior, the police station almost looked like an old, red brick schoolhouse. Inside, though, it was a modern office building. We walked through a reception area to a bank of elevators. "You had good grades, at least."

I shrugged. "It stopped being important."

Julia hit the button for the third floor and glanced at me with disapproving eyes.

"For some people, school's not important," she said. "For you, it is. You're too smart to waste what you've got."

"Maybe I'm not as smart as you think," I said. She shrugged.

"Maybe you're right," she said. I didn't care what people thought about me, but that stung. Before I could respond, the elevator pinged as the door opened, and we walked into a busy open-concept office. There were desks pushed against one another in four-person groupings. Gray partitions offered a modicum of privacy and blocked noise.

"This is where the magic happens," said Julia. "We've got twenty-four detectives on staff. Homicide gets the headlines, but we get the job done up here, too."

"Are you important?" I asked.

"Nope," she said, smiling just a little. "I'm a woman doing her job."

By the deference people paid her, I would have said Julia undersold her position. We walked to a small office tucked away in the corner of the floor, where she had a view of the street below and a coffee shop across the way. I looked out the window while she sat down.

"Have a seat," she said.

"I'm fine," I said, continuing to look out the window.

"Sit down, Joe," she said, her voice a little sharper. "I don't like people hovering over me."

I turned around and crossed my arms but didn't sit.

"Why am I here?"

Julia considered me for a moment before crossing her arms and matching my posture.

"You're here because I wanted to give you an update on Megan Young."

"She's dead, isn't she?"

"Yeah."

Other people might have lied or tried to soften the blow somehow. I liked that she had been honest. I walked to a chair in front of her desk and sat down.

"Did you find her body?"

"No, but we found her blood in the trunk of Christopher Hughes's car."

"So Christopher killed her," I said. She nodded. "Figures."

"It's not your fault," she said. "In case you were wondering."

"I know that," I said, narrowing my gaze at her. "It's your fault. It's Mr. Ballard's fault. It's the judge's fault. It's her mom's fault. It's everybody's fault but mine. It wasn't Megan's fault, either. You people let us live with a monster."

"You're right," she said, her voice calm. "Christopher Hughes is a monster, but he won't hurt anyone again."

I wanted to believe that, but I couldn't. My fingers curled into fists, and heat rose to my face.

"How do you know?"

"We've got a strong case," she said.

"Tell me about it."

Julia blinked a few times, but then she pushed her chair back. I expected her to walk around the desk and escort me outside. Instead she reached into her bottom right desk drawer and pulled out a thick manila folder, which she put on the desktop in front of me.

"I can walk you through this, but it's a little graphic. You sure you want to see it?"

"Show me how you plan to put him away."

"Okay," she said, opening the document. We glossed over the first few dozen pages of typed reports before getting to anything interesting. "Diana Hughes—Christopher's wife—reported that Megan Young went missing on Monday, April 3rd. The call came in at four in the afternoon when Megan didn't come home from school. Subsequent interviews revealed that Diana had been out of town the weekend prior and that Emily Young was the last person to see her sister. That was on

Saturday, April 1st, at 1:00 in the afternoon."

"I remember that," I said, nodding. "Diana was pissed. Christopher kept telling her that Megan would show up, but she never did."

Julia nodded and turned a few pages. "Uniformed officers talked to Emily, Christopher, and Diana Hughes. They also visited her school and confirmed that Megan hadn't been in class. They referred the case to our missing-persons section."

"I never talked to a missing-persons detective," I said.

"You wouldn't have," she said. "Mr. Ballard took you out of the house the moment Megan disappeared. The missing-persons detectives read through the reports written by the uniformed officers, and then they talked to Christopher and Diana. With Diana's permission, they searched Megan's room. They found staining on her bedsheets, which they determined to be seminal fluid."

"It was Christopher's," I said. "That's where he raped her. He raped me on the couch in the living room."

She paused and then nodded. "Detectives at the time couldn't prove it was Christopher's, but it gave them reason to conduct a deeper search. They also called me and Travis in."

"And Travis is your partner?"

"Detective Travis Kosen," she said, nodding. "We found a significant quantity of blood in the trunk of Christopher Hughes's car. That blood evidence allowed us to acquire search warrants for his businesses and other property he owns."

"I didn't realize he owned a business," I said. I swallowed and looked at my hands, feeling small all of a sudden. "Nobody told me. He had this huge home, and I didn't even ask what he did. That probably makes me stupid."

"Sweetheart, you had enough to worry about in that man's home," said Julia. Normally when someone called me sweetheart, they were being condescending or rude. She wasn't, though. She seemed to mean it as a term of affection. I looked away when she smiled at me, unaccustomed to that kind of attention.

"What did you find?" I asked.

"Nothing," she said. "Mr. Hughes owns three bars in the city and two gas stations in the county. We didn't find anything anywhere."

"So you've got nothing on him except the blood," I said.

She raised her eyebrows. "Until yesterday."

"What happened yesterday?"

"Diana Hughes started divorce proceedings against her husband after we interviewed her. She kicked him out of the house and packed up his stuff. Yesterday, she cleaned the garage and found his underwear stash."

She didn't clarify, so I had to ask the obvious question.

"What's his underwear stash?"

"We found fourteen pairs of panties in a box in his garage, including one of yours and one of Megan's. You two had written your names on the waistband. In addition, he had hair clips, bracelets, necklaces, key chains, and rings belonging to other girls."

I balled my hands into fists and exhaled through my nose.

"He kept souvenirs after he raped us."

"That's what it looks like," she said.

I felt violated all over again. My lower lip trembled, and I tried to say something, but I couldn't get it past my throat.

"You need some water?" asked Julia.

"I need a gun so I can kill him."

"Don't tell me that," she said.

"If he had fourteen pairs of underwear, that means he raped fourteen girls."

"That's possible," said Julia, nodding. "We haven't been able to determine the owners of the other garments yet. Emily identified a ring, though. It belonged to her sister. She only took it off at night. Combined with the blood in his car, the semen and other body fluids in her bed, and the panties—all of which we can tie to Megan via DNA—homicide detectives brought him in for an interrogation.

"This morning, he signed a written confession to the murder of Megan Young. In exchange, he'll receive life in prison. We took the death penalty off the table."

My hands trembled, and my heart pounded.

"What about my rape?"

Julia drew in a breath and averted her eyes from mine

momentarily. "Your rape was harder to prove. Without forensic evidence, it would be your word against his. We know what Christopher did to you, and we're convinced that a competent judge would believe you, too, but that's not enough to convict somebody."

"That's bullshit," I said, shaking my head.

"That's life."

"I don't buy it," I said, crossing my arms. "If Christopher is a serial rapist, why did he keep our stuff? That's stupid."

She tilted her head to the side. "He might be stupid."

"You're the sex crimes detective. If Christopher is stupid, and he got away with raping fourteen girls, what does that make you?"

She held my gaze. "I'm sorry for what happened to you. If I could take it away, I would, but I can't. This is something you'll deal with forever. I know a counselor who's helped a lot of young women in your position if you'd like to talk to her."

I looked out the window so I wouldn't have to meet her gaze. "Counselors can't help. I've talked to enough social workers and psychologists and counselors to last a lifetime."

"You want to talk to a friend?"

"I don't have friends," I said. "I don't need them."

"That's too bad," she said. "I like talking to my friends."

"Good for you," I said. She smiled as she stood.

"Come on, kid," she said. "I'll walk you out."

I followed her out of the office and to the elevator.

"So what's the plan now?" she asked as we waited for a car to arrive. "You've got a couple of years of high school left. Are you going to college after that?"

"I was going to, but Christopher Hughes ruined those plans. Now I've got to start over and plan something new."

She looked as if she wanted to ask me something else, but our elevator car arrived before she could. I got on and hit the down button, hoping she would stay on her floor. She followed me in.

"I've got to escort you to the door," she said. "This is a secure building."

I said nothing until the doors closed. We were alone.

"What do you want?" I asked.

"A perfect pina colada would be nice."

She wanted me to laugh, but I didn't.

"What do you want with me?" I asked. "Why are you following me and asking me questions?"

"We clarified that," she said. "I've got to walk you outside. Then you're on your own."

"I'm used to being on my own."

"I've learned," she said. "So what are you doing after high school?"

I didn't want to answer, but the doors opened on the floor beneath us. A bunch of people got on, so I had to step closer to her.

"I'll join the Navy. I'll be in there for four years, and then I'll go to college once I'm out."

"That's a good plan," she said, nodding. I waited for her to continue. She didn't.

"But what?" I asked. She looked at me and raised her eyebrows as if she were unsure about something. "That's a good plan, but what? What else do you want to say?"

"You won't join the Navy," she said, shaking her head. "You'll go to college. Then you'll become a cop."

I laughed. "Because your detective work is so inspiring?"

"Well, that would flatter my ego, but that's not why I said it. You think like us. You're sixteen, and you're already as cynical as every other miserable asshole in this building."

Two people laughed, but none of the other passengers looked at us. I ignored them all until we reached the bottom floor. The doors opened onto the lobby, and everybody got out. I stayed put, so Julia put her foot in the doorway to keep the elevator door from closing.

"I know what you're doing," I said.

"Trying to kick you out of the building?"

"Trying to make me like you."

She snorted. "If that's how you interpret this, maybe you should join the Navy, sweetheart."

"Yeah," I said, walking out. "Maybe I should."

She let me cross the lobby and get to the front doors before she called out.

"Hey. Joe," she said. I turned around and crossed my arms so she'd know I wasn't interested in talking to her.

"What?"

"I'll keep in touch."

"Terrific," I said, trying to keep the hope out of my voice. She smiled and then turned toward her elevator. I walked out of the building. Julia must have called ahead because a uniformed officer was waiting for me outside. He drove me back to school. I should have spent the rest of the day stewing on the police department's failure to protect me and Megan, but instead, I thought about Lieutenant Julia Green. I liked her, which didn't make sense. It didn't matter, though. She'd forget me. Everybody else did.

Only, she didn't.

She called me that evening at the girls' home to ask how I was doing. I told her I was fine, and then I hung up. She called again two days later and asked the same question. Once more, I told her I was fine, and then I hung up. On Saturday, she came by the youth facility I was staying in and picked me up. I had dinner at her house. Her husband made hamburgers, and I played tag with her kids. Three months later, she and her husband became my foster parents.

Some people were lucky. They met their families the day they were born. It took sixteen years of pain and hardship to find mine. When I walked into Julia's office, I didn't know what she'd become to me, but meeting her was the best thing that had ever happened to me. I loved her with everything I had, but I couldn't get over my bitterness no matter how hard I tried.

Because meeting her had come with a price no one should have to pay.

19

Before I made it home, Trisha, my station's dispatcher, called my cell. I wanted to pretend I hadn't heard the phone ring, but she wouldn't have called without reason. Since I hated talking while driving, I pulled off the road near a copse of trees. The sun was still up, but the shadows were growing longer, and a cool stillness was settling in to replace the day's warmth.

"Trisha, yeah," I said, leaning back. "What's up?"

"I'm sorry, but I need you to head back in. It's not an emergency, but it's important."

I groaned and shut my eyes as I leaned my head back. "What happened?"

"Got a missing-persons case. She's sixteen, and she disappeared Monday. I'd give it to Harry, but he's busy with the Megan Young case. With the fair going on, it's a zoo here, and I need a detective. You're it."

I rubbed my eyes and nodded. As much as I wanted to go home, unexpected calls were part of the job.

"All right. Give me fifteen minutes. I'll be back."

"Thanks, Joe. I'll let the family know you're on your way."

I hung up and then sighed. So much for my relaxing night with a drink. I called Susanne, my neighbor, and waited through six rings for her to pick up. Her voice sounded high and inquisitive. We only spoke for a few moments, but she agreed to feed and water Roger. Susanne had a strict no-dog-inside policy at her house, so he wouldn't stay the night with her, but she'd take good care of him until I returned.

I drove back to town. Already, there were lines outside the restaurants and bars as tourists waited for tables, while families carrying picnic baskets and foldable chairs made their way to the park. A young woman wearing a Waterford College T-shirt played the violin on the sidewalk. Her case was open in front of her, and a small group crowded around her to listen. The sound of a bluegrass band warming up floated on the breeze.

I parked outside my station and rubbed my eyes, wishing I were at home. Every police department in the world took missing-persons reports, and the vast majority of them worked themselves out when the missing person came home from his vacation, business trip, or extended stay at a friend's house. Missing young people were problematic, but nothing Trisha had said concerned me too much. I wouldn't be looking for an eight-year-old who got lost while hiking with her family; my missing person was a sixteen-year-old young woman. More than likely, she was at a friend's house.

Even still, I'd do my best to find her. Her mom and dad deserved that.

When I got inside, Trisha smiled at me and then pointed to a middle-aged couple sitting on chairs in the waiting room. None of the drunks had vomited in my absence, so the place didn't stink. Just a whiff of beer and body odor. It reminded me of my college dorm when my roommate came home late on Friday nights.

I walked to the couple with my back straight as I tried to project a reassuring, calm demeanor.

"I'm Detective Joe Court. My dispatcher told me your daughter is missing."

"Yes," said the woman. She was in her mid-forties and had brunette hair held back by a tie. She was tall and had an athletic frame. There were crow's feet around the corner of her serious, blue eyes. A pink handkerchief twisted between her right index finger and thumb. She was nervous, but she was trying to keep herself together. "We're worried."

"She disappeared Monday. We hoped she'd be back by now, but she's not here. Our lawyer said we should talk to the police."

The speaker was her husband, I presumed. He was about the same age as his wife, and he wore a white button-down shirt and black slacks. Similar to the woman beside him, he was tall and thin. He looked like a basketball player, albeit one with thinning blond hair and fine lines around his lips. He looked as if he smoked. Smokers always got wrinkles around their lips at young ages.

Interesting that they had contacted a lawyer before

they contacted the police. I didn't see that too often and didn't know what it meant in this case.

"Okay," I said, nodding and taking a step back. "Let's go talk somewhere a little more private."

They followed me through the bullpen and to the conference room. Surprisingly for a police station, our conference room was the most comfortable room in the building. It had a tall, coffered ceiling and elaborate mouldings around the door. There were no windows, but the previous owners had painted the ceiling a cheery blue and hung huge bronze pendant lights on chains, giving it a much airier feel than it otherwise might have had.

I gestured to the conference table. The couple sat down, and I sat across from them. First thing, I introduced myself again and got their contact information. They were Jane and Michael Maxwell, and they lived in a prosperous part of town popular with upper-middle-class men and women who worked in St. Louis but wanted a country home. I wouldn't have wanted the commute, but the home they bought for half a million dollars here would cost them two or three million just thirty miles north. Plus, our schools were good. I understood the appeal.

"So, Mr. and Mrs. Maxwell, tell me about your daughter. What's going on?"

"She didn't come home after school on Monday," said Jane. "We thought she had gone out with friends. They did that if one of them had a bad day. I called and left a message, but she didn't answer."

I took notes and then glanced up.

"When you called, did her phone ring, or did it go straight to voicemail?"

Jane shook her head and blinked before shrugging. "I don't know. Does it matter?"

"It tells me whether her phone was on," I said. "If it's on, we can track her with it."

"It went straight to voicemail," said Jane. "But that's not surprising, either. She turns it off at school, and she might have forgotten to turn it on again."

"Sure, I can see that," I said, trying to avoid letting my skepticism enter my voice. I looked down at my notes. "And what's her name?"

"Paige Olivia Maxwell," said Michael. "Olivia was my mom's name."

"And she's sixteen years old, right?" I asked, glancing up again. Both parents nodded. Paige's age made this difficult. If she had been eleven or twelve, I would have called every officer in the county to look for her. At sixteen, I needed to take a different approach. "How's your marriage?"

Jane didn't seem to react, but Michael shook his head and closed his eyes.

"Our marriage is none of your business."

I glanced at him and smiled, but I didn't allow it to reach past my lips.

"It tells me about her home life. If you suspected someone had abducted Paige, you would have come on Monday. You came today, though. That tells me her absence didn't worry you. You think she ran away, and at sixteen, she ran for a reason. I'm trying to figure out what that reason is. If you cooperate, it makes everything easier. Okay?"

Neither responded for a few moments. Then Michael leaned forward.

"Our marriage is fine."

I glanced to his wife. She sat still.

"Jane?" I asked. Her eyes darted to her husband.

"He's sleeping with his secretary. Paige knew about it, and she hated him for it."

"Oh, Jesus," said Michael, closing his eyes. He stood and then rested his hands flat on the table while leaning forward. "I screwed up, but this isn't my fault. Don't you dare blame me for this."

"Not your fault?" asked Jane. "Your daughter hates you, and so do I. I'd leave, too, if I had anywhere to go. If you kept your dick in your pants, we wouldn't be here now."

"If you didn't nag me so damn much, I wouldn't need a girlfriend."

We had the door shut, so I let them yell at one another for a minute in case one of them yelled something pertinent. Mostly, they traded personal insults. If this thing happened at their house often, I could understand why Paige had left. After a few minutes, I whistled to get their attention.

"Okay, so there's tension at home," I said. "Here's what we'll do. You will both go to opposite ends of our waiting room. You will refrain from speaking to one another. While in our waiting room, you will both write a list of your daughter's friends and acquaintances, her email address, contact information, internet passwords, and anything else that could help me find your daughter. You will also detail your whereabouts on Monday from the time Paige went to school until now. Include a list of men and women who can verify your account.

"While you two do that, I will search your house."

Michael stood straighter and crossed his arms. "Why do you need to search our house?"

"To look for signs of a struggle or signs of a break-in. Most likely, your daughter ran away for a few days. It happens a lot at this age. Ninety-nine percent of the time, the kid comes home safe and sound. If there are signs someone abducted your daughter, this investigation will change, but that only happens if I'm allowed to conduct a search. So do I have permission to do my job and search your home?"

"Yes," said Jane, nodding.

Michael closed his eyes and held up his hands. "If there were signs of a break-in, we would have seen them ourselves, Detective. You don't need to go to our house."

I nodded as if that made perfect sense.

"I appreciate that you've looked, but I am a professional investigator. There might be subtle things you missed. For instance, a lock pick will leave scratches on a deadbolt. Furniture that's been pushed out of place might leave indentions on the carpet. Body fluids often can be seen with specialized equipment even if an assailant cleaned them up. I respect your desire for privacy, but your daughter's life is more important. If someone abducted her, we need to find out now. If you'd like, I can get a warrant."

He stood straighter and drew in a breath. "No need for a warrant."

"I hoped you'd say that," I said, standing. "Now, I'll need your address and a key."

Jane recited her address as her husband removed a key from his key chain. Before handing it over, he looked at me.

"There are business papers in my office I'd like to remain private."

I considered him for a moment. He was hiding something.

"If it's legal and unrelated to your daughter's disappearance, there would be no reason for me to share it with anyone."

He seemed to accept that because he nodded and gave me his key.

"Thank you," he said. "Please find my daughter."

"I will do everything I can," I said. I escorted the couple to the reception area, where I told Trisha what was going on. She gave each of them a clipboard, pencil, and paper. I hoped they wouldn't kill each other while I was out. I drove my truck to their house north of town. The Maxwells lived in a big brick house in the middle of an immaculate grass lot. Dense forest surrounded the property, giving them some privacy from the similarly sized home next door. The neighborhood had a single exit onto the highway. If someone had abducted Paige, a neighbor might have seen the car.

I parked in the driveway and walked around the exterior of the house, searching for broken windows, doors, or other obvious signs of entry, but everything looked intact. The front and rear doors both had sturdy brass deadbolts free of tool marks or other blemishes, and none of the windows on the first floor were unlocked.

I unlocked the front door and walked inside. The interior was clean and modern. A pink backpack rested on the ground beside the back door. I picked it up and carried it to the kitchen table.

Inside, I found an iPad—password protected—three textbooks, pens and folders, and a daily planner. This was interesting. Paige's parents said she had gone to school on Monday, but if she had, she would have brought her bag. Why was it here?

I flipped through the planner. From what I could see, she was vice president of the Art Club, she exercised regularly, and she attended after-school practices for the school's competition government team—whatever that meant.

She had filled out the entire week, including large blocks to go out with her friends on Friday and Saturday night. I wondered whether she would have done that if she planned to run away on Monday. As I closed the book, I noticed a signature on the front page.

Paige Lewis.

She had just written it once on the organizer's front flap. I pulled out my phone and called Trisha.

"Hey, it's Joe. Are the Maxwells still there?"

"Yeah, they're still here," she said. "I had to put them in different rooms because Michael kept trying to start fights with his wife. I don't like to advocate divorce, but they seem like good candidates for it."

"That was my assessment, too," I said. "Can you find Jane and ask whether Michael is her father? Also, ask whether the surname Lewis is familiar."

Trisha paused for a second, probably writing that down.

"Sure. You want to wait, or do you want me to call you back?"

"Call," I said. "I've got more work to do."

Trisha said she would do as I asked, so I put my phone in my pocket and walked.

The Maxwells' open-concept first floor had a dining room, kitchen, and living room all open to the entryway, while private rooms lay off a main hallway to the east. I stuck my head in doorways until I found the first-floor home office. Dark wood paneling covered the walls while French doors led out to a patio in the backyard. There was a couch and a desk and six file cabinets.

Michael might have stored something incriminating in those file cabinets, but I didn't have time to search them. Instead, I focused on his desk. Most of the drawers held office supplies, but he had locked the lower left one. When he gave me permission to search the house, I doubted Michael expected me to break into his desk, but I needed to see what he had.

I reached into my purse for my lock pick set. When I had first become a detective, Harry had taken me to meet a locksmith to learn how to pick locks. I didn't realize how helpful it would be at the time, but it had become one of the most useful skills in my toolbox. It took about a minute to get inside and open the drawer. At one glance, I knew why Michael had installed the lock.

He had surveillance photos of his wife making the beast with two backs with a younger man. He wasn't the only one stepping out on the marriage. If I had to guess, Michael had hired a private detective to take the pictures so he could get a better settlement in a divorce. Things at the house were worse than I'd expected. If the parents were feuding, I didn't blame the kid for running.

Before leaving, I locked the front door. Trisha called back as I turned my truck on.

"The girl's name is Paige Maxwell, not Lewis. When I asked about her paternity, her parents screamed at one another. They're both sitting in holding cells right now."

That'd make it easier to find them later if we had to.

"So Michael is Paige's father?" I asked.

"Jane says so. Michael isn't so sure," said Trisha. "And congratulations. Your probing questions have turned my lobby into *The Jerry Springer Show*."

I laughed a little and nodded. "And the Lewis name?"

"Girl's got a boyfriend named Jude Lewis. They go to school together."

I wrote the name down and made a mental note to call him when I could.

"The house is a bust. Paige's parents are jerks, but nobody broke in here. I think she ran because she didn't want to be around her mom and dad. We'll hand out her picture at roll call tomorrow, but I'm not worried."

"What do you want me to do with her parents?"

"Did they get violent with one another?"

"Nope," said Trisha. "But they screamed a lot."

"Then let them go. I've not found anything that makes me think Paige's life is in immediate danger. We'll look for her, but I think she'll come home soon. If she doesn't, we'll escalate this."

"Can do," said Trisha. "Will you be around if her parents want to talk?"

"No. If they want to talk to somebody, tell them to call a divorce lawyer. I'm going home."

20

I drove to my station to fill out a report and left at about nine. The town's bar and restaurants had their doors open, and live music flooded the street. On the forty-foot walk to my car, I heard jazz, blues, and bluegrass. St. Augustine wasn't usually that cosmopolitan.

I yawned and drove but didn't get over ten miles an hour until I hit the outskirts of town for fear of hitting a pedestrian. Children ran everywhere, and many of them carried glow sticks. Four boys I passed were playing with them as if they were swords. I thought nothing of it until I saw a guy selling them out of his food truck. Falafel may not have sold well, but I had to give him some props for the glow sticks. Kids seemed to love them.

I pulled into my driveway at twenty after. Roger must have been at Susanne's house still, so I grabbed a flashlight from inside before walking along the side of the road.

My day had not been fun, and my bathtub was calling my name. Fair week had just started, and already I felt as if I had run a marathon. I needed a break, and nothing beat a warm bath and a drink for relaxation.

When I reached Susanne's house, Roger bounded off the porch to me. I knelt in front of him and felt some of my day melt away. His tail wagged so hard as he licked my face that his entire body moved. Susanne heard the commotion and came outside, holding a shawl over her shoulders.

"He's always so happy when you come home," she said.

"And I'm happy to be home," I said, standing but not taking my hand off my dog's shoulders. "Thank you very much for feeding him. Everybody is working overtime right now."

"My pleasure," she said. "It's nice to talk to someone during the day."

As someone who lived alone, I understood what she meant. I loved my privacy, and I loved being able to do what I wanted when I wanted, but sometimes, it was nice to talk to somebody. I made a mental note to visit more often instead of sending my dog.

"Thank you again," I said. "I'm hoping tomorrow is better."

"Have you eaten dinner, sweetheart?" she asked. "I've got chicken and dumplings if you'd like some."

I thought of the bottle of wine I had hoped to open at home, but then I thought about sitting down and talking to someone I liked. It had been a while since I ate dinner with a human being. Maybe Susanne wasn't the only one who needed a friend.

"I'd love chicken and dumplings," I said.

Susanne smiled, and her entire face lit up.

"Come on in. I'll make you supper."

Roger lay down on the front porch, and I walked inside. Susanne had eaten earlier, but she sat with me at the table and listened as I talked about my day. She told me about the garden she planned to plant, and then she told me that a tulip poplar fell in the woods behind my house. She and Roger had gone for a walk earlier, and she thought the tree would make fine firewood if someone cut it up and let it season for a year or two.

We didn't talk about anything special, but I felt better than I had when I walked in. When I finished dinner, Susanne insisted on taking my plate to the sink herself. I joined her in the kitchen.

"Thank you for dinner," I said. "I didn't realize how much I needed a night with a friend."

When she turned around, she beamed at me. "You're always welcome at my table, Joe. Girls like us need to look out for one another."

I smiled and looked down.

"That's true," I said, nodding. "Goodnight, Susanne. We'll see you tomorrow."

"I'm looking forward to it," she said. "Roger's got work to do around here. I can't chase those rabbits away myself. They eat my seedlings."

I laughed and started toward the front door. Susanne walked beside me.

"Roger's getting a little old to be chasing rabbits, but I'll send him over and see what he can do."

"We all get old," she said. "Few of us get wiser, though."

"You're right," I said.

"I know I'm right. I'm a member of that rarified group who's gotten wiser."

I smiled. "Thanks for dinner. I'll talk to you tomorrow."

She nodded and took a step back. Roger and I left the house and walked into the darkness. We lived out in the country, so I didn't worry too much about cars. Instead, I looked for bobcats. My dog thought he was tough, but he was a sweet boy at heart. A real predator—a bobcat, mountain lion, or something else—would tear him apart.

I put my flashlight on and whistled as we walked, hoping that would scare away any animals who saw us. I had enjoyed the evening, but I still wanted my drink. Roger, though, didn't want to hurry. He kept his nose to the ground, looking for something. Most of my neighbors had dogs; one of them had probably walked by and peed on Roger's favorite spots. It happened a lot.

Then he slowed down, and the hair on his back stood on end.

We were two hundred yards from my house. Few animals walked this close to the house, so I put one hand on Roger's back and the other over the firearm on my hip.

"Easy, boy," I said. "Everything's fine."

Several hunters in the last year had reported seeing a mountain lion in the area, but the Missouri Department of Conservation couldn't confirm that we had one. The prospect of having big cats back in the area excited their scientists, but they didn't live in the country like I did. As someone who walked through the woods, I would have preferred to avoid having a two-hundred-pound predator in my backyard.

I slipped my hand from Roger's back to his collar as a deep, guttural growl came from his throat.

"What's out there?" I asked, scanning the horizon. Nothing moved at first, but then a man darted from the trees across from my house. Roger's growl turned into a bark. I held his collar tight as he tried to lunge forward. Ninety-nine percent of the time, Roger was a sweetheart who loved everyone he met. If he thought someone was a threat to me, though, he became a maniac.

The guy jumped in a car and drove off. Roger wanted to chase him, but that wouldn't end well for anybody, so I held on until he calmed down. Then he looked at me with his big brown eyes and licked his nose. I scratched him behind the ears, and he leaned into me.

"You are my brave protector, Sir Roger," I said, looking into his eyes and stroking the back of his head. His tail thumped against the top of my thighs. I broke eye contact with him and looked at the spot where I had seen the man standing. Then I sighed. "Let's see what this guy wanted."

Roger and I walked across the street. He smelled a few things and peed on some high grass. I flashed my light at the ground and looked around. The guy would have had a clear view of my front porch and truck from where he had stood. That was creepy. During another time of the year, I would have asked my department to send extra patrols by the house, but the evening shift during fair week had drunk drivers to arrest and bar fights to contain.

I wasn't worried. Roger had good ears and a bark that carried for miles. If anybody came near the house, he'd scare him off. And if Roger couldn't scare him off, I was a cop, and it was a terrible idea to sneak up on a cop's house.

I grabbed my keys and crossed the street. The house looked secure. Not only that, Roger had stopped growling. Even still, I checked the backyard and the windows to make sure they were locked, and then I searched the house to make sure nobody had broken in. Roger and I were alone, though.

I locked the front door, poured myself a tall glass of vodka, and started my bath. Within five minutes, I was relaxing in the tub. A John Coltrane album played on the small stereo in my bedroom. It felt good to relax.

Unfortunately, my cell rang before I could even finish my first drink. I would have ignored it, but Roger whimpered. He did that when the phone rang. My ring tone bothered his ears.

I reached out of the bathtub, grabbed my pants, and fished my phone out of the pocket. Before answering, I pointed it at the dog. He cocked his head to the side.

"I'm doing this for you, dude," I said, glancing at the

screen. I didn't recognize the number, but I answered anyway. "Yeah. This is Joe Court."

"Ms. Court, I'm Angela Pritchard. I'm a reporter with channel three in St. Louis. How are you doing today?"

My eyes closed, and a groan escaped my lips as soon as she introduced herself.

"I have no comment."

"I asked how your day was."

"I have no comment."

She paused before clearing her throat. "Well, I'm working on a story involving Emily and Megan Young. I understand you knew them."

"For the record, I have no comment on Emily or Megan Young."

"How about off the record?"

I sighed. "Off the record…I have no comment. Please don't call me again. In fact, who gave you this number?"

"I understand you lived with the victims, so I know it's difficult to talk—"

"I have no comment," I said, interrupting her. "If you won't answer my basic question, I won't answer yours. I'm going to hang up now."

"I want—"

I ended the call before she could say anything else. Then I drank the rest of my vodka and sat up straighter. My bath no longer relaxed me. If nothing else, the call put my stalker in context. If one reporter knew I had lived with Emily and Megan Young, the others would, too. My stalker was probably a journalist looking for a quote for a story.

I tossed my phone on top of my clothes and looked to the dog. He perked up.

"Mommy's going to have another drink. You see anybody outside tonight, rip his nuts off."

21

The house was huge, more a monument to its former owner's ego than it had ever been a home. Its front facade looked like a bizarre mating of the Parthenon and a classic red brick schoolhouse.

Sherlock didn't understand the appeal of living in a house like that, but he had little in common with its previous owner. Christopher Hughes would have described himself as a visionary. Sherlock knew him to be a lecherous moron, though. To use the foster care system to identify vulnerable girls he could recruit to work in his whorehouses made business sense, but it was repugnant. Sherlock had complimented Randy Shepard on his role in the endeavor earlier, but he hadn't meant it. He and Hughes were lucky the police hadn't caught them and sent them to prison for life.

That wasn't Sherlock's concern that evening, though. He parked his twelve-year-old Mercedes in the circular drive out front and walked to the portico. The front lights popped on. Whether someone had seen him, or whether Christopher Hughes's ex-wife had installed a motion sensor, he couldn't say.

Before getting out of the car, he reached to the seat beside him for the hammer and tarp he had purchased earlier that day. This would be a long night. He should have picked up coffee before coming over. As Sherlock walked to the front door, he yawned and set his purchases on the ground before knocking.

Diana Hughes opened the door a few minutes later. She was younger than her ex-husband and better looking. Her straight black hair cascaded down to her shoulders, drawing his attention to her chest and the pink, silk robe she wore. Her hair was still wet from a recent shower, and her cheeks were flushed with heat. Her brown eyes locked on his. Her gaze was probing and intelligent. Why she'd married Christopher Hughes, Sherlock would never know.

"Yes?" she asked.

"I'm James Holmes," he said. "I'm your ex-husband's attorney. He's asked me to come and talk to you."

She crossed her arms. "I'm not sure how much I have to say to my ex-husband's attorney, but I hear the state plans to release him from prison soon. Is that your doing?"

"It is," he said, nodding. "Does that upset you?"

"Christopher deserves to die in prison for the things he's done."

"Many people deserve to die in prison," said Sherlock. "Part of my job is making sure they don't get their just deserts."

"And do you like this job?" she asked.

Sherlock allowed his eyes to travel up and down her

body. She was a remarkable woman.

"It has its perks."

Her lips parted as they drew upwards into a demure smile.

"Why are you here, Mr. Holmes?"

"Christopher asked me to come and kill you," he said, tilting his head to the side. "He wanted you to die screaming."

She didn't react for a moment. And then she took a step back. Sherlock took that as an invitation to come inside, where he kicked off his shoes. He had stepped in dog shit outside a detective's house earlier that day, and Diana wouldn't have appreciated him tracking dog droppings inside the house.

Polished marble covered the floor while a winding wooden staircase led to the second floor. An elegant bronze chandelier hung from the ceiling, bathing the room in a warm yellow light. Sherlock shut the door behind him, leaving his tools on the porch. They'd be fine for a while.

"How much did Christopher offer you to kill me?"

"Fifty grand," said Sherlock. "I balked at first, but then he said he wouldn't mind if I slept with you first."

She brought her hands to the tie that held her robe shut.

"Is there anything I could do that would persuade you to let me live?" she asked, untying the knot. The robe slipped open, exposing her athletic form.

"I can think of a thing or two," said Sherlock. He

kissed her and felt her body against him.

"I've missed you," she whispered as she pulled her lips away from his.

"I've missed you, too," he said, smiling. "Sorry I haven't been able to come by for a few days. Work's been keeping me busy."

She took his hand. "Come on. I want to show you what you've been missing."

She led him upstairs where they made love in her bedroom. Afterwards, as he held her close, she looked at him and sighed, their hands and legs intertwined.

"You are so much better than my ex-husband. I wish I had met you before I met him. Life would have been so different."

Sherlock looked around the spacious master bedroom. "You might not have had all this."

"I wouldn't have wanted all this," she said, kissing his neck. He thought she wanted another round, but then she pulled her head back. "So what did you leave on the porch?"

He grunted, remembering everything he still had to do that night.

"A hammer. Christopher said he hid money inside the wall in the master bedroom closet."

She nodded and looked to the closed closet door.

"He started as a builder, you know. He was a finish carpenter when I met him, but he had all these big ideas about opening his own business. When he renovated the closet, I assumed he was feeling nostalgic."

Sherlock nodded and swung his legs off the side of the bed. "Did you see my pants?"

"They're in the hallway," she said, stretching and arching her back. He wanted to make love to her again, but he had work to do first. He swung his legs off the bed and dressed in the hallway. Diana sat up in bed and held the blanket over her chest. "Come back to bed, honey. It's late."

"It's never too late for money, darling," he said, winking. She rolled her eyes and lay down again as he walked to the front door to retrieve his hammer and tarp. When he returned, Diana was in the restroom, showering. He laid the tarp on the floor and hammered the wall, breaking the drywall. The shower turned off, and Diana's voice called out.

"Are you breaking the walls open at midnight?"

"Christopher is my client. I have to find out whether he's lying."

Instead of answering, she turned the shower back on. Sherlock kept hammering and tearing away sheets of drywall. The tarp caught most of the mess, but he'd still need a Shop-Vac to clean the carpet. If Christopher had hidden a quarter-million cash in the walls, he wouldn't mind buying one at all.

After opening holes on every wall, he found what he had been looking for: plastic-wrapped straps of cash. He pulled them out. There were five bricks, each of which held twenty-five bundles of fresh twenty-dollar bills.

He carried them into the bedroom and tore open the

plastic on two of the bricks. A hundred thousand dollars cash spread over the bed. Another hundred and fifty thousand remained wrapped in plastic.

"Diana," he called. She came to the bathroom door a moment later with a towel wrapped around her ample chest. Her eyes grew wide.

"That's a lot of money," she whispered. "Christopher gave you this money to kill me?"

Sherlock nodded. "Yep."

She let her towel drop before lying down and pulling the money overtop herself and smiling.

"I feel like we should celebrate."

"I kind of feel like that, too," he said, unbuttoning his shirt. Once he had removed his clothes, he climbed onto the bed beside her. As they made love on their cash, she bit his ear and moaned.

"When Christopher gets out of prison, you've got to kill him."

He pulled his head away from her. "You want to talk about him now?"

"You're all I want to talk about," she said. "But if he's alive, he won't let us keep his money."

Sherlock cupped her cheek with his hand.

"You needn't worry about him. I'll never let him hurt you again."

"Are you going to kill him, then?"

Sherlock shook his head. "No, I'll let the police do that for me."

22

Roger's snoring woke me up a little before six the next morning. I tried to roll over and go back to sleep, but his snoring was still so loud it almost shook the bed. I tried putting a pillow over my ears next, but that didn't work, either. I thought about waking him up and kicking him out of the house, but he looked so content I didn't have the heart.

I grabbed a thick bathrobe from my laundry hamper and crept out of the room, being careful to avoid kicking the wooden stairs Roger used to climb to the bed. My vet had told me that dogs at his age declined quickly and that I needed to prepare myself, but I couldn't think about life without him. He was a dog, but he was my buddy. I loved him.

It was too early for such maudlin thoughts, though, so I changed into some yoga pants and a sweatshirt and ran on the trails in the woods behind my house. Hard alcohol at night and hard exercise in the morning made my life manageable. The exercise woke me up, and the liquor put me down. Combined, the two kept me from dwelling on thoughts I had no reason to dwell upon.

After forty-five minutes on those wooded trails, my lungs loosened, my legs grew tired, and sweat dripped down my forehead and into my eyes. Dirt and bits of dried leaves covered my arms, neck, and legs, but I felt well. When I got home, Roger stretched on the back porch, having come out of the doggy door. Then he yawned and lay down again. It was a tough life he led.

I fed Roger, made a pot of coffee, and sat down on the back porch to watch the world wake up. It would have been a pleasant morning had my cell phone not rung at ten after seven. I sipped my coffee and let the call go to voicemail without looking at the screen. When it rang again two minutes later, I groaned to myself and looked at the screen.

Green, Julia.

"Hey, Julia," I said, upon answering. "You rarely call this early. Everything okay?"

"Everything's fine," she said. "I needed to catch you before work. Are you alone?"

"Are you asking whether I picked up a man in the bar for a wild night of anonymous sex?"

Julia hesitated. "I didn't think you did that kind of thing."

"I don't."

Julia said nothing for a second. "Are you happy, sweetheart?"

"That's why you're calling? I like living alone. I've got friends, I've got Roger, I've got everything I need. That's all I have time for."

She sighed.

"I want you happy."

"I like my life," I said. "I'm not lonely if that's what you're worried about."

"That worries me, but it's not why I called," she said. "We need to talk about work."

I closed my eyes and clenched my jaw before speaking.

"Is this about Detective Ledgerman?"

"No," she said. "Not directly, at least. Our coroner's office has been working with Dr. Sheridan, your coroner. He sent over dental X-rays of the victim who died in St. Augustine. We compared those dental X-rays to ones of Megan Young and got a match."

I blinked and drew in a breath. "The detective on the case here has been operating on the theory that a pizza delivery driver killed her in some kind of failed robbery. He won't appreciate hearing that."

"I'm sure he'll get over it. The story is already going national. We've got a truck from CNN parked on Forsyth Boulevard right now. Christopher Hughes's attorney filed a petition of habeas corpus last night on Christopher's behalf. Christopher's confession complicates things, but he didn't kill Megan Young."

"He may not have killed her, but he hurt people."

"I know," she said. She paused. "He's getting out. A rep from the governor's office called last night, and somebody from the DOJ called this morning. If we don't move to vacate the charges against him, there'll be riots."

The Girl in the Motel

I blinked and drew in a deep breath. "He's in prison for a crime he didn't do. I get it. When are you going to charge him with rape?"

"We're not," she said. "The prosecutor thinks he's spent enough time in prison. The county is going into damage-control mode. Hughes's current lawyer claims we coerced his client into signing a confession he didn't understand. He's already filed a civil lawsuit against the county and state. The world's watching us. We don't want a riot on live TV. The county is already in negotiations to settle."

"I see," I said, nodding as a cold chill passed through me. "So they'll throw the police under the bus and pay Hughes millions. That sounds about right."

"It sucks," said Julia. "Everything about this is wrong. I want to kill the guy as much as you do, but we can't. He's been in jail twelve years, but he's getting out today. It's already on the docket. Andy—the prosecutor—will drop all the charges against Christopher at nine this morning. He'll be a free man by noon. With luck, he'll take his money and move to Hawaii or Florida. He'll be someone else's problem."

"I don't want to kill him. I want to see him in prison."

She paused. "I'm sorry, but it won't happen."

"I'm sorry, too," I said, clearing my throat. "Thanks for calling. I need to get ready for work."

"No, you don't," she said. "Take the day off and come home, sweetheart. Your father and I love you, and we're here to support you."

She meant it, too. I could hear it in her voice. My eyes grew moist, so I blinked until a tear fell.

"I appreciate that, and I love you guys, too," I said. I coughed so she wouldn't hear the catch in my throat. "But it's fair week. If I stay home, someone else has to work a double shift. That wouldn't be fair for anybody."

She sighed. "Okay. If you need me, call me anytime. I'll have my cell phone with me all day."

"I know. I'll call you later."

Before she hung up, she told me she loved me again. For a moment, I sat there, watching the trees sway in the breeze and listening as the birds sang. Then I drank the final sip of my coffee and petted Roger's head. My throat felt tight, but I couldn't let this bother me. I coughed and blinked away the tears that threatened to fall.

I'd go to work, and then I'd come home and get drunk. People might frown at that, but I didn't care. Life was about survival. You either made it through the day, or you didn't. I'd make it to tomorrow, and then I'd make it through the next day and then the next day. Because that was who I was. I was a survivor. Christopher Hughes couldn't hurt me anymore, and I planned to make damn sure he didn't hurt anyone else.

23

I showered, got dressed, and threw a ball to Roger for a few minutes before heading to work. It wasn't even eight in the morning, so St. Augustine was just waking up. A bar owner was hosing off the sidewalk in front of his establishment on Main Street, and a few tourists sauntered to diners and restaurants for breakfast.

My phone call with Julia had thrown off my schedule, so I had missed the morning roll-call meeting once again, which wouldn't endear me to either my boss or anyone else in the station. I skipped my usual stop at Rise and Grind and went to work, where I found my boss —Travis—in the conference room along with Detectives Delgado and Martin. All of them sat around a table strewn with documents and photographs, most of which focused on Megan Young. When he saw me, Delgado's face went red.

"You missed roll call again," he said. "That's two strikes. What do you think happens at three?"

"I'm not sure. Maybe I'll turn on the news and learn I screwed up a murder investigation because I refused to listen to a colleague."

Delgado didn't get the chance to speak before Travis escorted me out of the room. When we reached my desk, he crossed his arms.

"What did you hope to accomplish with that conversation?"

"I had hoped Delgado and Martin would listen and pull their heads out of their asses," I said. "Megan Young was my case before they took it. I was right, and they were wrong. If I were still on the case, we'd be days closer to finding our murderer. We might have even been able to save our department some embarrassment. Instead, I'm sidelined to working the speed trap. Is that what I'm wasting my time on today?"

He paused before speaking.

"You're close to insubordination."

"I don't care. Delgado and Martin can do the job, but I'm better. I'm not bragging; I'm stating a fact. You know it, and I know it. That should be my case."

He sat on a nearby desk. "You're too close to it."

I shook my head and tried to keep my voice level and strong.

"My proximity to the case gives me insight other people can't possess. From what Harry tells me, those two clowns in the conference room were ready to start waterboarding a pizza delivery driver yesterday. They should have been following up on Megan Young. Instead, they wasted everybody's time and harassed some poor kids trying to make a buck at their after-school jobs."

Travis drew in a breath and raised his eyebrows while

looking down.

"Delgado and Martin had their own ideas about the investigation. They were wrong, but I'm not sure what I would have done differently."

"Then you would have screwed up, too," I said. "I had already asked Dr. Sheridan to check the victim's teeth against Megan Young's records. Delgado told him not to. Even if the guy doesn't like me, even if he thinks I'm an idiot, he should have let the process work."

Travis uncrossed his arms and rested his hands on either side of him. His eyes locked onto mine.

"You're right. They should have listened to you," he said. "Since they didn't, we all have to deal with the consequences. This isn't some personal vendetta, though. They talked to witnesses who saw a pizza delivery driver at the Wayfair Motel at the time of Megan Young's murder. They followed the evidence and did their jobs."

"They should have let Dr. Sheridan do his job, too," I said. "And this is personal, Travis. Delgado has had it out for me ever since I became a detective. He's patronizing, misogynistic, and mean. I've tried to talk to him about it, but he ignores me. If we had an HR department, I'd talk to them. But we don't have an HR department. We've got you. You're the boss. He's your employee. Deal with him."

Travis looked down. He bit his lip before speaking.

"You remind me of Julia when you say things like that."

"Then respect me as much as you respect her and do something about an asshole under your command."

He looked up and raised his eyebrows while nodding.

"I'll talk to him. Meantime, I need you to work a missing-persons case. Boy's name is Jude Lewis. Parents came in early this morning."

I walked around my desk, opened the top drawer for a notepad, and then flipped through pages of interview notes.

"He's Paige Maxwell's boyfriend. Her parents reported her missing last night. I think they ran off together."

"I see," said Travis, standing. "Talk to the parents. Trisha has their contact information."

"Does this mean I'm off the speed trap?"

He nodded. "You're off the speed trap. You're too close to the Megan Young case, so I stand by my decision to take you off it. That said, I'll make sure you have access to Delgado and Martin's reports. Maybe you'll see something they don't."

"Helen Keller could see things they don't."

Travis nodded and then stood. "Respect goes both ways, Detective."

I softened my voice. "Yeah. Message received."

"Good," he said before walking away.

I spent the rest of the morning talking to Doug and Karen Lewis, Jude Lewis's parents. When I told them Paige Maxwell was also missing, they seemed relieved. They knew Paige had difficult circumstances at home, so they weren't surprised that she and Jude might have gone away for a while.

Even though I suspected the two of them were

together and safe, I dug into both of their lives. I looked into their bank accounts and found that they had both withdrawn several hundred dollars. I checked on their cell phones and found that both were off and inaccessible. Then I talked to their friends. Nobody admitted knowing where the two kids were, but their friends all agreed to call me if they heard from them. Next, I called two dozen hospitals to make sure they hadn't admitted anyone who matched the description of Paige or Jude. And last, I contacted the Missouri Highway Patrol to ask them to look for Paige's white Ford Focus.

Beyond that, I couldn't do much. If they wanted to hide, we wouldn't find them. More than that, nothing I had found told me they were in trouble. They were two kids in love, and they wanted a break from the stresses of their lives. I couldn't blame them. If we hadn't found them by the week's end, I'd worry, but for now, the two of them could have their fun.

I left the high school where I had interviewed Jude's friends at about noon, and my stomach was rumbling. On a normal day, I would have picked up a sandwich at Able's Diner for lunch, but I didn't want to wait in line—not when I had other options, at least. I pulled out my phone and called Trisha at work. When she answered, there was a commotion in the background. That wasn't too uncommon in a police station.

"Hey, it's Joe. I'm going to run by the grocery store and pick up lunch. You want anything?"

"Lunch? No," she said, sounding surprised. "I need

you to get down here."

"Something wrong?"

"Yeah," she said. "Get down here. Lights and sirens."

My old truck didn't have lights or a siren, but I turned my key in the ignition. "I'm on my way. See you in a few."

24

When I reached my station, a few dozen protestors stood on the sidewalk out front. Some chanted, while others booed. Two men in suits stood at the top of the steps while Sasquatch and two other St. Augustine uniformed officers tried to keep the crowd at bay. Four news crews —including one from CNN—filmed everything.

I parked and got out of my car, not knowing what the hell was going on until one of the camera crews turned toward me. Then a familiar-looking woman sauntered toward me from a news van near the street. Her hair, makeup, and clothes were impeccable, and she walked with a quiet confidence born from years of practiced performance. She held her hand out.

"Angela Pritchard," she said. "We spoke on the phone. I'm glad to meet you."

I glanced at her and then to the crowd.

"Pleasure's all mine," I said, ignoring her outstretched hand and walking toward the building. Pritchard's smile didn't waver, but she couldn't keep her annoyance out of her eyes. I didn't care. I directed my focus toward the two men on the steps. James Holmes and Christopher Hughes. My heart pounded against my chest. Julia had told me Christopher would get out, but to see him on the streets again made a knot grow in my gut and my fingers tremble. My throat felt tight, and I could feel my breath grow shallow.

Even twelve years after I had last seen him, even with a gun at my hip and a badge on my belt, he terrified me. I tightened my hands into fists so he wouldn't see me tremble as a cold sweat formed all over my body.

Travis, my boss, came down the steps and pushed his way through the crowd toward me. Most of the protestors let him go, but one shoved him back. Sasquatch pulled the boss from the crowd while the other officers blew their whistles and removed collapsible batons from their belts.

"Everybody stop. We're not doing this on TV," I said, hurrying forward. The crowd, for whatever reason, parted around me. Sasquatch and the boss were heading up the steps. I grabbed Officers Simpson and Ortega by their elbows and backed them away from the crowd. The civilians yelled but didn't follow. Our officers took the hint and kept going up the steps. Then I looked to Sherlock and Hughes. "You two, inside."

"You don't get to order us around, miss," said Sherlock. "We're not like your jackboots."

I looked over my shoulder to the crowd. They hadn't picked up rocks yet, but several of them carried signs on wooden poles. This would get ugly if they used them as cudgels.

"Inciting a riot is a crime," I said. "And I doubt you

got a permit for this demonstration. We don't have the manpower here to keep you safe, so I'd get inside if I were you."

Sherlock protested, but Hughes put a hand on his lawyer's elbow. Then he turned to the crowd.

"Detective Court has a point," he said, looking over the heads of the crowd to the camera crews just beyond. "I'm here to put my life back together. Sheriff Travis Kosen will receive punishment for his crimes in time, but that's not my concern. I'm here to talk to my foster daughter. Thank you for your support, but please respect my privacy and the privacy of my family. I will release a formal statement through my attorney later."

After speaking, he held his elbow toward me as if he wanted me to escort him inside. Even the thought of touching him made me feel nauseated, but I was a professional. I ignored his elbow and walked in front of him and pulled open the glass door to let him into the lobby. He and his lawyer took the hint and walked in.

Travis and our other officers waited for us. My boss leaned against the front desk and crossed his arms. He was trying to play it cool, but the muscles of his jaw were tight, and an artery on his forehead throbbed with every beat of his heart. His skin was flushed, and there were tight beads of sweat on his neck.

Christopher Hughes looked delighted by the attention. He looked around the room before focusing on me.

"You've done well for yourself, Joe," he said. "I'm

glad."

"Don't talk to her," said Travis, stepping in front of me. I didn't care for chivalry, but I appreciated his presence. I might have gone for the knife tucked in my belt if I had been alone. "As the elected sheriff of St. Augustine County, I'm here to answer your questions and listen to your concerns. You have my full attention. I can bring in the county prosecutor or county attorney for questions if we need them."

"As my client stated outside, Sheriff," said Sherlock, "we're not here to confront anyone. We're here as a courtesy to notify your department that my client intends to move to the county. The government has ruined his life for twelve years. He wants to move somewhere quiet and comfortable. St. Augustine is perfect for his needs.

"Due to the circumstances, my client has unique security requirements. The state has dropped all charges against him, but the courts can't silence rumors. Already, my client has received dozens of threats. We would appreciate if you could investigate them."

"We're busy," I said, speaking without waiting for my boss to give an answer. "Why don't you use some of that settlement money you're getting from St. Louis County to hire a private security team? It might be easier that way."

Travis held up a hand to prevent me from saying anything else.

"We try to keep everyone in our county safe. If someone has threatened you, we'll investigate that threat to the best of our abilities."

"I know you will," said Sherlock, nodding. "All the same, we'd feel much more comfortable if Detective Court gave these matters her personal attention. Considering the lawsuit my client has filed against you, Sheriff, we'd like someone else to conduct those investigations."

My face felt hot, and every muscle in my body trembled. For years, I had dreamed of confronting Christopher. I thought I'd tell him how he hurt me and how I had overcome all that pain. I'd tell him he made me stronger than I ever could have been before. Seeing him in front of me, though, made nightmares I thought I had forgotten real. My muscles trembled, and I felt like a thousand tiny spiders were crawling up my back. I couldn't stop moving my fingers, so I crossed my arms tight and hid my hands beneath my biceps. My heart raced.

"You don't get to tell me what to do," I said, looking to Christopher and hoping my voice didn't catch in my throat. "I'm not a little girl anymore."

"We know that, Detective," said Sherlock before his client could say anything. "Consider it a token of our esteem that we've made this request."

Travis stepped in front of me once more, this time blocking my view of Christopher. My shoulders slumped, and my heart slowed. My colleagues would wrestle Christopher to the ground if he so much as looked at me wrong, but he still made me feel ill.

"As Detective Court's commanding officer, I decide

what she will or will not investigate," said Travis. "I will take your request under advisement, but I cannot guarantee I will act upon it. Police work is complicated and ever changing. I will assign my officers to the assignments I feel best fit their capabilities and schedules. Clear?"

"Sure," said Sherlock, smiling that vapid, empty grin of his. He looked to Christopher. "I believe we've said what we need to say."

Christopher peered around Travis's side to look at me. "I'd like to talk to Joe in private, if I could."

Most of my colleagues didn't know what Christopher Hughes had done, but Travis did. Hughes and Sherlock did, too. Travis crossed his arms and shook his head.

"Not today," he said. "Not in my station. I think it's about time you left."

"Are you sure?" asked Christopher. He licked his lips. My stomach and throat tightened, and I balled my hands into tight fists. "I'd say Joe and I have a lot to talk about. She's the only family I have left. Plus, if she plans to investigate the threats made against me, it would be helpful if she and I could establish rapport now."

I drew in a long breath. As much as he scared me, I was still a police officer. I was in control here, not Christopher. I counted to five and forced the muscles in my legs, back, and shoulders to relax.

"It's all right, Travis," I said. "He's right. He and I should talk."

Travis hesitated and looked at me. "You sure?"

I nodded. "I am."

"All right," he said. "Trisha, please escort Mr. Hughes and Mr. Holmes to the conference room."

"Just me," said Christopher. "My attorney can stay in the lobby."

"I don't think—" began Sherlock, taken aback.

"Shut up, James," said Christopher, glaring at his lawyer. "I'd like to talk to my foster daughter in private."

"Fine," I said. "We'll talk in private. No lawyers."

Travis didn't like it, but he nodded to Trisha. She led Christopher through the bullpen to the conference room. I followed, but Travis caught my forearm before I could take more than a few steps. Christopher stopped to watch us with a curious smile on his face. My boss lowered his voice.

"Leave your firearm at your desk," he said. "Trisha and I will wait outside the room. If he provokes you—and he will try—do the right thing and walk away. You have nothing to prove."

The advice was sound, but I pulled my arm away as if I were angry, anyway. Christopher raised his eyes. He might have even smiled a little. Good. That was the reaction I wanted. Even now, the memory of what Christopher had done made me quake, but he hadn't broken me. He thought I was a terrified child. I wasn't, and I planned to use his ignorance against him. The more emotional I seemed, the more likely he would drop his guard. This was theater now.

"This isn't about proving anything," I said. I lowered

my voice so Christopher couldn't hear us. I pounded my index finger on a nearby desk as if I were angry. "Sherlock's private investigator went looking for Megan and Emily a week ago. Days later, they were dead. Somehow, Christopher is involved with this. He thinks he's invulnerable, so he'll be cocky and stupid. He thinks I'm the same little girl he assaulted fifteen years ago. He thinks I'm volatile, angry, and easy to manipulate. I can use that. I will break him before he has any idea what I'm doing. Now hold out your hand and try to look annoyed."

Travis's eyes locked on mine. He blinked a few times and then held out his hand. I clenched my jaw and then shook my head before removing my firearm from its holster and handing it to him.

"Happy?" I asked.

He pulled back the receiver to remove the round I had chambered that morning. Then he slid out the magazine.

"Your weapon will be here when you're out."

"You're a dick, Travis," I said. He raised his eyebrows in surprise, but I winked and turned around before he could say anything. When I saw Christopher again, he had an amused smirk on his face. That disappeared, though, and he gestured toward the conference room.

"After you, Mary Joe," he said.

"Just Joe," I said, stepping past him. Inside the conference room, I walked to the far side of the table, putting it between us—just as someone scared of the man opposite her might. Christopher pulled the door shut and checked me out as if I were a prostitute. He did everything but smack his lips.

"You've grown up, Joe," he said.

"Why are you here?" I asked, crossing my arms.

He held out his arms as if he wanted a hug, but he was smart enough to stay well away from me.

"It's been twelve years. I wanted to see you."

"I'm not afraid of you," I said. "You used to scare me, but you can't hurt me anymore."

He took a step toward me. I took a matching step back as a shiver passed through me. Christopher smiled. I wanted to knock that grin off his face, but I couldn't. Not yet, at least.

"I'm glad you're not afraid."

"Please leave me alone," I said, my voice a whisper. He laughed and took another step forward. He smelled like mint toothpaste.

"You have turned into a gorgeous young woman," he said. "You know, I wouldn't have made it in prison if not for you. Every time life got hard, I thought about you and the things we did together."

I walked to the head of the table.

"Stay where you are," I said. "You make another move, this meeting's over."

He held up his hands and nodded. "You're in charge, sweetheart. I thought you'd like to know the impact you had on my life. That's all."

"Terrific. You can leave now."

He smiled and paced the room but stayed away from

me.

"You weren't the only beautiful girl on my mind, though," he said. "I was so sad to hear about Megan and Emily. It was hard to forget Megan's gorgeous green eyes."

In an instant, I knew I had him, but I couldn't let him see that.

"I'm not scared of you," I said, forcing a tremble into my voice. The smug asshole smiled.

"Sure you're not," he said, walking around the table, stalking me like an animal. I took a step back. "Do you remember that night you pissed the bed? I didn't even have to touch you."

If I lived to a thousand, I'd never forget that night. He had made me feel helpless and scared and weak. Travis had good reason to take my gun. I would have drawn it if I'd still had it. I swallowed hard enough that my throat moved.

"If you're just here to reminisce, it's time to go," I said. He stopped walking and then sighed.

"You're right. My lawyers and I have many people to visit today. I'll see you around, Joe."

"I'm looking forward to it," I said, my lips straight and thin. He left the room, almost dancing. Trisha and Travis both came in, but I held my finger to my lips, stopping them from speaking until Christopher was far enough away he wouldn't hear us. Then I looked to Trisha. "I need the autopsy report from Megan Young."

Trisha looked to Travis. He blinked and then crossed

his arms, confused.

"Why do you need the autopsy report?"

"I need to check something," I said. "And tell me you were recording my conversation."

"We filmed it," he said, nodding. "Why?"

"Give me the autopsy report, and I'll tell you."

"Okay," he said, glancing to Trisha and nodding. "We'll give you access to it."

Travis and I followed her out of the room and to the front desk. Christopher Hughes and his lawyer were just leaving to the adulation of the crowd outside. I knew I'd be seeing footage of that on the news later, but I didn't care. I had him.

We didn't have the physical autopsy file—although we could have requested it from the Medical Examiner's Office. Instead, we had a digital document complete with pictures and video. Since booting me off the Megan Young investigation, Travis had limited my access to that file until now. I scanned through it at Trisha's computer with my boss at my side.

"What are you looking for?" asked Travis.

I ignored him until I came to the medical examiner's written description of the body.

"Christopher said she had beautiful green eyes," I said. "According to Dr. Sheridan, she had brown eyes, but she wore green-tinted contacts at the time of her death."

"Okay," said Travis. "Why is that significant?"

"I don't know what kind of health insurance kids in foster care had twelve years ago, but it wouldn't have provided colored contact lenses," I said. "He's seen her."

Travis considered this and then nodded. "Even if that's true, he couldn't have killed her. He was in prison at the time of her death."

"Then he hired someone to kill her," I said. "Plenty of professional shooters take pictures of their victims to prove they did the job."

"If we confront him, Hughes will say his memory was faulty, or that Megan came to visit him in prison or that he got lucky and guessed."

I lowered my chin. "Are you his defense counsel or the sheriff now?"

"I'm your commanding officer," he said. "The comment is revealing, but we can't build a case on it."

I leaned closer to him and lowered my voice so no one else in the station could hear me.

"Maybe not, but it's a start. If you give this case to Delgado and Martin, they're just going to screw up again."

Trisha snickered, but when Travis looked at her, she straightened and took a step away. Then he considered me.

"You've got history with both the victim and Christopher Hughes, but you've also got insight into this case. Starting tomorrow, you're back on it. Find something to put Christopher Hughes in prison for the rest of his life."

This was the case that had persuaded me to become a cop, and I'd do it right. I'd follow the evidence wherever it went, even if that meant looking away from Christopher. For now, though, he was my best lead.

"If Christopher ordered this murder, he did it from prison," I said, looking at my boss. "You want to drive to Potosi with me and see what we can stir up?"

Travis shook his head.

"If Hughes ordered a murder from prison, he had help from a corrections officer. I'll go to the prison. You will go home and sleep. Then you will return tomorrow and work."

"I'd rather go to the prison with you," I said, standing straighter.

"You might be the only person in history to say that sentence and mean it," said Travis. "If a prison guard helped Hughes order a murder, things will get political. We'll get the lawyers involved, and I'll work with the DOC's internal affairs team. I need you working the case here. I'll waste my time with the bureaucracy."

"When you put it like that, a nap doesn't sound so bad."

"I'm glad my sacrifice doesn't go unnoticed," he said, nodding toward the station's front door. "Now get out of here. Some of us have work to do."

25

Sherlock waved and smiled for the cameras, but inside he seethed. No matter what Christopher said to her, he had been reckless to hold a private meeting with Detective Court. Worse, it was pointless. They gained nothing by talking to her, and they risked revealing something important. This was the problem when working with morons: They did stupid things.

Christopher smiled at everyone and shook a bunch of hands. He even tried to take an interview from a reporter. That wasn't happening. Sherlock might not have been able to prevent him from meeting with Detective Court, but no way in hell would he let him talk to a reporter on his own. If Christopher wanted a nationwide audience, Sherlock would arrange it. He'd handpick the interviewer, he'd specify the questions she could ask, he'd negotiate payment, and he'd control the situation.

For the time being, Christopher wasn't just a client: He was an asset Sherlock had to protect—and exploit.

Sherlock put a hand on Christopher's back and led him toward the limousine he had hired for the day. The vehicle and driver had cost almost a thousand dollars, but it was a necessary expense. He and Christopher had business to discuss, and the limo gave them privacy and comfort a regular car couldn't provide. When they reached the vehicle, Sherlock opened the rear door and pushed his client inside before he could do something else stupid on live television.

"What the hell are you doing?" asked Christopher. "I was having a good time. I thought we could get a corn dog. There's a spring fair going on if you didn't notice."

"I noticed," said Sherlock, sitting beside his client and pulling the limo's heavy door shut behind him. He looked at the driver. "Take us to the Wayfair Motel. We passed it on the way into town."

As soon as the driver nodded and pulled away from the curb, Sherlock hit a button to close the glass partition that separated the front from the rear of the vehicle. Then he stared at his client.

"You wanted to move to St. Augustine, you wanted to see Sheriff Kosen, and you wanted to get your face on TV. None of that was a good idea, but you insisted," he said, locking his gaze on Christopher's. "Talking to Detective Court wasn't part of the deal."

"Relax," said Christopher, straightening his shirt. "Nothing happened. I wanted to make sure she remembered me."

"Did she?" asked Sherlock.

"Oh, yeah," said Christopher, laughing. "That little bitch is terrified of me."

Somehow Sherlock doubted that. He hadn't seen fear

in her eyes; she had been angry.

"What did you tell her?"

"Nothing," said Christopher. Sherlock stared at him without blinking until the other man sighed. "I asked how she was doing. I wanted to gauge whether she was a threat. She's not. She's nothing. She almost pissed herself when she saw me. I could have ripped off her clothes and had her on the conference room table, and she wouldn't have told nobody."

"She wouldn't have told anybody," said Sherlock, wiping his eyes. "If you want to go on television, you should at least speak well."

He cocked his head to the side and smirked.

"What are you, the grammar police?"

"She's the real reason you want to stay here, isn't she?" asked Sherlock. Christopher said nothing. Sherlock closed his eyes and shook his head. "This is stupid."

"Are you calling me stupid?" asked Christopher. "Where I'm from, people would cut you for less than that. Nuts to navel. I've seen it happen. Your guts spill out on the ground, and you die in your own shit and piss."

"If they're willing to murder someone over an insult, that's why they're in prison," said Sherlock. "They're stupid. And if you think threatening your lawyer makes sense, you're even stupider than they are."

Christopher narrowed his eyes and balled his left hand into a fist.

"If I smack you around some, you still going to think

I'm stupid?"

"You're not in prison anymore. The rules out here are different," said Sherlock, lowering his voice and leaning forward. "In prison, you might have been some kind of big shot, but out here, you're nothing. You don't even have any friends but me."

Christopher had the eyes of an animal. Sherlock gave him fifty-fifty odds he'd lash out. Instead, he laughed.

"You've got balls," he said. "I didn't know that about you."

"You're my meal ticket, Mr. Hughes. In exchange for payment, I—and the men who work for me—will provide you services to the best of our considerable abilities. That does not mean you get to insult me. Now, will you allow me to do my job, or are you going to be stupid again? I'd rather know right away so I can plan."

Christopher stopped smiling. Sherlock reached his hand to his belt and the knife holster he kept concealed there. The weapon had a curved ceramic blade and a hilt so he could draw it like a pistol. It was ugly, brutal, and sharp. He carried it as a weapon of last resort and because he could conceal it beneath his suit jacket. No client had ever given him reason to draw it, but Hughes could be the first.

"You're my employee," said Christopher. "You don't get to talk like that."

"I'm the only person standing between you and life in prison," said Sherlock. "I'll treat you with respect, but this is a two-way relationship. Do you trust me?"

"You got me out," said Christopher, nodding. "You didn't have to do that."

"No, I didn't," said Sherlock. "I did anyway, though, because I knew I would get paid. You still plan to pay me, don't you?"

"Yeah," said Christopher. "You'll get your money."

"Good. Then you'll continue to get my advice and services."

Christopher grunted. "Let's talk about those services. My wife's still breathing. I asked you to take care of her."

"As your counselor, I'd advise you to stop requesting that I kill your ex-wife," said Sherlock. "First, she's great in bed, and I like her a lot more than I like you. Second, if she goes down, every detective in St. Louis County will look right at you. Third, you don't kill people if you don't have to. Killing her is a risk for which there is no commensurate reward."

For a moment, Christopher didn't react. Then his hands shot out and grabbed Sherlock by the lapels of his jacket. His breath was hot on the lawyer's face.

"How do you know my wife is good in bed?"

Sherlock's heart pounded hard. With the partition up, the limo driver couldn't see anything they did. That worked out well for everybody. Sherlock slipped the knife from his belt holster and brought it to his client's throat. The tip dug into the soft flesh, scoring it until a drop of blood appeared.

"I've tried to be polite," said Sherlock. "Let go of my jacket. If you don't, I'll open your throat."

Christopher didn't move. If anything, his expression grew uglier.

"I know what you're thinking," said Sherlock. "You're wondering whether I'm fast enough to kill you before you overpower me. It doesn't matter. If I die here, the men who work for me will find you, cut off your testicles, shove them down your throat, and then leave you in a field to bleed to death. Do you understand?"

Christopher blinked and nodded before relaxing his grip. Sherlock lowered the knife.

"Now that we've got that out of our system," said Sherlock, "can we talk like normal adults?"

"You didn't have to cut me," said Christopher, bringing his hand to his throat and then looking at the blood on his fingers. Sherlock pulled a handkerchief from the inside pocket of his jacket and handed it to him.

"No, I didn't, but it got your attention," said Sherlock. "We're in a delicate situation. I'm negotiating with the state of Missouri and St. Louis County to compensate you for your illegal incarceration. With the media play this is getting, we've got the entire country on our side. If you do as I say, we'll keep that goodwill and leverage it into a settlement that will make you a wealthy man."

Christopher's eyes flicked down to Sherlock's hands before traveling to his face again.

"How wealthy are you going to make me?"

"Eight figures, I'm hoping. And who knows? Maybe you could get a book deal or a spot on Court TV."

Christopher leaned back in his seat, his eyes distant. "I'd like to write a book."

"People like authors," said Sherlock, leaning back in his own seat and feeling his shoulders relax. If he could keep his client in check, this might still work. Christopher would die, but with luck he wouldn't screw things up beforehand.

The limo pulled to a stop outside the Wayfair Motel a few moments later. Christopher rolled down his window.

"This is a shit hole."

"Yeah," said Sherlock, "but a lot of girls who work at the strip club across the street perform outcall work. If you've got the money, you'll be able to get a blow job—or whatever else you want."

He looked thoughtful and then nodded.

"They good looking?"

"I wouldn't know," said Sherlock. "I don't frequent strip clubs or prostitutes."

"That's right," he said. "You're nailing my wife."

"Ex-wife," said Sherlock, reaching into his briefcase for an envelope thick with hundred-dollar bills. He handed it to Christopher, who whistled. "This is your stop. Get some girls and have fun. Afterwards, hit the town. People need to see you."

"Why?" asked Christopher, thumbing through the money.

"Because I have a project in the city."

Christopher nodded. "So you need me to establish an alibi."

Sherlock looked to the strip club. The bouncer must have seen the limo because three girls came out.

"With ten grand, I expect you to establish three or four alibis."

Christopher chuckled and looked to the girls walking toward their car.

"I like the way you think," he said, opening his door. "Catch you later. This is going to be fun."

Sherlock watched as Christopher crossed the street and embraced the girls. They may not have known him, but they recognized a man on the prowl.

Sherlock had work to do, so he hit a button to open the partition. The frosted glass slid down, and the limo driver glanced back.

"Where to, sir?"

"My office in St. Louis," he said, already taking out his cell phone. He closed the partition again and dialed the number of Diana Hughes. She answered after two rings. "Hey. I might be late. I've got to meet people at my office to talk about your ex-husband. I have to kill him sooner than I expected."

26

I drove home but slowed almost to a stop before reaching my driveway. There was a gray full-size SUV in my driveway, and my living room windows were open. Travis had been my adoptive mother's partner in the St. Louis County Police Department for almost ten years. They still kept in touch and talked about me often. This was why Travis had told me to go home. He knew my parents had come in.

I parked in the driveway next to my dad's vehicle and stepped out, expecting Roger to come barreling toward me. He didn't, so I whistled and waited. Again, he didn't come. Julia must have taken him for a walk. She liked to do that, and he liked having new people around.

I walked to the front porch and smelled baking bread. That was Dad's hobby. He had been a fireman for thirty years. Living at a firehouse twenty-four hours a day with a bunch of other men hadn't always been easy. When he first joined up, he didn't know how to keep a house—and a firehouse was a home for the men who worked in it—so one of the other guys taught him how to cook, and a second taught him how to bake bread. He had a gift in the kitchen and had made some of the finest dinners I had ever eaten.

I stopped and took a deep breath. Then I caught a whiff of cinnamon and vanilla and browned butter. Those delectable smells weren't coming from bread; Dad was making coffee cake, one of my favorites. He had made it for me the day I graduated from high school and the day I finished the police academy. Even years later, whenever I smelled coffee cake, I felt like I was home.

I tossed my purse beside Julia's on the table in the entryway.

"Dad," I called. "I'm home."

"Hey, honey," he said, peeking his head into the hallway from the kitchen. My home had the same layout it had when its builder constructed it a hundred years ago. A hallway ran down the middle of the building, and rooms branched off to the left and right. The kitchen was in back so the stove wouldn't warm the rest of the house on hot summer days.

I walked down a hardwood floor that had held fathers and daughters for over a hundred years, and I felt a still calmness flood through me. I felt content and connected. My dad and Julia kept me grounded, even when the world around me came unmoored. I was lucky to have them in my life. I couldn't always say that aloud, but it was true all the same. They were my family, not by genetics, but by choice. That made them even more precious.

When I reached the kitchen, Dad tossed me a cotton

apron and turned his attention to a cutting board on the mobile island in the middle of the floor. I slipped the loop of the apron over my head and tied it around my back as Dad chopped an onion. When he looked up, he smiled.

"I like this kitchen island," he said. "Is it new?"

"New and old," I said, nodding. "Wood came from an ash tree on the neighbor's property. He had to cut it down before the emerald ash borer killed it. It's a bug. I dried the wood in the shed out back and then built an island from it."

He grinned.

"I'm glad someone taught you how to do all that. Your mother and I don't have a handy bone in our bodies."

"I know," I said, nodding and trying not to smile. "I've seen bookcases you've tried to build."

He glanced up. He wasn't smiling, but he was close.

"If you've got another cutting board, I need diced carrots and celery. Assuming that's not too much trouble, smartass."

I smiled and then went to the cabinet beside my fridge.

"Did Julia take Roger for a walk?"

"Yeah," he said. He paused for a moment. "You know, it hurts her feelings when you call her Julia and me Dad."

It was an old discussion but still a sore point. I put my cutting board on the counter beside the sink so I could chop and answer without having to look him in the eye.

"She knows I love her," I said.

"That's true. She knows."

The way he said it let me know he had hoped to hear something different. I blinked and then cut the ends off the carrots.

"You're the only dad I've ever had, but I've had a mom. Julia's not her."

Almost the moment the words left my lips, the front door opened, and I heard Roger's nails on the hardwood floor as he walked inside. I looked down the hallway to see Julia stepping inside. Roger bounded into the kitchen, stopped beside me so I could scratch his cheek, and then devoured a carrot peeling that had fallen on the floor. He looked happy. I wished life were that easy for me, too.

When I looked at my dad, his eyes held just a hint of sadness.

"Please don't let Julia hear you say that," he said.

Before I could respond, Julia walked into the room. She wore jeans, a white shirt, and a navy blazer. Her brown and gray hair just swept the top of her shoulders. My foster mother was a fox. I had seen pictures of my father when he and Julia first dated, and to this day, I didn't understand how they had gotten together. Dad was funny and kind, but Julia was way out of his league. They loved each other, though.

"Don't let me hear you say what?" she asked.

I cleared my throat. "Nothing special. I was

complaining about work. Travis has been a taskmaster these past couple of days."

"I see," she said, going to the fridge and taking out a glass pitcher full of iced tea. "Your dad's right. We're not here to talk about work. We're here to relax. Roger's looking good."

I looked to the dog, and he walked toward me and sat down, his mouth open in a gaping doggy grin. The hair on the tip of his muzzle had grown gray, and he had a noncancerous tumor on his belly, but he looked good. My vet had said the tumor wasn't anything to worry about unless it impeded his ability to run, but I still worried. I didn't like to see him growing old.

I patted his cheek and then scratched his ear the way he liked. His tail thumped behind him.

"He's a good boy," I said, looking from the dog to Julia. "He's getting old, but he's healthy for now. My vet has warned me that dogs his age decline quickly."

"Spend as much time with him as you can," said Julia, kneeling beside him and petting his head. Roger soaked in the attention. It was hard not to smile at a happy dog.

For the next hour, Dad and I made dinner—a chicken, pepper, and potato casserole—while Roger and Julia sat at the kitchen table. We chatted about my adoptive siblings, and about my house and all the projects I had ongoing. For the entire time they were in the house, we didn't talk about Christopher Hughes or my case.

For a brief afternoon and evening, life was normal

again. The worried knot in my stomach unraveled, and I laughed at Dad's jokes and held Julia's hand under the table. I hadn't realized how much I needed that until Dad stood up and carried our dinner dishes to the sink.

According to the clock on my microwave, it was ten to nine. I stretched my arms overhead and yawned.

"It's getting late, guys," I said. "I need my beauty sleep. I've got a big day tomorrow."

Dad slowed, and Julia looked at the table in front of us.

"What's Travis have you doing?" she asked.

With one question, the world came crashing back. I looked down at my hands.

"Julia," said Dad, his voice low. "We agreed not to talk about work."

"She's my daughter," said Julia. "I want to make sure she's okay."

"I'm okay, guys," I said. "I'm fine. Work is going well. I've been working a missing-persons case, but tomorrow I'll work on Megan Young's death again."

Julia said nothing, but Dad crossed his arms.

"I wish Travis hadn't put you on this case."

"He needs the help."

"You shouldn't be on that case," said Julia. "I can call Travis tomorrow and talk to him. If he needs help, I can lend him one of my detectives."

I blinked and then forced myself to smile.

"I appreciate your concern, but I'm fine," I said. "This is my case, and I'll see it to fruition. I don't want to talk about it anymore."

Both nodded but said nothing. As we cleaned up, Julia tried reviving a discussion we had started about books, but that went nowhere. Then Dad brought up Roger and a friend who had a similar dog who lived to fourteen. I hoped Roger would make it to eleven or twelve, but I couldn't see him living another four years—and if he did, he wouldn't be healthy. As much as I loved him, even I knew his best days were behind him.

Our conversation sort of tapered off after that. At nine-thirty, I walked them to the front door and gave them both hugs. I told them I loved them and that I'd call if I needed anything. As I watched their taillights disappear, all the warmth and hope I had felt just a few minutes earlier evaporated. I didn't feel sad. It was more fatigue than anything else.

I petted Roger and then went to the kitchen for a glass, which I filled with ice and vodka. Afterwards, I stared at the drink. Alcohol made life easier to bear. If I had enough drinks, I didn't mind that my house was falling apart, or that I didn't have many friends, or that my job sucked the joy out of life. I didn't care about anything when I was drunk.

I picked up the drink and then brought it to my face. The liquor smelled sharp but clean. It was good vodka. That was part of how I justified it. I had arrested lots of drunks on the job. When they bought vodka, it came in giant plastic bottles, and it smelled like paint thinner. I drank the good stuff. That made me better somehow.

As I stood there, I felt moisture form on the exterior of my class, I heard the ice crack as it melted, and I watched as a bead of condensation dripped to the floor. I didn't want that drink, but if I kept holding it, I would finish it. Then I'd finish another and another until I passed out.

I didn't want that. I wanted to feel something real—even if for just a night. Before I could stop myself, I poured my drink into the sink and then looked to the dog.

"You want to sleep outside tonight?"

Roger cocked his head at me, confused. I needed to get out of the house, so I patted his cheek and then went upstairs for my badge and firearm. With the fair going on, there was plenty of work tonight. I was sober and ready to do it. I took the dog outside and watched him climb into the doghouse I had built in the backyard. Then I locked up and got in my truck.

I didn't plan my route when I headed out, but somehow I knew where to go. I drove to the Wayfair Motel. With all the attention the media had given Christopher Hughes, Travis had assigned a uniformed patrol officer in a marked cruiser to sit in the motel's parking lot to keep him safe. I parked beside her and rolled down my window. Officer Alisa Maycock did likewise.

"Hey, Joe."

"Hey, Alisa," I said. "Anything going on tonight?"

"You're looking at it," she said, nodding toward a closed door at the end of the building. During fair week, people often congregated outside to drink and smoke, but tonight, the lot was empty. Alisa's cruiser had a lot to do with that. "Nobody's been in, and nobody's been out."

"How much longer do you have on your shift?"

She glanced at her watch. "Two hours. I'm here until midnight."

I nodded. "Why don't you go home? I'll take over. I need the break."

"You need a break, so you came into work?" she asked, raising her brow.

"Yeah," I said, not wanting to elaborate further. Alisa considered and then nodded.

"If you want the most boring job on the planet, it's yours for the next two hours."

"Thanks," I said. "Have a good one."

"You, too," she said, before rolling up her window. Within five minutes of arriving at the Wayfair Motel, I was alone in the parking lot. I stared at Christopher's door, almost hoping he'd come out. For twenty minutes, nothing moved. Then I drummed my fingers on the steering wheel. I hadn't thought this out. If I had, I would have brought coffee.

At the hour mark, I wondered whether I should have stayed at home and gotten drunk. It would have been more fruitful than sitting in a truck for two hours. At eleven-thirty, an old minivan pulled into the lot. It was late, but this was a packed motel. I thought nothing of it until the drapes in Christopher's room shifted a moment later, and his head appeared in the window. He scanned the lot, and I slouched low, hoping he wouldn't see me over the dashboard. He was looking for Alisa's cruiser.

"What are you up to?" I asked, my voice low.

Within seconds of scanning the lot, Christopher opened his door and climbed into the front seat of the minivan. I transcribed the van's license plate as it pulled out of the lot. Then I turned on my truck. I should have called this in, but that would have taken time. Plus, I would have had to explain why I was in the lot instead of Alisa. Travis wouldn't appreciate me taking over a uniformed officer's shift without consulting him first, but since I already had, I figured I might as well keep going. If I found something, I'd call it in, but for now, I could do this on my own terms.

I put my truck in gear and headed out, uncertain where the hell I was going.

27

May 2008

According to the experts, my therapist was the best in the city for young women, but I didn't give a shit. I wasn't a depressed little girl upset because her boyfriend broke up with her, and I wasn't stressed about getting into the perfect college. Nobody bullied me, and nobody harassed me online. I didn't have the same problems as everyone else, so I didn't need the same therapy as everyone else.

Sometimes I got scared late at night, and sometimes I had nightmares. Once, I even thought I saw Christopher Hughes in a tree outside my window. He was in prison, so I knew he wasn't there, but still, I hadn't been able to shake the feeling he was watching me, laughing at me, waiting so he could have his chance to hurt me again.

Talking wouldn't help that. My problems were my own, and I had solved them on my own. I had installed a deadbolt outside my bedroom door, and I slept with a baseball bat beside my bed. No one would hurt me again. I had taken care of that. My Louisville Slugger gave me all the therapy I needed.

Still, Julia insisted that I see a therapist every week.

She meant well, so I went along. She thought if I could just talk about what Christopher had done, I could process things and find closure. But closure was bullshit. If therapy taught me anything, it taught me that.

Still, therapy had one upside, at least: For two hours every Friday afternoon, I got out of school. Julia even took me for coffee afterwards. We didn't get a lot of time alone, so I looked forward to it most weeks. As I sat and sipped my chocolate chai latte after my latest session, Julia picked up her coffee mug and looked at me over the rim.

"Did you talk today?"

"No," I said. "Dr. Collins keeps pressuring me to talk about Christopher, but I don't need to talk about him. I lived through what he did. I don't need to rehash it."

Julia nodded and sipped her drink. "Many people think talking our way through trauma helps us get over it."

"So you've told me," I said, putting my drink down. "Here's the thing, though: I don't want to get over what happened. Christopher made me stronger."

Julia put her drink down. "There's a difference between being strong and brittle."

I rolled my eyes. "I spent an hour hearing that shit from my therapist, and I don't need it at home, too."

Julia looked up from her drink. "So this coffee shop is home now?"

I rolled my eyes again. "You know what I mean."

"I do," said Julia, reaching across the table to touch my wrist. She squeezed. "I love you, too."

"That's not what I meant," I said, shaking my head.

"Then I take it back."

I opened my mouth and then laughed. "You're impossible to talk to."

Julia smiled. "Your dad says that, too."

Neither of us spoke for a moment. "Doug is my dad, isn't he? I've never had one before."

"He'd love the job if you'll give it to him."

"I guess it's his," I said. We both went quiet again. I cleared my throat. "I'm thinking about becoming a cop after college."

Julia nodded and drew in a breath. "You're smart, observant, and well spoken. I think you'd make a good one."

"I will," I said.

"You're humble, too. I think that's your best quality."

"My humility is amazing," I said, smiling and looking down. Neither of us spoke, but then I locked eyes with the woman across from me. There was no pretense there. She didn't want anything from me. I liked that about her. "You don't have to keep driving me to therapy. I think I'll quit."

Julia nodded. "If you don't like Dr. Collins, we can find you someone else."

I shook my head and looked away. "Dr. Collins isn't the problem."

"Then what is?"

I drew in a breath and then another before sighing. "Every therapist I've been to thinks I'm broken and that they can put me back together just by talking. I'm tired of that."

Julia nodded and sipped her coffee. "What do you think?"

"There's nothing wrong with me," I said. "I'm not weak, I didn't wake up on the wrong side of the bed, and I'm not going through typical teenage depression. Dr. Collins doesn't even want to understand what happened. She wants to fix me and move on."

"I see," said Julia, nodding and sipping her drink. I waited for her to say something else, but she didn't, and that just pissed me off. Even though I was a teenager, I knew what she was doing. Silence was hard to deal with, and she knew it. Somehow, sitting with another person without saying anything was more intimate than even the most intimate conversation. I didn't like silence. Julia knew if she stayed quiet, I'd talk, just to fill in the lull in conversation.

And yet, even knowing that, I couldn't stop talking. Something inside me begged to come out. In that moment, I loved Julia, and I hated her. She knew what she was doing and what she was dragging out of me.

"Christopher Hughes drugged me so I wouldn't fight him, and then he put himself inside me. Afterwards, I tried to get help, but nobody did shit until another girl died. Do you know what that's like?"

"No," said Julia. "I can't imagine what that's like."

"I don't have to imagine. I lived it," I said, my voice rising. A couple at a table nearby looked at us, but Julia didn't belittle me by asking me to calm down. She nodded. My throat felt tight, and my skin felt hot. I felt like a balloon full to the breaking point. One more puff of air, and I'd pop. I waited for Julia to say something. Instead, she reached across the table and touched my hand. I ripped my arm back.

"I'm not human to them," I said. "I'm a puzzle to solve. That's it. I sit in their office for an hour, and they poke and prod me like a science experiment, and then they get a paycheck. I'm tired of people thinking they can fix me. There's nothing wrong with me. I want everyone to leave me alone."

Julia didn't react for a moment, but then she nodded.

"I understand."

I waited, expecting more. She looked at me with a serious but caring expression on her face.

"So you won't make me go anymore?"

She picked up her mug and sipped. Then her eyes went distant.

"I'll make you a deal," she said, putting down her coffee. "You can stop going to the therapist's office when you remove the deadbolt from your door, and when you can make it through a week without crying at night."

I shook my head, feeling my cheeks and throat grow hot.

"I don't cry at night."

"Yeah, you do," she said. "It's not every night, but it's three out of four. Doug and I take turns staying up in case you need somebody."

I lowered my chin. "You listen outside my door to hear if I cry?"

She picked up her coffee and shook her head.

"We live in an old house. The walls are thin."

I opened my mouth. It felt like the worst kind of betrayal.

"I can't believe you listen at night. That is so wrong."

"Get used to it. It's what families do, and you're a part of our family. We will always be here when you need us, even when you don't want us to be."

I shot to my feet, knocking my stool over.

"I can't talk to you right now. I'm going to the car."

"Okay," she said, nodding and sipping her drink. I hurried out and almost ran into somebody near the door as cascading waves of revulsion and anger washed over me. There was something else there, too, something in the background that made my eyes tear up. All those nights, all that time, I had felt as if I were alone behind that heavy wooden door...and I hadn't been. I'd had someone listening the entire time.

Half an hour later, Julia came to the car. I didn't know what to say, so I said nothing. I gave her the longest hug of my life though. She thanked me afterwards and told me she had needed that.

That night, I didn't cry myself to sleep as I had the previous two. Instead, I went downstairs. Doug was on the couch in the living room, eating Fruity Dyno Bites cereal from a soup bowl and watching Letterman.

"Hey, kiddo," he said. "You doing okay?"

"Yeah, I'm fine," I said, sitting on the end of the couch opposite him. For a few minutes, I watched TV with him, but then the show went to commercial, and he patted my knee.

"Make sure you turn the TV off when you go to bed," he said. "It's getting late for me."

He picked up his bowl and started for the kitchen. I almost let him go, but then I cleared my throat.

"Hey," I said. He stopped near the doorway and looked at me. I couldn't hold his gaze, so I looked down. "I don't want you to make a bigger deal about this than it deserves, but I want to call you Dad instead of Doug. Is that okay?"

He said nothing until I looked up. Then he smiled and nodded. "Yeah, kiddo. That's okay."

I swallowed a lump in my throat. "Goodnight, Dad."

He walked back to the living room. I didn't know what he was doing until he grabbed a blanket from the loveseat and tossed it to me.

"It's cold down here, sweetheart. You'll want that."

"It's not cold. You're just eating cold cereal. Does Julia know you're eating on her couch? She'd be pissed."

He looked down to his bowl. "I won't tell if you won't."

"You gave me a home, so I guess I can keep your secret."

"I'll be forever in your debt," he said, winking as he walked out of the room. I watched until he disappeared, and then I focused on the TV again. I cried after that. I wasn't sobbing or anything, but it was a steady cry. I didn't cry a lot, so I was glad no one else was around to see it.

When I went to bed that night, I locked my deadbolt, but I didn't put on the chain. My therapist would tell me that didn't matter as long as I kept the deadbolt engaged, but it mattered. As I lay in bed, and as my eyes adjusted to the dark, I thought about why I had cried on the couch. It made little sense at first, but then it did. I had cried because my dad loved me. It was as simple as that.

For the first time in my life, I was home.

28

Smoke and the soft murmur of whispered conversation hung in the air. Warren Nichols hunched over his drink at the end of a long scratched and scarred wooden bar. The nearest person sat three seats away from him, transfixed by a cell phone. Behind him, two guys played darts.

Aside from the bartender, no one had spoken to him for more than an hour. That was why he liked Ray's Tavern. Warren didn't go there to meet friends or make new ones. He went there to get drunk. Warren preferred to be alone nowadays. He had a daughter with whom he almost never spoke and an ex-wife who called every time she needed money. Sometimes he gave it to her, but sometimes he didn't. Sometimes she slept with him as a thank you, but most nights she told him to work one out on his own.

Pictures of his ex-wife and daughter had both ended up in the folder given to him by James "Sherlock" Holmes. If he didn't go along with Sherlock's plan, they would die. He wouldn't have minded if Sherlock and his goons knocked off his ex, but he couldn't let anything happen to his daughter, despite their differences. More

The Girl in the Motel

than his garage and shop, she was his legacy and his hope for a better future. One day, if he lived long enough, her kids would call him grandpa. The thought of someone hurting her made him sick.

And so he had gotten drunk at Ray's every night since then. After he had enough to drink, he'd walk two blocks home, where he'd pass out on his couch. If he went along with Sherlock's plans, no one would hurt his daughter. Maybe he'd even get rich like Sherlock had said. At this point in his life, he didn't much care.

Warren had stage four colon cancer that had metastasized to his lungs and liver. It was incurable. His doctors gave him a year, maybe two if he were lucky. No matter what happened, he was going to his grave sooner rather than later. He hoped he wouldn't take his kid with him.

A cell phone rang somewhere in the bar. It was only when the bartender glanced at him that Warren realized the sound was coming from his own pocket. He finished his drink and then pointed to his empty glass as he fished the phone out. Candace, his daughter, had made him buy the phone two years ago when she went to college. Only a handful of people knew his number, and he only liked one or two.

He didn't recognize the number identified by his caller ID, but he answered anyway. He wanted a fight, so he ran a finger across the screen and then put the phone to his ear.

"Eat shit," he said, speaking before the other person

on the line could say anything.

"Is that how you talk to an old friend?"

The voice sounded familiar, but Warren took a moment to place it.

"Christopher?" he asked.

"Yeah. My lawyer gave me your number. Didn't think you'd hear from me, did you?"

In fact, Warren had expected a call any day now. Christopher would expect to pick up business where they had left off. He didn't know everything had changed.

"Good to hear from you, brother. I saw you on the news today. I don't get to talk to too many celebrities."

"Hell yeah, I'm a celebrity," said Christopher, snorting. "My lawyer's gonna make me rich, too."

"You're already rich," said Warren, nodding his thanks to the bartender as he refilled his glass. "What do you need?"

"What do you mean, what do I need?" asked Christopher. "I got out of prison, and I'm calling an old friend. What the hell is wrong with you?"

Warren ran a hand over his head and sighed. "Sorry, man. I've had a long day. I'm glad you're out. We should get a drink."

"Hell yeah we should get a drink. You'll buy, too. I've been gone for twelve years. I deserve a drink with my friends."

"Yeah," said Warren, nodding. "We'll get everybody together. Steven ain't around anymore, but Randy and Neil are still in town."

"Where's Steven?"

"Dead," said Warren. "Shot by somebody."

"Who would kill Steven?" asked Christopher. "He was a good guy."

"I don't know," said Warren, already picturing in his mind Sherlock's goons. "It's a scary world."

Neither man said anything, but then Christopher cleared his throat.

"We've got to talk. I'm in the backseat of a minivan on my way to St. Louis right now."

"We're talking now," said Warren.

"In person," said Christopher. "We've got to talk business. I need to get back to work. You still got that garage?"

"Yeah."

"Meet me there in an hour," said Christopher. "I'll get money from the county, and I've got a few ideas about how I can best reinvest it."

"One hour," said Warren, reaching to the bar for his drink. He gulped it down and then grimaced as the liquor tore into his throat. "I'll be there."

"See you there, brother," said Christopher. He hung up, and Warren stared at his now empty glass. The bartender came over, carrying a bottle of Wild Turkey.

"You want another?"

Warren shook his head and searched through his phone's address book. The bartender stepped away and mixed drinks for the guys playing darts. Warren found the number he wanted and called.

"Sherlock," he said. "It's Warren Nichols."

"You're slurring your words. Are you drunk?" said Sherlock.

"I am," said Warren shifting on his seat so he could pass gas. He grimaced as his entire stomach tightened. At least he hadn't shit blood today. Colon cancer was a bitch. He'd miss his daughter, but he looked forward to being done with everything. He had lived enough. "You got a problem with that?"

The lawyer kept his voice tight and controlled.

"I assume you have a reason for calling me."

"Christopher called, just like you said he would. He wants to meet me at my shop in an hour."

"You agreed?" asked Sherlock.

"You'll kill Candace if I don't cooperate," he said. The bartender cast him a curious glance, but Warren was many drinks past caring who heard him talk. "So yeah. I set up a meeting."

"Good. Go to your shop. My team and I will meet you there," said Sherlock. "We'll talk about your drinking later. I don't like to be in business with drunks."

"Like I care about your business," said Warren. "Now go do your thing. I'll see you later."

He stood on unsteady feet and put a twenty on the bar, wondering whether he had just signed his own death warrant. That didn't sound so bad.

Sherlock hung up and looked to Diana. She bit her lower lip. The covers and their clothes lay on the ground. Her soft skin had the perfect amount of padding for a thirty-five-year-old woman, and he slid an arm over her waist and drew her close.

"You're going to leave, aren't you?" she whispered.

He nodded. "Yeah, but if you're still naked when I come back, I'll make it worth your while."

She walked her fingers down his chest and to his lower abdomen. "I could make it worth your while to stay."

He wanted to give in, but he shook his head and slid off the bed. She gave him a disappointed pout.

"Sorry, darling," he said. "Work is calling."

"What kind of work?"

He smiled and walked to the bathroom. "I'm going to kill your ex-husband. Then I'll come back here and screw you until neither of us can walk."

She purred. "That sounds perfect."

I didn't know where the hell I was going, so I followed the minivan. Since the Wayfair Motel and the nearby strip club and truck stop had a steady stream of traffic to and from the interstate, I kept several cars between us on the road. We headed north toward St. Louis. Along the way, I took out my cell phone and called my station. The front desk rang three times before someone picked up. People were shouting in the background.

"What's your emergency?"

The voice belonged to Jason Zuckerburg. He was a thirty-five-year veteran of the St. Augustine County Sheriff's Department and could have retired with a full pension. He liked the work, though. In an emergency, we could put him out in the field, but he preferred working a desk now.

"I don't have one," I said. "I'm calling the back line. This is Joe Court. What's going on?"

It was a dark night, and there were few cars on the road, so I kept my eyes in front of me at all times to avoid hitting anything. I let the minivan get about a quarter mile ahead of me so I could just see its taillights.

"Shit, sorry, Joe," said Jason. "We're a little hammered here. Didn't see your ID on the screen."

"What's going on?" I asked.

"Bar fight at Tommy B's spilled out into the street. Three drunk soccer moms from St. Louis decided they wanted to get in on the action, so they started swinging, too. So far, we've got three in the hospital and nine in shackles."

I nodded and squinted at the road in front of me, thinking I had lost my minivan. I hadn't, but it had sped up. The speedometer in my old truck only went to eighty-five, and I neared that speed now. Hopefully we wouldn't be speeding up too much more because I didn't think my forty-year-old Dodge could take it.

"That's surprising," I said. "Alcohol usually brings

out the best in people."

Jason grunted. "What do you need, Joe?"

"I'm in my truck, and I need you to run a license for me."

I read him the plate number, and then I heard him type for a moment. Then I heard him warn somebody in the lobby that he'd charge her with destruction of government property if she vomited in the drinking fountain. There were a lot of things I enjoyed about law enforcement, but none more so than the sheer glamour.

"Your minivan is owned by Anita Willits of Festus, Missouri. Looks like a solid citizen. She has no prior arrests and no outstanding warrants. Vehicle has been registered to her since 2015. She's got a class-E license with an S endorsement."

Meaning she had a chauffeur's license and could additionally drive a school bus. The minivan didn't belong to one of his friends, then; Christopher had called a car service. He could have been going anywhere. This might be a long night.

Before I could thank him, something crashed on the other end of the line. A lot of people shouted after that. Jason swore under his breath.

"You okay there?" I asked.

"Idiot threw a chair in the waiting room, so Sasquatch broke out a Taser. We've got it under control, but I've got to go."

"Good luck," I said. He grunted and hung up. Jason was one of the more jovial members of our department.

He had gray hair and a kind face. During the holiday season, he put on a Santa Claus outfit and handed out presents to kids at the local food bank. I didn't get to see him flustered or angry too often. Then again, we didn't get too many thrown chairs in the lobby, either.

I tossed my phone to the seat beside me. We were nearing the outskirts of St. Louis, and I had about a quarter of a tank of gas left. My old truck guzzled gas, so I'd have to stop if we kept going too much farther. I shifted on my seat, took a deep breath, and readjusted my grip on the old rubber steering wheel.

"Okay, Christopher," I said. "You can pull off any day now."

29

Alonzo pulled the hood of his sweatshirt over his head and huddled over the tailgate of his pickup, squinting in the faint light. The evening was cold, and the alley was dark. He had an old revolver inside his pocket. A gangbanger on Natural Bridge Road had sold it to him for fifty bucks just twenty minutes ago. Soot coated the weapon's grip, barrel, and chamber. Judging by the smell, somebody had fired it recently. More than likely, someone had already used it in a homicide. Maybe multiple ones.

That was part of the reason he'd bought it.

Gangbangers didn't always take care of their toys, though, which made the weapon dangerous. If the cylinder and barrel had become misaligned, a round could get stuck in the chamber and blow his hand off; if the electrical tape the previous owner had wound around the grip slipped, his accuracy could be off; or if soot or other debris made the trigger stick, the weapon might not fire. He couldn't take that kind of risk.

Alonzo put the revolver on the tailgate of his pickup and then grabbed his kit from the passenger seat. He had spent the first six years of his adult life as a Marine. After that, he had become a cop, a job he thought he'd have until he retired. When he first became a cop, he imagined he was a knight who patrolled the streets and helped men and women in need. He saved people. Most people didn't need saving, though. Alonzo didn't know what they needed, but they didn't need him.

He slid the cylinder from the pistol's barrel and sprayed every moving part with a solvent made for firearms.

He had liked being a cop. It made him feel powerful, and he got to bust a lot of heads, but the job didn't leave him with a lot of money for the work he put in. He wanted more. That's where Sherlock came in.

Alonzo scrubbed the weapon clean and then adjusted the cylinder so it aligned with the barrel. The gun only needed to fire once, so it didn't need to be perfect.

Tonight Sherlock had given him an easy task: kill everybody in a room and get out. Alonzo didn't like killing people, but the money made it worthwhile. Not only that, he didn't kill innocent people. Nobody would miss the people he planned to shoot tonight. Hell, the city ought to throw him a parade for what he was about to do. Now he just needed to get it done.

Where other neighborhoods in St. Louis had gentrified, Hyde Park had changed little since Christopher Hughes had last been in it. Christopher tapped the driver on the shoulder and pointed toward a well-lit building that looked like a gas station. A chain-link fence surrounded the property. There were cars everywhere. In contrast to the surrounding neighborhood, Warren's garage looked as if it were prospering. Good for him.

"That's it," said Christopher. "You can drop me off out front."

His driver nodded and darted her eyes around the neighborhood. She looked scared, and he couldn't blame her. It wasn't the best neighborhood in town, but if she stayed in the car and kept driving, she'd be fine.

The danger would come at stoplights. If somebody liked her minivan, she'd lose it. Even in north St. Louis—one of the most dangerous neighborhoods in the country—murders were rare events. Carjackings happened a lot more often.

That wasn't Christopher's concern, though. He wanted to see an old friend and to talk business. Sherlock got him out of prison, but somebody needed to bring the lawyer down a few pegs. You couldn't screw a man's wife without getting the shit beaten out of you. Warren may have been too old for a recreational beatdown, but he'd know people who were up for one. This would go just fine. Everybody would have a good time tonight.

Almost everybody, at least. Sherlock needed to find out who held the power in their relationship.

I parked on the side of the road about a block from a mechanic's shop. A brick three-story building cast a long shadow on the road to my left, cloaking my old truck in darkness. It was a dark night, and none of the nearby overhead lights worked. A flashlight would have been nice, but I didn't want to give my position away by turning mine on. I'd rather stumble on the broken sidewalk than get shot by a paranoid Christopher Hughes.

As I got out of my truck, the orange tip of a cigarette burned to my right. Three young men sat on the front steps of a row house not too far away. As the breeze blew toward me, I caught a whiff of flavored tobacco, but there was something else there, too. It wasn't marijuana; it almost smelled like oregano, which made me think it was synthetic weed.

At the moment, I was more interested in my safety than their drugs, so I crouched against my truck and kept my hand over the firearm on my belt. The herbalists didn't seem to care I was in the area. They kept talking and passing their cigarette back and forth. Hopefully they wouldn't become a problem.

I was out of my jurisdiction, but I crept forward anyway, being careful to stay in the shadows cast by nearby buildings. If Christopher wanted to have a normal conversation with someone, he could have picked up a phone. If he didn't like phones, he could have met someone for coffee. If he didn't like coffee, he could have hosted someone in his motel room.

He hadn't done any of that, though. Instead, he

waited until the police car in front of his motel disappeared, and then he snuck away to visit a mechanic's shop in north St. Louis in the middle of the night. A man who wanted to catch up with a friend would meet him in a bar, while a man looking to score some weed would ask around at a club. Normal people didn't take midnight meetings in auto body shops. I didn't know what Christopher planned, but he had something going on.

I looked over my shoulder to make sure the smokers I had seen earlier weren't following me. Even with my eyes now adjusted to the gloom, I could barely see them. One of them waved. I considered flashing a badge at him to see what he'd do, but instead I turned and faced the garage again.

The garage wasn't too far away, but it was lit well. I didn't know how I would sneak up there and listen to whatever was going on inside, but I didn't have a choice. No matter what Christopher Hughes said in interviews, he wasn't the victim in all this. He was a predator, and predators never changed. They just got smarter. If we left Christopher alone, he'd be running underage prostitutes through St. Augustine by week's end.

I wouldn't let that happen.

30

Christopher's nervousness spiked the moment he saw the minivan pull away. He could call another and have it pick him up within a few minutes, but he wondered whether meeting his old friend at this time of night in this neighborhood was such a good idea. He liked Warren, but he hadn't seen or talked to him in twelve years. A man could change in twelve years.

He looked at the phone Sherlock had given him. It was like a computer with a touch screen, like something off *Star Trek*. Before going to Potosi, he had owned a top-of-the-line cell phone from Motorola. It had set him back almost five hundred bucks in 2004. They called it a flip phone, and it didn't have a big screen. It only made calls and stored a few dozen numbers, but he didn't need anything else. Now, his phone checked his email, fed him news, and kept all his contacts in one spot. If he could figure out how to make calls with it, he'd be golden.

His finger hovered over an app for Uber. Twelve years ago, if you wanted somebody to pick you up in St. Louis, you called River City Cabs or a friend. Now, you hit buttons on a phone, and a stranger would pick you up within minutes. The world had changed while he had rotted in Potosi. Sometimes, he wondered whether he should take his money and go. He could move to the Bahamas, live large, and nail a bunch of island girls.

It sounded perfect, but Christopher knew he'd never be able to survive a life of leisure. Even as a kid, he had hustled. He'd bought Ding Dongs from one friend's lunch for a dime and sold them to another for a quarter. In junior high, he had downloaded pictures of naked girls from the internet, put them on a floppy disk, and sold them to his friends, ten pictures for a dollar. Beaches were for vacations. He lived on the streets. After twelve years behind bars, he planned to live it up.

As he walked toward the garage, Christopher smelled grease and pneumatic fluid. Before he had gone to prison, Christopher had marveled at Warren's immaculate shop. The world may have shifted, but at least that hadn't changed. Inside the garage, Warren's mechanics had put away every tool, swept the floors, and lowered the lifts so customers could drive right in the next morning to get their oil and filters changed. The fire extinguishers beside each lift looked out of place, but the fire marshal had probably ordered Warren to put them in.

Christopher stepped through an open garage door and then into the front office to his left. Near the front window, two couches faced one another. A television hung on the wall. Warren sat behind the receptionist's desk. His face was gaunt, and his hair had grayed. In the dim light of a desk lamp, his skin had a greenish pallor.

He looked sick.

"Hey, Warren," said Christopher. "You okay? You don't look so good."

"I'm dying," he said. "Cancer. My doctor gave me a year, maybe two."

Christopher opened his eyes wide and stood straighter.

"Aww, man," he said. "I'm sorry, brother. I didn't know."

He drew in a breath and nodded before looking over Christopher's shoulder and nodding. Then he looked at his former business partner again.

"I'm sorry, too, Christopher. This ain't personal."

Before Christopher could say anything, someone pressed a gun against his back.

Scott Gibson loved the dark. It was his element. He felt powerful in the dark, working in the shadows. A Ranger school washout, Scott had been a good but not exceptional soldier in the Army. He had spent the last six months of his enlistment riding a desk, but that wasn't so bad. Nobody had shot him, at least.

Now, he worked in the field again. After leaving the military, he had become a cop. He had driven through neighborhoods, talked to people, threw knuckleheads in jail, and then went home. It was a paycheck, nothing more.

Now, he had a good job. He was a private investigator with one of the best defense attorneys in town. The money was better, the hours were shorter, and the work was a lot more fun. He didn't have to deal with drunks or meth heads so high they might attack him as soon as they saw him. Now, he took pictures of parking lots, he interviewed witnesses, he helped people out. It was detective work without all the bullshit rules.

And, sometimes, like today, Sherlock gave him special projects. Gibson took his hand from the steering wheel and reached to the rifle on the passenger seat. He had stolen the vehicle that evening from a used-car lot owned by one of his boss's clients. The client wouldn't call it in. He wouldn't want the attention, not for a twenty-five-year-old Buick he'd be lucky to get five hundred bucks for. Hell, somebody probably stole it to begin with.

When Gibson finished with the car, he'd leave it outside a bar on a busy street with the windows open and the engine running. Somebody would take it out for a joy ride, saving him the trouble of disposing of it himself. Until then, though, he watched and waited.

The rifle was a Colt AR-15 he had purchased four years ago from a guy in the parking lot of a gun show in Mississippi. When this job was over, he'd have to destroy it. He hated to lose the weapon, but it was the safe thing to do considering the work he had ahead of him.

He was the insurance man on this job. While Alonzo killed Christopher Hughes and Warren Nichols, Gibson would shoot anybody who ran out of the building or neighboring houses. They couldn't afford potential witnesses on a job like this. Christopher was far too high profile.

So Gibson waited in the dark, watching the building through a pair of infrared binoculars from about half a block away. It didn't take him long to realize he wasn't the only person watching that night. Someone—a woman, by her shape—was skulking about across the street, trying to get close to the shop while still staying hidden.

Christopher Hughes must have pissed her off. He had a gift for pissing off women. She gave him one more thing to worry about. Gibson opened his door and then slipped out into the night, where he knelt beside his vehicle, using his engine block as both cover and support. His rifle didn't have an infrared scope, but he didn't need one to mark the girl. She was just visible in the shadows.

He focused his scope's reticle in the center of her chest and took a deep breath, slowing his heart rate and timing the shot so he could pull the trigger between beats. She was maybe three hundred yards away.

"Sorry, honey," he whispered. "You're about to have a bad day."

He brought his finger to the trigger and squeezed.

31

Even in the dark, I felt somebody's eyes on me. I didn't like this one bit, but I didn't have many other options. If I called for backup, the city would send officers out, but they'd come in marked patrol vehicles, and they'd tell the entire world we had eyes on the garage. We needed to find out what Christopher Hughes had planned, and we needed to do it now before he hurt someone.

I drew in a deep breath. There were half a dozen cars parked beneath the canopy in front of the garage. They'd give me concealment, but an awful lot of space separated us. I couldn't stay in place, though, because I was too far from the building to see or hear anything.

My heart thudded in my chest. Police work in St. Augustine didn't afford me much chance to practice my surveillance skills, so I felt like a high school kid sneaking home after hours. I hesitated in the dark and then drew in a breath.

"Now or never, Joe," I whispered to myself before digging my feet into the ground and sprinting forward. Nobody shot at me as I ran, and once I reached the other side of the street, I pressed my back against the nearest car. After that, I leapfrogged from one car to another, bringing myself closer to the building until I heard voices inside. The garage was maybe thirty feet away, separated from me only by a Mazda station wagon. The voices inside were clear but low. I held my breath and listened.

"I'm sorry, too, Christopher. This ain't personal."

The voice came from inside. Then a gun fired, and pain exploded down my side.

Christopher lifted his arms as a weapon pressed against his spine. This never should have happened. Prison had made him hard and strong. In prison, a man was either predator or prey. After twenty-four hours outside, he had grown soft.

"You don't have to do this," he said, his voice low as he turned his head to the side, hoping to glimpse the gunman. "I can make you money. I'm rich, and I'll be even richer."

"You can't afford me," said the gunman, pressing his weapon harder into Christopher's back. Christopher searched his memory, but he couldn't recognize the voice. "If you want to survive through the night, tell me where you keep your money."

Christopher looked to Warren, hoping for some kind of tell. The aging mechanic wouldn't meet his gaze. Coward. Christopher wasn't young anymore, but he was tough. He had gotten into fights in prison and held his own. He wouldn't die here.

Christopher swallowed and stepped forward, more to see what the gunman would do than to give himself room. The shooter matched him step for step. Twenty years ago, he would have whipped around and knocked the gun out of the shooter's hand. Now, that move would get him killed.

Christopher's breath was shallow as he considered his options. He was dead if he made the wrong move. His gut was tight, and his skin felt hot. No matter what else happened tonight, people would die. Nobody betrayed him like this. First, though, he had to get himself out of this mess. He needed help.

"Hey, Warren," he said, hoping to catch his old friend's attention. "I'll take care of your daughter like she was my own if you shoot this son of a bitch."

Warren didn't hesitate. He had a gun in his hand almost before the words left Christopher's mouth. Christopher dove to the ground, bracing himself for the shots. He hoped Warren survived, but even if he didn't, Christopher would fulfill his end of the bargain.

Then a woman's scream outside changed everything.

I gasped and dove over the car, putting its engine block between me and the direction the shot had come from. The round had grazed my left arm before slamming into the vehicle. Adrenaline poured through my system, crowding out the pain and any thoughts of my mortality. I took slow, deep breaths as warm blood trickled down my arm and to my wrist.

I blinked and popped my head up, hoping to catch movement on the street. The gunman fired again. This shot buzzed by my ear. I lifted my weapon and returned fire in a three-shot burst. The shooter crouched behind an old Buick and used its hood to stabilize his rifle. I couldn't hit him at this distance, but I needed to keep him back.

Pain radiated from my side with every breath as I pulled out my phone to dial 911. A half dozen shots rang out from the garage and slammed into the car. I dove and scrambled to the rear of the vehicle, dropping my phone. My phone skittered away. I must have kicked it by accident. I swore to myself and sucked in great lungfuls of air.

Whoever these people were, they had surrounded me. That didn't leave me with any options. I needed to fight my way to safety, but first I had to even the odds.

I fired toward the building to drive the shooters back. Then I sprinted to the open garage door. My feet barely seemed to touch the ground. Once I got inside, I vaulted toward the nearest cinder block wall and watched outside, hoping the shooter near the Buick was stupid enough to emerge. He didn't, but he didn't shoot at me, either—probably because he feared hitting his friends.

This spot gave me better cover than the car outside, but the bad guys outnumbered and outgunned me. Worse, my phone was gone, which meant the cavalry wouldn't come unless a neighbor called in the gunshots, something they may or may not do in this neighborhood. I was on my own.

I slid to my left. Blood trickled down my arm from where the first gunshot had grazed me, making the grip on my weapon slick. I was losing a fair bit of blood. It wouldn't be long before I got lightheaded. With at least two active shooters after me, that was bad.

My lungs sucked in deep breaths as I tried to think my way through this. Between the Glock 26 in a holster on my ankle and the Glock 19 in my hand, I had twenty-five rounds remaining. I wouldn't overwhelm anybody with that kind of firepower, which meant I needed to change the game.

I looked around me and found a fire extinguisher on the floor. The idea formed in an instant. It was either the best idea I'd ever had, or the worst. I grabbed the fire extinguisher and crept to the left, toward an open door.

The garage's reception area and front room were across the hall. Nobody lurked in the hallway.

God, please let this be a good idea.

I heaved the heavy fire extinguisher across the hall and into the room.

"Whoa," came a voice. I didn't know whose it was, nor did I care. My Glock 19 barked as I ducked and fired. The first round pinged off the extinguisher's side, but my second hit it dead center. Carbon dioxide spewed everywhere, filling the room.

I ran, but so did a guy from the office. He hit me in the hallway, almost knocking me down. As I staggered back, he sprinted down the hallway toward a back exit. He was out of the fight, which meant I had one fewer asshole to worry about.

Then glass shattered as another figure threw my fire extinguisher through the shop's front window. The fog inside the room lifted, and I raised my firearm to take aim as a man dove through the broken glass of the front window.

A man in mechanic's overalls coughed from the ground. A pair of gunshot wounds pockmarked his chest, but he didn't have a gun in his hand. Blood pooled around him and dribbled down his chin.

"Shit," I said, between breaths. He looked like a civilian caught in the crossfire. I wanted to give chase to the men who had escaped, but the mechanic would die unless I did something.

"You'll be okay, buddy," I said, holding a hand to his wound and pressing hard. Blood kept pouring out. I shot my eyes around the room. Even a roll of duct tape would help. It fixed everything. Surely they'd have it in a big garage.

Tires screeched outside. I looked through the shattered remains of the front window. A rifle inside the car lit up the night. Rounds slammed into the shop. I dropped to my belly and crawled on the ground toward the receptionist's desk for cover. The mechanic's blood coated my shirt, arms, and pants like I was in some macabre horror movie.

Every muscle in my body tightened, and my fingers trembled as I searched the desk and ground around it.

"Where's the goddamn phone?" I shouted. "Where's the phone? There's got to be a phone."

Rounds thwacked into the desk as I popped up. A rolling office chair spun into the wall as a round struck it on the back. I grabbed the landline from the desktop and dove to the ground again as a fresh volley rang out. I pounded 911, but it didn't make a call. Then I hit buttons at random, hoping something would work.

"How do I get an outside line?"

The mechanic said nothing. He was dead. Unless I moved, I'd die, too. I squinted in the light until I found a button with a shield on it. I pounded that, and the damn thing dialed. In some faraway dispatch center, a 911 operator answered.

"Officer needs assistance. I'm under fire, and I lost my phone. There's at least one casualty. Trace this call and send all available units to this address."

The dispatcher said nothing for a moment. Then gunfire shattered the momentary quiet, getting the dispatcher's attention. She routed every officer in the area to the garage. I thanked her and popped my head up as tires screeched. A sedan peeled away in a cloud of gun smoke and burned rubber.

Three young men walked toward me. One of them held a pistol cocked to the side. I raised my weapon, crossed the waiting room, and then stepped through the front window. My arms were black with blood in the moonlight.

"Police officer!" I shouted. "Drop your weapon now."

The men hesitated. Then each ran in a different direction. I stayed there, holding my pistol in front of me as if I were trying to subdue a suspect.

Then my shoulder trembled, and pain lanced through my arm as my adrenaline waned. I dropped my arm to my side. Gradually, I realized that my hands hurt, but only when I looked down did I realize that I had shards of glass in my palms.

I wondered how I'd gotten that. Somewhere in the distance, a siren shattered the sudden quiet around me. Blue and white lights sped toward me from up the street. I dropped my firearm and then fell onto my ass. In six years on the job, I had never fired my weapon on duty. Now I had, and not only had I fired it, I had also tried to kill somebody.

Eventually, the importance of this evening would catch up to me. My world would change. I'd change. But for now, all I could do was hurt.

32

The next few hours passed as a blur. The first officers on the scene checked out the mechanic, but he was already dead. His blood covered my arms and chest, but I never even learned his name. That seemed wrong.

Paramedics cut the arm off my jacket, saw the gash from a bullet, and drove me to the emergency room at Barnes Jewish Hospital, where a nurse helped me change into a clean robe. After that, she cleaned the glass from my arm and hands and gave me an IV for antibiotics and pain medication. The paramedics thought a piece of shrapnel might have lodged in my arm, but the bullet had just grazed me. A physician gave me a dozen stitches before leaving the room.

Forensic technicians with the city's crime lab came in next. They took my blood-soaked clothes as evidence and swabbed my hands for gunshot residue. Once they left, Julia and two city detectives came in.

Julia gave me a quick hug and held my hand as the detectives interviewed me. I was honest about everything. The detectives took my statement and asked a few questions, but I didn't know who'd shot me, whom I'd shot, who'd run off, who had driven the Buick, or who had come to my rescue.

The detectives left about an hour after they arrived, but Julia stayed. She squeezed my good shoulder and sighed.

"I called Travis on the way over here," she said. "You weren't on duty tonight. Why were you following Christopher Hughes?"

I closed my eyes and allowed my head to sink deeper on the pillow.

"Somebody needed to."

"Maybe. According to Travis, he put a uniformed officer on Hughes's room. You sent her away."

I counted to sixty in my head before opening my eyes. Julia crossed her arms and stood at the foot of my hospital bed.

"I needed to do something. If I stuck around my house, I thought I'd drink. I didn't want to get drunk."

For a moment, Julia's gaze was hard, but then her expression softened, and she closed her eyes.

"You told your father your drinking was under control," she said.

"It is," I said.

Julia sat down near my legs and put a hand on my knee.

"How many days a week do you drink alone?"

"We're not going there," I said, shaking my head. "I'm fine. I never drink alone."

"Roger doesn't count," she said.

The Girl in the Motel

I crossed my arms—which didn't feel great considering someone had shot me—and looked away.

"Every night?" she asked. "Every other?"

I cocked my head to the side. "That's none of your business."

She nodded. The look she gave me was so pitiful that I almost snapped at her.

"Your father and I would have stayed the night."

"I only have one bed, and it only has room for me and Roger."

She looked at me and smiled, but there wasn't a lot of warmth in it.

"We would have slept on the couches," she said. "We're here for you. The harder you try to push us away, the harder I'll push back. You know that."

"I've learned that," I said. "But I don't need a lecture."

"What do you need?"

I looked up at the ceiling. "I need to be alone."

Julia drew in a breath and sighed. "All right. If that's what you want, I'll go home, but I'll call you tomorrow."

I nodded. She held my gaze for a moment. The look she gave me was soft and loving and kind. I didn't know how to return it, so I looked down and swallowed. Before she left my room, I coughed.

"Hey," I said. She paused and looked at me. I wanted to tell her I loved her, and that I needed her, and that I had no one else in my life like her. I didn't know how to express everything she deserved to hear. So I didn't try. I hoped she understood. "Thanks for coming down."

She smiled. I couldn't tell from her expression whether she was disappointed or whether she had just expected me to say something different.

"I'll call you tomorrow."

She left, and I stared at the ceiling. A doctor came in a while later. He wanted me to stay overnight in the hospital where they could administer IV antibiotics, but I told him I'd rather have someone shoot me again than stay overnight. By his nonplussed expression, he had expected that answer. He warned me that, due to the blood all over my clothes and my open wound, that I'd need HIV tests at four weeks and then at three months. He also warned me to refrain from unprotected sex until both tests came back clean. At least the latter I could manage.

I left the hospital at four in the morning and took a cab back to my truck. Uniformed and plain-clothes police officers swarmed around the body shop. I thought about staying and watching them work, but I needed to go home. Besides, they already had my contact information and statement. If they needed me, they knew where to find me.

The horizon was a clouded dark gray as I turned into my driveway. It was a quarter to six. The spring sun would burn off the morning gloom in a few hours, but for now, the gloom fit my mood. The moment my door squealed open, Roger came bounding toward me from his house in the backyard. He had long trails of saliva down his muzzle, and the hair on his back stood at attention. He looked mangy and angry, and he immediately put himself between me and the road. Something had him spooked.

I stroked his back, locked my truck, and looked out across the property. With everything going on, it wouldn't have surprised me if a reporter had parked across the street hoping he or she could get an interview when I came home. It had happened before when I picked up a big case. If I had to guess, Roger had scared him off.

I went inside, gave the dog water, called my boss to let him know I'd come in late, and then crashed on my bed. News reporters could wait. Sleep couldn't.

33

Sherlock's feet dug into the plush carpet as he paced the conference room floor. His investigators, Alonzo Morrison and Scott Gibson, sat on the other side of the table. Both held coffee mugs and had bags under their eyes. The moment they had shown up on his doorstep that morning, their faces told him they had failed. Thankfully, they had kept their heads about them enough to dispose of the evidence.

"How many people saw you?" asked Sherlock.

Alonzo shifted on his seat. "Christopher Hughes and Warren Nichols for sure. The girl outside may have seen me, but I don't know."

Sherlock ran a hand across his face. "Hughes, we can deal with. He's weak. The girl's trouble, though. She's a detective in some podunk town south of here. She shouldn't have been there."

"What should we do?" asked Gibson.

Sherlock walked to a window and looked out over the bustling streets of Clayton. When he rented this office, it had seemed perfect for him. It was respectable and clean. The location had plenty of parking and foot traffic. Even his white-collar clients wouldn't have minded meeting him there. He wondered whether this cushy office and life had made him grow too soft.

Ten years ago, his employees wouldn't have failed. They would have killed Joe Court already and tied up Christopher Hughes so they could burn him with cigarettes during an interrogation.

"If Detective Court is watching Christopher, she's a danger to us. She's got to go."

"I won't kill a cop," said Gibson. "Even one from some podunk county. Job like that has legs that follow you to the grave."

He was right. Killing a cop wasn't like knocking off a gangbanger. Nobody cares if you shoot a gangbanger. You shoot a cop in St. Louis, though, and you'll have a thousand of the most motivated, vindictive, and evil sons of bitches on the planet beating the bushes looking for you. Nobody needed that hassle.

"We can't kill her, but we've got to take her out somehow. You guys were cops. How would you get her off the case?"

Alonzo almost said something, but Evelyn, the office assistant, walked into the room before he could speak. Sherlock tried to mask his annoyance.

"Evelyn," said Sherlock, forcing a polite smile to his face. "Yes?"

"Christopher Hughes is on line two," she said. "He says it's an emergency. He sounded stressed."

Given that a trained killer had tried to murder him the night before, he had every reason to sound stressed.

Sherlock nodded and then walked to the conference room's phone.

"Thank you," he said, hitting a blinking button to answer. Evelyn nodded and left. "Christopher, it's Sherlock. I've been working on your case all morning. The St. Louis County executor is considering my proposal for a settlement. If he accepts, it'll be six million dollars."

Christopher paused. "You said they'd offer me eight figures."

As much as Sherlock wanted to call him a greedy asshole, he couldn't piss him off that much yet.

"It's a considerable sum of money."

Christopher paused again and then sighed. "Yeah, yeah, whatever. You're my lawyer, right?"

"Yeah," said Sherlock, nodding.

"So that means I can tell you anything, and you can't tell anybody."

Sherlock hesitated. "There are exceptions to attorney-client privilege, but it's a strong protection. If you say you plan to commit a major crime, I'm obligated to go to the police. If you tell me you've already committed a crime, I can't share that with anybody."

"Good," said Christopher. "Because I need your help. Somebody tried to kill me last night."

Sherlock glanced to Alonzo and Scott.

"Are you sure?" asked Sherlock. "Why would someone try to kill you?"

Alonzo rolled his eyes. Scott just grinned.

"Cut the shit," said Christopher. "You understand

who I am and the business I ran. My old crew turned against me. I tried to meet a friend last night, and this guy just comes out of nowhere and tries to shoot me. Then somebody else showed up with a gun. I can't trust anybody else."

"You called the right person," said Sherlock. "I'll take care of you. Where are you right now?"

"A shitty hotel on the south side of St. Louis."

"Good," said Sherlock. "Stay there. I can set something up for you, but I'll need time. You got a gun?"

"Yeah. I got it from Warren last night. He's dead, so he didn't need it."

"Okay," said Sherlock, nodding to himself. "Keep your gun handy and keep your eyes open. I'll set something up and call you back as soon as I can. I won't let anything happen to you. You're my meal ticket, Mr. Hughes."

Christopher laughed. "All you care about is money, isn't it?"

He liked sex with Christopher's ex-wife, too, but it didn't seem like the right time to bring that up.

"Makes me trustworthy," said Sherlock. "I got your back. Okay? Hang tight, and I'll get you somewhere safe as soon as I can."

Christopher thanked him and then hung up. Sherlock pocketed his phone but said nothing while he processed the conversation. Christopher didn't seem to understand what had happened the night before. Good.

"He say anything about us?" asked Scott. Sherlock

shook his head.

"No, he didn't," he said. "You guys take a walk. I need a few minutes to think."

Alonzo and Scott left, giving Sherlock the privacy and quiet to think. Joe Court was as big a problem as Christopher Hughes. He had known it from the moment he took the case. Somehow, Christopher had convinced himself that Detective Court wanted him and was playing hard to get. Never mind he had raped and tormented her when she was a teenager. He'd never leave her alone, and she'd never leave him alone.

Now, Sherlock had to deal with both. He had driven by the detective's house twice so far in the last few days. It was remote. The nearest neighbor—an elderly woman who lived alone—was about a quarter mile away. Detective Court didn't have a traditional security system. Instead, she had a massive dog who barked at everything that moved.

He needed to figure out how to use all this.

The plan coalesced in his mind over twenty minutes of pacing back and forth. If he pulled it off, he'd kill two birds with one stone. If he failed, he'd have enough money that he wouldn't care.

He picked up his phone again and dialed Christopher's number.

"Christopher," said Sherlock, drawing in a deep breath once the ex-convict answered. "I made a lot of phone calls and set up a safe house. One of my clients has a mother who lives outside St. Augustine. It's an old, shitty house. It's remote, but it's defensible. Nobody will look for you there."

Christopher sighed. "Thank you, Jesus."

"Thank your lawyer, not Jesus," said Sherlock. "You understand how many favors I had to call in for this?"

"I owe you," said Christopher. "This is above and beyond. When do I go?"

"Tonight," said Sherlock. "After dark. Can you use that cell phone I gave you to call for a car?"

"Yeah," said Christopher. "Uber. I remember."

"Good. Call an Uber and have the driver drop you off about a block from the house. Bring as much cash with you as you've got. The old lady wants ten grand, but she'll take whatever you can give her. She's got a dog. He's big, but my client says he's a sweetheart. He won't bother you if you bring him something to eat."

"I'll give him a sandwich or something," said Christopher. He paused. "You sure I should wait until tonight?"

"Yeah," said Sherlock, nodding. "You go early, the old lady'll shoot you. She's paranoid."

"Okay," said Christopher, his voice low. "What next, then? I can't stay at some old broad's house forever."

"No, you can't. That's why you've got to disappear. I don't know who's after you, so we need to get you out of town. I can help, but it will cost money."

"How much?" said Christopher.

Sherlock paused. "A lot. You'll get a new ID, a new passport, new everything. I've got a guy who works in the

Canadian Embassy in Washington. They're legit, but they're expensive. Hundred grand."

"Jesus," said Christopher. "I don't have that kind of money."

"You had a quarter million hidden in the walls of your ex-wife's house," said Sherlock. "I can front you a hundred grand, but you better find going-away money fast."

Christopher swore under his breath and then went silent for ten or fifteen seconds.

"All right," he said. "I've got money, but it's at a bank in a safe deposit box."

"Then I'll get it," said Sherlock. "I'm your lawyer. If you trust me with your life, you can trust me with your money."

Christopher swore again. "I don't like this."

"Nobody likes this," said Sherlock. "We've got to improvise. What's it going to be? You trust me and survive, or do you sit in a hotel room until your old business partners slit your throat?"

Sherlock counted to five before Christopher spoke.

"I trust you. I've got four safety deposit boxes in banks in Clayton. They don't have keys. They've got passcodes. You got a pen?"

He recited a long string of numbers, which Sherlock wrote down.

"What's my cut?" asked Sherlock.

"It's all about money with you, isn't it?" asked Christopher.

"Yeah. We're both businessmen. My organization is providing you a valuable service, and I think we should get paid for that. You understand. Five hundred ought to do it."

"Five hundred grand," said Christopher. "That's a lot of money."

"You can't expect me to do this for free."

"For five hundred, I don't want to owe you anything else. That's it. Five hundred, you get me out of the country, and we're done."

"It's a deal," said Sherlock. He read off Joe Court's home address. "That's where you need to go. Show up at between one and two in the morning. Lights will be off. The dog will probably bark, so throw him a piece of ham or something. That'll shut him up. The old lady's expecting you, but she'll be in bed. She will unlock the back door. You can sleep on the couch."

"I don't like this," said Christopher. "Sneaking around doesn't feel right."

"Sorry if you don't like sneaking, but it's either this or die," said Sherlock, forcing a measure of annoyed sharpness into his voice. "Make your own arrangements."

"I didn't mean to sound ungrateful, but this is my life we're talking about. It's important."

"Yeah, it is," said Sherlock, softening his voice. "Which is why you called me. Nobody will come after you at the old lady's house. In a week, you'll be sipping margaritas on the beach in the Dominican Republic. In the meantime, I'll get your money and put this together.

Keep your head down, and we'll get through this. All right?"

"Yeah," said Christopher, his voice stronger and more confident than it had been just a few moments earlier. "You're a real friend. I can't thank you enough for this."

"Pay me, and we'll call it even."

"You're a cold bastard," said Christopher, laughing. "That's what I like about you."

"Stick to the plan, and you'll stay alive."

Christopher thanked him again before hanging up. Sherlock rubbed his eyes. In fourteen hours, Christopher Hughes would sneak into Detective Joe Court's home. She'd shoot without hesitation.

Sherlock knew no one who deserved it more.

34

I woke at about noon. My entire body ached, and my head pounded as if I were hung over. Roger must have heard me get up because he ran into my bedroom and licked my hand as I swung my legs off the bed. The sweatpants and shirt I had picked up at the hospital felt rough and scratchy. My arm hurt, but it didn't burn or itch—two signs of infection the doctors at the ER had warned me to watch for. That was nice.

I drank a glass of water before showering and getting dressed. The doctors at the ER had given me some antibiotics and painkillers, so I took both and drove into work. I should have taken the day off. If I did that, though, I'd sit around all day thinking about the shooting. The round that grazed my arm could have hit my chest, or it could have nicked a major artery.

As a police officer, I knew the risks that came with wearing a badge. I had never lost a colleague while in St. Augustine, but a couple hundred police officers per year died in the United States in the line of duty. Despite the risks, I put on my badge every morning because I believed in the work I did. People needed help, and I gave it. Nothing I did could bring a murder victim back from the dead, but I could give a family justice.

I didn't like the thought of almost dying while chasing Christopher Hughes. He had taken enough from me. He didn't deserve more.

Trisha stopped me as I walked into the station. The waiting room was empty, making it a rare quiet moment during fair week.

"I heard what happened to you in St. Louis. You don't need to be here."

"I've got paperwork to fill out," I said. "I either do it here, or I sit home alone. The ambience here is nicer."

"I'm glad you're okay."

"Me, too. Thanks," I said, starting toward my desk. Before I could go more than a few feet, I stopped myself. "Have you seen Travis this morning?"

"He's with a detective from St. Louis. They're trying to track down Christopher Hughes to ask about the shooting."

"So Christopher's gone to ground?"

"Best we can tell, yeah. We tried his hotel this morning, but he's not there. His lawyer claims he hasn't seen him, either. He'll show up. He's suing St. Louis County. There's too much money at stake."

I nodded. Even after thinking about it, I didn't know what happened last night. The shooters could have been trying to kill me, but they could have been after Christopher Hughes. They might have even targeted the shop's owner. The investigating officers would figure that out. As a witness, I needed to stay away from it.

"Those missing high school kids ever show up?" I asked.

Trisha shook her head. "Not that I know of."

Now that was troubling. If they had been adults, I would have suspected they had eloped and gone on a honeymoon to spite their parents. Missing teenagers should have returned by now. They didn't have enough money to disappear this long.

"And no one's even seen their car?"

Trisha shook her head again. "Not that we know of. Highway Patrol has issued a statewide notice on the car. If it's in Missouri, we'll find it."

I nodded, already thinking. "If they're gone too much longer, we'll bring in some help. If you need me, I'll be at my desk. I've got paperwork to fill out."

She smiled and nodded. Her phone rang almost the moment I turned my back. No rest for the weary during fair week. I looked forward to having free time again.

I walked to my desk and checked my messages. My boss had called and left me a voicemail, which told me I was on desk duty pending an investigation into my shooting in St. Louis. It was a formality considering I had only fired my weapon after being fired upon, but it was important. The rules mattered. I wasn't above them because I carried a badge.

While all that was going on, Travis, officers from the Highway Patrol, and detectives from both St. Louis County and the city were trying to find Christopher

Hughes. They could have him. He may not have killed the garage owner, but he was there when it happened, and he had gone there to commit some kind of crime. Once they found him, they'd book him on felony murder charges. He was toast.

I spent the afternoon writing reports. Those missing teenagers worried me. Desk duty or not, I planned to follow up.

I started by calling Paige Maxwell's and Jude Lewis's parents. Neither had heard from their children or their children's friends. Next, I called the principal at their school, who said the kids hadn't attended since their disappearance. Next, I called the local bank and learned neither had used their debit cards or withdrawn money from the ATM since going missing. After that, I checked their social media accounts, but neither had posted anything since their disappearance.

On the off chance they were sitting in a holding cell somewhere out of state, I called law enforcement agencies in Illinois, Arkansas, Kentucky, and Tennessee. Nobody had seen the kids, and there had been no reports of traffic accidents involving their vehicle.

After striking out all afternoon, I stood up from my desk with my stomach rumbling. It was a little after five. I hadn't wasted the day, but it felt like it. The swing shift would come in soon. They didn't need me.

I got my things together, told Trisha I'd see her tomorrow, and then headed out. On my way home, I stopped by a grocery store and picked up a twelve pack of a pale ale I liked, two rice bowls with chicken and teriyaki sauce from the prepared food section, and a big bag of ice.

At home, Roger met me on the porch and bowed in front of me, his signal that he wanted to play. I put my groceries away and tossed him a ball until he calmed down.

Years ago, I couldn't tire him out no matter what I did. We'd run through the woods for an hour in the morning, and then he'd want me to throw him a ball or a stick all day. Now, if he followed me jogging in the morning, he'd go—maybe—a quarter mile before turning around, and he'd only chase a ball a few times before having to sit.

Every day, I saw fresh signs of his aging body, but every day, he gave me a new reason to love him. I couldn't ask for more from a friend.

It was about six when we finished playing. I figured I might as well exercise, so I changed into some athletic gear and then hit the trails in the woods near my house. Roger didn't follow far, but he came with me at first. Then a squirrel caught his attention, and he ran home.

I worked up a sweat, came home, and had my dinner on the front porch. Roger sat at my feet. It was a comfortable night, but it was lonely. I figured I had done enough drinking while alone these past few days, so I changed into some clean clothes and went to a bar on the edge of St. Augustine.

I wouldn't take a friend to The Barking Spider, but I

knew it would be the least crowded bar in town during fair week. It had two pool tables, a bar, and cheap tables and chairs through a big, open room. Someone always smoked no matter when I came in, and the jukebox seemed to play only Def Leppard.

I parked on the edge of a full lot and went inside. There weren't many seats left, but the room wasn't so crowded that I had a hard time making my way to the bar where I found a single open stool near the bathroom. Everyone around me seemed to be talking at once, so I couldn't hear what anyone said. It was just enough noise to leave me alone with my thoughts.

As I sat down, the bartender nodded a greeting as he filled a plastic pitcher with Bud Light.

"What can I get you?" he asked.

"Jack and Coke with a shot of Wild Turkey on the side."

He raised his eyebrows for a moment and then poured. I downed the shot and slipped him a ten before looking at the surrounding room. I rarely drank bourbon, but it seemed to fit the decor better than a shot of vodka would have. Plus, The Barking Spider's vodka tasted more like rubbing alcohol than something a human being should have ingested.

The shot hit me about five minutes later, and I felt my shoulders relax. After two more shots, my mood lightened even further. I drew from the energy of the crowd. For the first time that day, I didn't think about Paige Maxwell or her boyfriend, Jude Lewis; I didn't think about Christopher Hughes, or Megan and Emily Young; I didn't think about the shooting last night or the dead mechanic. I felt normal.

After about an hour, a man about my age sat beside me and smiled. I knew most of The Barking Spider's regulars, and this guy didn't fit in. He wore jeans and a T-shirt and polished black shoes. He didn't even try to hide the wedding ring on his left ring finger.

"Hey," he said. "Can I buy you a drink?"

"No thanks," I said, already feeling my words slur.

"It's all right," he said, motioning toward the bartender. "Two shots. Whatever the lady's having."

The bartender poured, and the tourist pushed one to me. I pushed it back. My pleasant buzz subsided.

"No, thank you," I said, forcing myself to smile as I reached to my purse for my wallet. I looked to the bartender. "I'll cash out now."

"It's just a drink," said my new friend. He smiled. "Come on. It won't hurt you. Have a drink with me. You're the prettiest girl in the bar."

"No, thank you," I said.

He put his hand on my leg and squeezed my thigh above the knee. His smile never wavered.

"I just bought you a drink. At least have the courtesy of being nice."

I looked down. "Remove your hand, please."

He took his hand away but then leaned his torso toward mine, crowding me.

"It's just a drink, sweetheart," he said. His smile

wasn't so friendly. "I'm not asking you to sleep with me. I'm alone. You're alone. I'm asking for you to have a drink with me. No pressure."

I looked to the bartender again. "Leo, call me a cab, please."

The guy beside me leaned closer so that I could feel his breath on my cheek. His eyes traveled down my neck and then my chest.

"I'll drive you home. I've got a car outside."

Leo, the bartender, grabbed a phone but stayed close.

"Buddy," he said. "Joe asked you to leave her alone. You should listen."

The tourist smiled at me. "A pretty girl named Joe. I like that."

I had spent a lot of evenings in bars, so men had pushed drinks on me before. As long as they backed off when I declined, I didn't mind. Men who didn't understand the word *no* pissed me off.

"When I was fifteen, a guy like you pushed a lot of alcohol on me. Then he raped me when I passed out," I said, my voice a whisper. "I'm not a kid anymore. I've got a Glock 19 in my purse, a Glock 26 in a holster on my ankle, and a badge on my belt. If you don't back off, you will see one of the three, and I can't guarantee which one it'll be. Your choice, but the odds are high you'll get some gratuitous holes in you if you don't leave me alone."

He held his gaze on me for a moment and then leaned back.

"Piss off, bitch," he said, reaching to the bar for his shot. He downed it and then walked away. Leo watched him and then leaned close so we could talk over the din of the room.

"You still want that cab?" he asked. I nodded, having lost my buzz.

"Yeah. I need to get out of here."

"Want a drink before you go? Consider it a thank you for not shooting him."

I looked to the bar where the asshole had left the shot he ordered me. I picked it up, downed it in a gulp, and then shook my head as I stood on legs wobbly from booze.

"No, but thanks," I said, taking deep breaths and willing the room to stop spinning. When I felt I could walk to the door without tripping over my own feet, I took a deep breath. I felt a little better. "I'll wait outside."

Leo nodded and leaned a little closer. He lowered his voice.

"Maybe next time leave your firearm home when you're not on duty."

"I'm not armed," I said. "I don't drink and shoot. It doesn't work out well for anybody. See you later."

He straightened. "See you later, Detective Court. Your cab should be here soon. Have a good night."

I thanked him and then walked out, hoping I wouldn't puke on the ride home.

35

The house was remote, and the front porch sagged. Christopher had seen worse, but he had seen better, too. He was almost surprised it didn't have a car on cinder blocks in the front lawn or an old washing machine beside the rocking chairs on the front porch. Hopefully Sherlock would get his ass in gear and put together a workable escape plan because he didn't want to stay here any longer than he had to.

The Uber driver had dropped him off about a quarter of a mile from the home. Christopher felt the weight of Warren's weapon in his pocket. It was a revolver, and it had six rounds in the chamber. He hadn't fired a gun in almost thirteen years, which was a problem. Shooting wasn't like riding a bicycle. A kid learns to ride a bike when he's ten, and he could pick up a bike twenty years later and ride just fine.

To shoot a firearm well, though, you needed fine motor control, muscle memory, and keen eyesight. Your stance had to be perfect, your weapon had to be clean, and the environmental conditions had to be right. At any kind of distance, rain and wind could throw off what would be an accurate shot. An experienced shooter could compensate for the environmental conditions, but that took practice he hadn't been able to put in.

The house was far from town. Maybe if he stuck around long enough, he could set up a backstop somewhere and get some target shooting in. He'd leave the country and retire somewhere nice, but he didn't know where that'd be. No matter where he ended up, though, chances were that he'd be safer with a gun than without one.

As he walked closer to the house, a dog barked inside. It wasn't the high-pitched yip of a Chihuahua, but the deep, throaty boom of something much larger. He was glad Sherlock had warned him about the animal. And he was glad he had the firearm. Something that size could rip his arm off.

When he reached the home, he stopped and looked around. A big oak tree shaded the lawn and front porch while hostas decorated the home's foundation. The clapboard siding looked clean, and the windows were intact. A good contractor could have made it perfect for fifty or sixty grand, but it wasn't a dump.

"Home sweet home," he said, stepping onto the porch. The dog inside stopped barking. Sherlock didn't like dogs, but they sure made effective alarms.

The road in front of the home was straight for a quarter of a mile in either direction, affording him sightlines only blocked by trees. There were deep woods behind the house. If he put a car on the other side of those woods, he'd have an effective escape route, and with that dog, he'd know when anyone unwanted approached within a couple hundred yards. Sherlock had chosen well.

He put his hands in his pockets, one over his revolver and the second over a stack of seventy hundred-dollar bills. This place would be just fine.

I rolled over in bed and felt the world spin. My head pounded, but I wasn't hung over: I was still too drunk for that. Roger had just sprinted out of the room so fast he ran into my dresser, almost knocking over a lamp. Now, he was barking his head off at something outside.

I swung my legs off the bed. Once my feet touched the hardwood, the world came into focus and stopped spinning. I wouldn't have wanted to drive anywhere, but I was sober enough to walk. That was something. My throat felt dry. I could still taste the bourbon I had been drinking at the bar. Sweat dampened my sheets and pajamas.

Roger had run through the pile of clothes at the foot of the bed, scattering everything I had worn earlier that day. I picked up my pants and shirt and tossed them in the hamper before leaving my bedroom. Roger ran from the front window. He bowed in front of me and then yawned.

"Do you want out?" I asked, rubbing my eyes. He stretched, bowing again. It was his way of saying yes. I grumbled and walked to the kitchen. "If you had to pee,

The Girl in the Motel

you could have just told me earlier, asshole. You didn't have to wake up the entire world."

Roger maintained his characteristic silence until I opened the back door. Then he sprinted out into the night while I filled a glass with water. The sky was pitch black.

"It's way too early for this shit, honey," I shouted toward my open kitchen door. I heard nothing in response, so I stuck my head outside. When Roger had to go to the bathroom, he stayed in the yard. I couldn't see him at all. "Roger?"

Then I heard him growl from the front of my house. Roger didn't growl like that at squirrels, rabbits, or possums. Someone was there, someone he found threatening. With everything else going on, he was probably right. A little precaution would go a long way to keeping me safe. I went to the front hall closet and grabbed my Mossberg pump-action shotgun before running to the yard after my dog, all the while hoping this was just a stupid reporter.

It wasn't a dog. It was a Goddamn horse, and it came sprinting around the house straight toward him. Christopher took his hands out of his pockets and backed off.

"Easy, boy," he said, hoping to placate it. The animal stopped running about twenty feet from him. The fur on its back stood straight, and it leaned its weight on its front legs. Its mouth was open. The sound it produced was primal and menacing.

Christopher reached into his pocket for his revolver while taking stutter steps back. The dog matched his movements and slunk low along the ground, growling deep in its throat. This couldn't have been right. The old lady knew he was coming. If she had a dog this vicious, she should have locked it up.

Somebody called from behind the house. The dog stopped growling and cocked his head to the side. Christopher had owned dogs growing up. Dogs growled when scared, but this dog didn't fear him. He was protecting his home. If he ran far enough from the house, maybe the dog would stop.

Christopher took shuffling steps backwards until he hit the oak tree he had seen earlier. As he slid around it, the dog growled once more and crept to the side, cutting off his avenue of escape.

"You son of a bitch," he whispered, reaching into his pocket for his revolver. "Don't make me do this."

"Roger?"

"He's out front," said Christopher, not daring to raise his voice for fear of provoking the enormous animal. His revolver cleared his pocket as he backed around the tree. That at least gave him some cover for the moment. In his experience, most dogs could outpace him in a straight-line foot race, but they had a harder time cornering.

As Christopher tried to maneuver the tree between

him and the dog, he saw movement near the side of the house. It was a woman, and she carried a rifle.

"Roger," she called. He recognized her voice and felt his stomach drop. Christopher stopped moving and focused. It was Joe Court, and she wore flannel pajamas. Their eyes locked, and she raised her weapon to her shoulder. His stomach plunged into his feet.

Sherlock hadn't sent him to a safe house; the son of a bitch had sent him to Joe Court's house.

Christopher had just gotten played.

36

It was later than he had expected, but Sherlock pulled his old Mercedes to a stop at the top of the circular driveway in front of Diana Hughes's home. For a few moments, he sat there, gripping the steering wheel and thinking. It was after two in the morning. He liked seeing Diana, but he didn't want to be there.

Before he could leave, the light beside the front door popped on. Diana hadn't expected him, but her alarm had a motion sensor to let her know when someone reached the top of her driveway. It would have been annoying had more traffic stopped to turn around at her place, but her neighborhood had ample places to turn around. Someone moved behind the frosted glass of the front door.

Then she opened it. Even without makeup, even wearing just one of his old, long T-shirts, even without wanting to be, she was gorgeous. Sherlock had never loved anyone in his life. He cared about his parents, and he had told a girl in high school that he loved her, but that had been to get beneath her dress on prom night. His feelings for Diana were different. He wanted her happy, and she wanted him happy, too.

The Girl in the Motel

That was why he hated this moment.

As he opened his door and stepped out, the pistol in his pocket felt heavy. Scott Gibson had given it to him earlier for this occasion. Tonight, it would do a job, and then it would disappear again.

Sherlock trudged up the steps to the front door. Even from three feet away, he could smell Diana's alluring scent, an intoxicating mix of lavender and various kitchen spices combined with just a hint of clean sweat. She smiled at him.

"Didn't expect to see you tonight," she said.

"Did I wake you up?"

She nodded and stepped forward to put her hands on his chest. The movement caused her shirt to rise and expose the creamy skin of her upper thighs. "Yeah, but you can make that up to me."

She bit her lower lip. Sherlock didn't stop himself. He put his arms around her and kissed her and felt her body press against his. Then he picked her up, kicked the front door shut, and carried her to the bedroom. There, they took off each other's clothes and made love on her king-sized bed.

As he held her afterwards and felt her body heat against him, he closed his eyes.

"Christopher got away last night."

She sighed and nodded. "I heard."

"I hoped that we could capture him and persuade him to tell us where he had stashed his money."

She put a hand flat on his chest and gave him a soft,

warm smile. "If we're together, we don't need his money. I've got more money than we can spend. It's yours."

He nodded and looked at the ceiling. "I talked to him today, though, and convinced him that I could smuggle him out of the country if he paid me well enough. He spilled it all. He had four safety deposit boxes in banks in Clayton."

Diana pulled away. He didn't look at her. He couldn't look at her.

"I checked them out," he said. "There should have been ten million dollars in them, but every one was empty."

Diana didn't respond.

"So I talked to the bank manager," he said. Sherlock paused. "He said you had come and emptied them years ago."

Diana said nothing, but he could feel her hand on his side, tickling his ribs.

"Do you have the money?" he asked.

Again, she said nothing. So he rolled onto his side to see her face smiling at him. She pursed her lips and made a shushing sound as she cupped his cheek.

"We need that money," he said. "I don't care if you stole it. We need it."

The moment the words left his lips, he felt something hot pierce his side. He drew in a sharp breath. In a flash, Diana had pushed him onto his back. She kept a hand on his cheek and shushed him again.

"Hush, sweetheart," she said. "No more talking. I

don't want this to hurt more than it has to."

Sherlock looked down and found the handle of a knife sticking into the left side of his chest. He tried to sit up, but Diana put her hands on his shoulders, keeping him rooted in the spot.

"Don't move. I've put that knife into the intercostal space between your fourth and fifth ribs. If my aim was right—and I'm sure it was—the tip is now inside the left ventricle of your heart. If you move, it will only get worse."

He felt something cold pass over him.

"What are you doing?" he asked.

"I might ask you the same thing," she said. "You've never carried a firearm into my home before, but tonight you did. It was for me, wasn't it? If you wanted me to tell you where I put my ex-husband's money, you could have asked."

"I would have," he said. "I didn't get the chance."

"That admission betrays a much bigger problem," she said, reaching down to the knife she had plunged into him. "If you're worried about this, you can calm down. I was an ER nurse for several years. The left ventricle will seal small puncture wounds as it contracts. It will only leak blood when it relaxes. I've seen people survive hours with wounds like this. You'll be just fine until I sweep the blade to the left and open you up."

"You stabbed me," he said.

"Yeah," she said, nodding. "Sorry."

He closed his eyes and swallowed. "Please take me to

the hospital. We'll say we had an accident."

"Oh, honey," she said, exhaling. "That's not going to happen. You don't trust me. I love you, but I can't be in a relationship with someone who doesn't trust me."

Sherlock licked his lips and said the only thing that came to mind.

"I love you, too."

She smiled at him. Her eyes were almost teary.

"You don't know how long I've waited for you to say that, baby," she said. "Love is one thing, though. Business is another. Tonight, you brought a gun into my home so you could threaten me and take money I earned. If you had just asked, I would have shared it with you. I would have shared my whole life with you. Everything I owned would have become ours. I would have given you the keys to the kingdom if you had just asked."

"I'm sorry."

"Me, too," she said, sliding off the bed and getting a silk robe to cover her still naked body. Sherlock slid to the side of the bed, hoping he could reach his clothes and cell phone. Diana clucked her tongue and shook her head. "The more you move, the more likely you'll tear open the hole in your heart. That's a bad idea."

Sherlock took a deep breath and lay back.

"All right. What do I do?"

"Stay there," she said, pulling the sheet over his legs. "Mr. Gibson will come for you."

"Scott?" asked Sherlock. She nodded.

"He works for me now," she said, walking into her

closet. She came out a moment later carrying a belted gray dress on one hanger and a long green dress on another. "Which do you think I should wear?"

"The green one shows off your body," said Sherlock. "I always liked that one on you."

She held the dress to her chest and then tossed it on the bed before going back into her closet.

"Green it is," she said. "And thank you. If I had known you had liked it, I would have worn it more often."

Sherlock watched her slip her robe off. She noticed and winked at him before closing the door.

"It was you, wasn't it?" he asked. "All this time, I thought Christopher ran the business, but it was you."

She stepped out of the closet and then walked to her dresser for undergarments. As long as he could keep her talking, he was alive. St. Louis had excellent hospitals just a few miles away. They'd have cardiac surgeons on staff twenty-four hours a day. If he could persuade her to take him there, he could survive.

"Yeah," she said. "Christopher provided the seed capital, and he always thought he was in charge, but he couldn't rub two thoughts together if he tried. I did the work. I ran the girls. I held them when they cried, I selected them from the foster care office, I introduced them to Randy and helped him turn them into assets we could use. Then I used those little friends of Christopher's to launder our money. My ex-husband was disgusting. He deserved to die in prison."

"I underestimated you," he said. "I wish I had known you better."

"Me, too," she said, slipping a bra over her shoulders.

"So what now?" asked Sherlock. "You kill me and then run away with Christopher's money?"

"No," she said, shaking her head. "You set up a terrific business deal with Mr. Mendoza. After some discussion, he's agreed to continue the arrangement with me. I will become St. Louis's largest distributor of cocaine and sundries. My financing was in order. Yours wasn't. It was a real shame."

She walked to the bed and picked up her dress.

"Is this is formal enough to wear while meeting a new employee?" she asked. "I can't look too flirty."

"It's beautiful," he said. "You're beautiful."

She smiled at him, but instead of the usual affection he saw, he found anger.

"Flattery won't help. You fucked up, baby. You can't walk away from this."

Her expression was flat as she walked to the bathroom to get ready. He slid to the right, ever mindful of the knife in his chest. It hurt, but he didn't feel as if he were dying. Even still, he trusted Diana's medical judgment. If he could get to a phone and call 911, he'd have a chance. If he couldn't, he was dead.

When he reached the side of the bed, he heard a soft beep. Diana came from the bathroom wearing that green dress that hugged her body so well.

"Mr. Gibson's here," she said, crossing the room. She

knelt beside him and looked into his eyes again. He saw affection and real love staring back. "Believe it or not, I love you. I'm sorry, but this is business."

She reached to the knife. It was just a quick movement, but he gasped and felt the change come over him as the blade slit his heart open. She pulled the knife out. Sherlock's skin felt hot as blood rushed out of him. He tried to speak, but the words caught in his throat. She kissed his lips and stroked his hair, staining her beautiful dress with his blood.

"It's okay, baby," she whispered. "I'm here. I'm not going anywhere."

He tried to reach up and squeeze the life out of her throat, but he couldn't get his fingers to work right.

"I'm here," she whispered, batting his hands away as if he were a child. "Just listen to my voice and let yourself drift away."

His vision grew white and then black. His eyes felt heavy, but he needed to say something before he died. She leaned close as he whispered.

"Go ahead, love," she whispered. "I'm here."

"You deserved him, bitch," he said. "Christopher. You deserved him."

It filled him with joy to see the pain in her eyes as his closed for the last time.

37

I had expected to find a reporter with a video camera on the front lawn. Instead, I found Christopher Hughes hiding behind a tree. He was pointing a revolver at my dog. I put my shotgun to my shoulder and took aim.

"Christopher, drop your weapon!" I screamed.

He looked at me as if he were lost. My finger slipped past the trigger guard and to the shotgun's trigger. Around here, people used shotguns to hunt game birds and deer. I didn't use mine to hunt animals, though. I kept mine to defend my home. It had a rifled barrel, and it shot one-ounce lead slugs at almost two thousand feet per second. Few animals on Earth could survive a well-placed shot from a weapon like that.

Human beings were not one.

"Drop your weapon!" I shouted again.

"You won't shoot me in the back."

Before I could process that, he had already turned and run. And he was right. I wouldn't have shot him in the back. I would have chased him and tried to tackle him, but I wouldn't have shot him. My dog, though, didn't play by the same rules I did. The moment Christopher ran, so did Roger. They reached the far side of the road in front of my house at the same time. Roger got in front of him and growled, but Christopher couldn't slow down enough to avoid a collision.

They fell in a mass on the ground. Roger yelped, and Christopher grunted. I sprinted after them, holding the rifle against my chest with both hands. Christopher got up first, but Roger wasn't slow to follow. They ran again, this time disappearing into the woods across from my house.

Where Roger could move well on trails, his short legs had difficulty in the weeds.

"Roger, freeze!" I screamed. It was one of the most important commands I had ever taught that dog. It kept him from running into the street after other animals, it kept him from chasing cars, it kept him from treading on glass when people threw bottles on the side of the road. It had taken weeks to get the command right. He should have stopped everything he was doing and come to a complete stop.

He didn't, though. The excitement was too much.

He pushed through the thick underbrush at the edge of the wood to the clear, virgin forest inside. There, his speed was his undoing. Christopher turned and fired the revolver behind him. A round buzzed past me while another thwacked into a tree. The third brought about a yelp that broke my heart.

Roger tumbled and rolled on the ground before coming to rest against the base of a big tulip poplar.

Christopher stopped running. I couldn't see well in the dark, but I raised my shotgun to my shoulder. I wanted to check on my dog, but I couldn't yet.

"Drop your weapon!" I shouted.

"He was coming after me," he said. "Your dog would have bitten me. He was crazy."

"Toss your weapon down and lay on the ground."

Christopher glanced at his weapon and then to me.

"I shot your dog," he said. "You'll kill me if I do that."

My heart pounded as adrenaline coursed through me.

"Drop your weapon. If I wanted you dead, you'd be dead."

He considered me for a moment and then dove behind a tree. I ducked and scrambled to my left as he fired. Dried leaves crinkled and sticks popped beneath me as my torso hit the ground. Christopher ran. I held my breath and pushed myself to a kneeling position. My left elbow was on my left knee, stabilizing the barrel of my weapon as I lined up a shot.

Christopher turned as he ran and raised the gun, just as he had toward my dog. I didn't give him the same chance Roger had. I squeezed the trigger. The heavy pump-action shotgun pounded against my shoulder, rocking me back. I chambered another round and lined up another shot as Christopher fell to the ground. For a few seconds, nothing moved. Roger whimpered, but I couldn't go to him yet.

"Get up, motherfucker," I whispered, holding the

barrel of my gun in Christopher's direction. "Run. I dare you."

I counted to ten and then to thirty, just watching for movement. When Christopher didn't get up, I crept toward him. He was, maybe, thirty feet from me, and when I reached his body, I saw why he hadn't moved. I had hit him square in the back, just below his shoulder blades. Likely, it had clipped his heart. I felt his neck for a pulse, but he wasn't breathing.

The man who had raped me all those years ago, the man who had ruined my life, was dead. I had killed him. I had dreamed about killing him, but I'd never believed it would happen. A wave of disgust came over me. I spit on his corpse and then kicked him in the ribs.

"Fuck you, Christopher," I said, kicking him again. His body barely budged, so I kicked him again, almost wishing he would cry out in pain. He didn't. He was dead. I kicked him until my leg grew so tired I couldn't kick him again. Then, Roger whimpered once more, bringing me back to the present.

I leaned my shotgun against a tree and knelt beside my dog. He licked my hand and mewled as I cradled him. Christopher had shot him in the chest near his shoulder. Nothing I could do would stop the bleeding, so I petted him once more and then stood.

"I'll be back, sweetheart," I said. "Mommy loves you. I'll be right back."

He whimpered again. I wanted to stay with him, but he needed help. I sprinted home and picked up the phone in my kitchen. My first call was to 911, but my second was to Roger's vet. He agreed to come out. Before going back out, I grabbed clean towels from the kitchen, a flashlight from near the back door, and my shoes.

When I got to my dog again, his breathing had slowed, but already I could hear sirens in the distance. He lifted his head as he saw me, and I held him and pressed towels against his wound, hoping the bleeding would stop.

"Please don't die, honey," I whispered. "Please stay with me. You're my buddy. I need you."

As I held my dog, a squad car skidded to a stop in front of my house with its lights blaring. I waved my flashlight around.

"I'm here," I shouted. "In the woods."

A man came running toward me. It was Sasquatch. His eyes were wide.

"That your blood all over your shirt or someone else's?"

"It's Roger's," I said. "I'm fine. Christopher is somewhere."

More officers came within minutes. I lost track of things for a while until Travis knelt with me and tried to pry me away from the dog.

"No," I said. "He's mine."

"It's okay," said Travis. "Your vet is at the road. We've got a back brace. Sasquatch and Vince will carry him. They'll make sure he's okay. You and I will go to your house, and you'll change into some clean clothes. Your mom and dad are on their way. Everything's okay."

Travis put a hand on my elbow and helped me stand. Roger was alive, but he didn't look good. He wasn't moving much. Sasquatch and Vince transferred him to a back brace and then carried him toward the road. I looked around me. There were a dozen officers with me in the woods, and they all had flashlights or lanterns.

"Trisha's at the house. Your neighbor, Susanne, is there, too," said Travis. "They'll get you cleaned up. We'll figure this out."

I nodded. Travis kept a hand on my shoulder as we walked.

"I shot Christopher," I said.

"I know," he said. "Your lawyer is already on the way. Some detectives from the Highway Patrol will try to talk to you at the house. Don't tell them anything until you've talked to your lawyer first."

"I spit on him," I said, drawing in a breath. "Then I kicked him. I wanted him to hurt."

Travis said nothing until we reached the edge of the road.

"I'll take care of you. Your mom and dad will be here soon."

As Travis had said, Trisha and Susanne met me on the front porch. I was a little shell shocked, but I didn't feel drunk anymore. The two of them stayed outside my bedroom while I changed. Afterwards, Trisha bagged my blood-stained clothes as evidence and then gave me a hug before leaving the house. Susanne made coffee and then sat with me on the front porch until Dad and Julia arrived.

They had to park up the road, but they ran from their car when they saw me. Julia threw her arms around me. Dad put a hand on my back.

"I killed the son of a bitch," I whispered.

"I know," said Julia.

"It's over," I said. "It's over."

"He'll never hurt anyone again."

And she was right. Christopher wouldn't hurt anyone again. I had made sure of that. Part of me screamed that I should have felt sick to my stomach, that I should have felt guilty.

But I didn't.

For the first time in years, I didn't feel afraid. When I went to bed, I wouldn't have to check beneath my bed or in my closet to make sure he wasn't there. I wouldn't have to leave a loaded shotgun in my front closet to protect myself. I didn't have to leave a light on in my hall in case he came in the night.

For the first time in years, I was no longer Christopher Hughes's victim. I was me. Just me.

I was free.

38

Since Christopher had never made it past the tree in my front yard, the police stayed out of my house. Dad and Julia made coffee for them, though, and played host while I slept in my room. At about six, Dad woke me up and said Roger was out of surgery. He had lost a lot of blood, but the vet thought he would live. I almost cried.

Roger had saved my life. I couldn't ask for a better friend. I ordered the largest rawhide bone I could find on the internet and had it overnighted to the house so he'd have a treat when he came home.

After that, I slept until about nine. By that time, the emergency had passed, so detectives from the Highway Patrol had begun focusing on laying blame. They started by interviewing me. Travis had warned me not to talk without having a lawyer present, but I had nothing to hide.

The detectives spent about two hours with me. They asked a lot of questions, but I had few answers to give them. Those officers left at about noon. After that, Dad drove me to The Barking Spider so I could pick up my car. Then, I went to the animal hospital to see my dog. He didn't wake up, but he was doing okay. That was all that mattered. Long term, this would take a toll on his health. I didn't know how much longer he had with me, but he was mine for as long as he drew breath.

My vet had patients to see, so I didn't stay at the animal hospital long. Instead, I went by the grocery and picked up food. I didn't know what Dad wanted to make for dinner, so I grabbed beans, ground beef, tomatoes, and everything else he'd need to make chili and cornbread. When I got to the house, there were two marked police vehicles in my driveway. One was from St. Augustine, but the other was from St. Louis County. I groaned and then parked on the grass so I wouldn't block anybody in.

This didn't promise to be fun.

Inside, I found my dad, Julia, and Travis in my living room staring at two people I didn't know. There were empty coffee cups on the end tables, so they had been there for a while. I stopped in the front door and then looked to Travis.

"Hey, boss," I said. "Sorry I wasn't in. I was checking on my dog."

Two strangers, a man and a woman, stood. The woman was in her late forties and had short brunette hair, and she wore a fashionable navy blazer over a white shirt. The man was younger than her but not by a lot. He wore a black suit and black tie as if he were going to a funeral.

The woman held out her hand.

"Lieutenant Beth Rampbell," she said. "The

gentleman with me is Detective Ezra Garza. We're with the St. Louis County police."

"Beth and Ezra work homicide," said Julia. "They're here to talk about James Holmes."

I furrowed my brow and looked at them. "Christopher Hughes's lawyer?"

"Yeah," said Beth. "Someone murdered him."

"That doesn't explain why you're interested in my daughter," said Dad.

Ezra looked at him. "Mr. Holmes had words with your daughter on at least one occasion. In addition, he filed a harassment complaint against her with our department after a meeting in his office in Clayton."

"I'm sure he had words with many people," said Dad, standing and crossing the room. He put himself between me and the detectives. "The man was a lawyer. That's what they do. They file complaints."

I put my hand on my dad's arm.

"It's okay, Dad," I said. "They're just doing their jobs. Why don't you and Julia go around back?"

Dad looked at me and raised his eyebrows. "You sure?"

"Yeah," I said. "Travis is here. If they get out of hand, he'll shoot them. Then you, Julia, and I can bury the bodies together as a family while he leads the other cops away. It'll be a bonding experience for all of us."

The detectives from St. Louis didn't look amused, but Dad smiled a little. He and Julia held hands as they walked through the kitchen to the back door. I focused on the two officers.

"Okay. I did not kill Mr. Holmes, and I do not know who did. Until you showed up, I didn't know he was dead. I had no reason to want him dead, and I did not blame him for the actions of his client."

"Let's back up," said Beth. "You were involved in a shooting in St. Louis. Tell us about it."

I looked at Travis for advice. He nodded, so I sat on the couch and repeated to them the story I had told the city detectives two nights ago. When they pressed me for details, I told them they could talk to the actual detective assigned to that case. They didn't like that answer, but it shut them up.

"Has Mr. Holmes ever come to your house?" asked Ezra.

I shook my head. "Not that I know of."

"That's an interesting answer," said Beth, sitting down and then resting her elbows on her knees. "It's kind of weaselly."

"In what way?" asked Travis, sitting beside me. The lieutenant looked at him.

"It's the answer a politician would give. If we find evidence that Mr. Hughes came to the house, you haven't committed perjury, but you have misled us. It's weaselly. Will we find evidence that he's been here?"

"Not with your head up your ass," I said.

"Joe," said Travis, touching my elbow, his voice low. I straightened and shut up. "It's the perfect answer. She means she hasn't asked him here or invited him here. If you find evidence that Mr. Holmes has been to this house, it would surprise us both."

"Are you her lawyer now, Sheriff Kosen?" asked Ezra.

"I'm her commanding officer," said Travis. "You wouldn't have driven all the way out here to ask questions you could have asked over the phone. You came out here because you thought you'd make an arrest. What have you got?"

Ezra looked to his boss. Beth reached into her purse for a notepad.

"At five this morning, a jogger reported seeing an attractive blonde woman drag a body from the bed of an old red Dodge Ram pickup truck and dump it on the shore of Creve Coeur Lake. The truck had a license plate that began with PL2," said Beth, looking up from her notepad at me. "You have an old Dodge Ram pickup truck with a license plate that begins with PL2."

"I do," I said, nodding. "And thank you for calling me attractive. I appreciate that."

Ezra locked his eyes on mine. "You have the only old Dodge Ram pickup truck in the state with a license plate that starts with PL2."

I looked at Travis. His smile was bemused, but he looked away before I could say anything. I looked at the two detectives.

"What's this jogger's name?"

"Your attorney will get that information as part of the discovery process," said Ezra. "We found him credible."

"Judgment isn't your strong suit, is it?" I asked.

Ezra sat straighter. "We followed the evidence, Ms. Court. A witness saw your truck at the site of a body dump, and you have a history with the victim. How do you explain that?"

"I don't think I have to," I said.

"We'd prefer if you did," said Beth.

I looked to Travis. "You want to take this?"

He blinked a few times and then cleared his throat. "Detective Court was here with me at five this morning. She wasn't in Creve Coeur."

"See, that's a problem," said Ezra, smiling. "If you're her lover, too, your word won't carry the weight you think it does."

I shouldn't have laughed, but I did anyway. Travis sighed and shook his head.

"Something amusing?" asked Beth.

"Yeah," I said.

They waited for me to clarify, but I wasn't in the mood to help them. Beth crossed her arms and looked from me to Travis and then back again.

"Enlighten us," said Beth. "What were you two doing at five this morning that kept you so busy?"

"Well," I said, thinking for a second. "I was in bed. It had been a long night. I don't know what Travis was doing, but if he says he was here, I trust him."

Beth narrowed her eyes. Travis spoke before she could say anything.

"Christopher Hughes came to Detective Court's home last night. He shot the detective's dog before discharging his weapon at her. Detective Court defended herself and killed him. There are at least a dozen witnesses from my department who can verify Detective Court's location. If my officers don't convince you, there were several detectives from the Highway Patrol here, too. At five this morning, the truck your credible witness described as being near Creve Coeur Lake was in the parking lot of a bar called The Barking Spider."

Neither Beth nor Ezra said anything for a moment. Then Ezra looked to Travis.

"You could have told us about the attack on the phone, Sheriff Kosen. It would have saved us a trip."

"You could have told me why you needed to see my detective. Instead, you tried to ambush her. You wasted everyone's time."

Ezra started to retort something, but Beth put a hand on his shoulder, stopping him.

"We've got three dead men connected to you," she said. "Warren Nichols, Christopher Hughes, and now James Holmes. If you didn't kill them, I'm guessing you have a good idea who did."

I leaned back and shook my head. "I killed Christopher, but I don't know the other guys. But on the plus side, there's a good chance you'll have more evidence soon. Something tells me your shooter isn't done yet."

39

Beth and Ezra stuck around for about twenty minutes longer, but I couldn't get them to tell me much about their investigation so far. And that was part of the problem.

We had five bodies tied to this case—Megan and Emily Young, Christopher Hughes, Warren Nichols, and James Holmes—and four different law enforcement agencies with jurisdiction over various parts of the investigation. Our departments communicated with one another, but we didn't have a central information clearinghouse. It was a mess.

Ideally, stakeholders from each department would sit down and share information, but every department had different procedures and reporting mechanisms. We talked about evidence in different languages. Not only that, we'd have massive egos and the department politics of four different government agencies to contend with. With this many bodies on the ground and the media attention this case was already getting, somebody would take one on the chin. Cases like this ruined careers.

And I was glad to stay out.

The detectives left after our interview. Julia and I took a walk while Dad made dinner. At six, we sat down together around my kitchen table as a family. It was comfortable. I joked and laughed. Roger would come home once he recovered. I'd go back to work. Life would go on.

But things were different. Christopher Hughes had ruined my life, but he hadn't taken it. With his death, I felt like I had it back. I laughed easily, I smiled freely, and I felt happy.

At about seven, we finished dinner. Julia and Dad drove home. They offered to stay the night, but I felt okay. Christopher's death had transformed my world. I wanted to face it on my own. Once Julia and Dad's car disappeared, I sat on the porch and drank a soda as the stars rose. A beer would have tasted good, but I decided against it. I liked the thought of having a drink, but I didn't need one.

That was a new feeling, too. I didn't feel like I had to run from anything. For the past twelve years, I had walked around with an ever present sense of unease, a feeling of wrongness that followed me everywhere I went. It was my shadow, and I drank to make it go away. But now I couldn't see it anymore.

So I sat and rocked and thought. At about eight, I saw a pair of headlights in the distance. I lived far enough in the country that few people drove by my house. If you were on my street, you had a reason to be on my street. And this vehicle did. It was a news van from a station in

St. Louis. As I watched, it pulled into my driveway and then turned around so it could park on the side of the road nearest my house.

Angela Pritchard stepped out of the front passenger seat. She wore a red dress with a scoop neck that showed a scant amount of cleavage. Her hair seemed to flow like water in a soft, evening breeze. A man in jeans and a yellow sweater vest—her producer, more than likely—stepped out of the driver's seat and joined Angela near the side of the van. Their cameraman—a younger guy with scruff on his chin and unruly curly hair—opened the rear sliding door and stepped out.

The cameraman and the producer pulled a pair of tripods with lights from the van and set them up facing the woods across from my house. As the crew prepared for their shot, Angela walked down my driveway toward me. Her smile almost looked genuine, but something in her eyes told me it wasn't. She waved as she got near.

"Detective Court?" she asked. "Angela Pritchard. We met the other day outside your station."

"I remember," I said, nodding. "Can I help you?"

She looked toward her crew and then to me. Her smile faded and turned into a concerned expression.

"I heard about the shooting near your home. I'm so sorry. Are you doing okay?"

"Fine. What do you need?"

"My producer and I were hoping we could get shots of the area for a piece we're producing on Christopher Hughes and James Holmes. Did you know they called him Sherlock? We found that out this afternoon. I thought it was interesting."

"I have met Mr. Holmes," I said. "Someone told me his nickname."

Her fake smile came back. "Since I'm here with a camera crew, I'd love to get your side of things."

"I don't have a side."

"How about a statement?" she asked.

I shrugged. "Off the record, Christopher Hughes was a monster. The world's a better place without him. His lawyer wasn't much better."

Angela lowered her chin. "Are you sure I can't quote you on that, Detective?"

"Please get off my lawn," I said.

She walked toward her van but then stopped.

"We'll still film. It's a county road. I checked before coming out here."

"That's right," I said, nodding. "It's a story, and you're reporting it. You're doing your job. I don't blame you, but I don't want to be a part of this."

"I can respect that," she said. "If you change your mind, we'll be here for about an hour. I'd love to talk to you."

"Not going to happen, but thank you," I said. "Good luck with your story."

I stood and walked inside before she could respond. The moment my feet hit the hardwood floor, I braced myself for an impact that never came. It was habit. Every day when I walked in that door, Roger would careen toward me. Now, there was nobody to greet me. I missed my buddy, but he'd be back soon.

I closed my door and told my voice-activated sound system to play the blues. Almost immediately, I heard the strumming of a guitar. Then Lightnin' Hopkins began begging his baby not to go. Hopkins's voice was harsh, as I expected, but the music sounded warm and rich and comforting in a way few things were. I had always liked the blues. More than that, I liked the stories those songs told. The blues singers of old refused to let oppression or segregation silence their voices. The emotion was real and raw. It was human in a way modern music wasn't. I liked that.

So I sat and listened and relaxed and felt my day disappear. The news van left, and I put on a trashy TV show. I didn't watch TV often, but people at work talked about *The Bachelor* often enough that I felt like I knew the cast. Most of the girls vying for the bachelor's attention seemed nice enough, but the actual bachelor seemed like a jerk more interested in playing the girls against one another than meeting someone. From the conversations around the water cooler at work, I gathered that was part of the show's appeal.

I grabbed a beer from my fridge and watched until ten. Then I flipped to channel three. The evening's lead story focused on a thunderstorm bearing down on the area, but I knew the second story right away. The screen split into two parts. The left showed an image of two newscasters in the studio while the right showed a satellite image of St. Augustine and the surrounding area.

"Breaking overnight, a terrifying scene involving a detective with the St. Augustine County Sheriff's Department who was forced to take drastic action against a man with a gun. It happened outside her rural home near the community of St. Augustine. And that's where we find our own Angela Pritchard. She's attempting to learn more about this terrifying story. Angela, good evening."

The screen shifted so that the newscasters and the map disappeared, replaced by a live shot of Angela Pritchard on Main Street in St. Augustine. Dozens of people milled around her, most of whom seemed oblivious to the camera. Two kids made faces, but Pritchard ignored them and nodded to the camera.

"Tom, Lisa, good evening. As you see behind me, young men and women are enjoying St. Augustine's annual Spring Fair. One of St. Augustine's own is not, though. Last night, at around two in the morning, Detective Mary Joe Court received a most unwelcome visitor when Christopher Hughes showed up on her property with a firearm.

"Even twenty-four hours later, details are still a little sketchy. From what I can gather, though, Detective Court's heroic bullmastiff alerted her to a potential intruder on the property. When confronted, the intruder, Christopher Hughes, opened fire upon Detective Court's dog and her person. A chase ensued in which Christopher Hughes was shot."

The screen split again with the newscasters on the left and Angela on the right.

"Is this the same Christopher Hughes who was released from the Potosi Correctional Institute?" asked one of the news anchors in the station. Angela held an earpiece against her head, nodded, and drew in a breath.

"It is. As you can imagine, the story is complicated. I've done some investigating, and what I've found is shocking."

I sat straighter and held my breath.

"Christopher Hughes and Detective Court knew one another well. In fact, twelve years ago, Detective Court lived with the Hughes family as a foster daughter. While in his care, she accused him of sexual assault. No sexual assault charges were ever filed."

My fingers trembled. My beer slipped through my hands, and the bottle bounced on the hardwood floor. Cold liquid spread onto my feet as my breath caught in my throat. This was why she had wanted to hear my side of the story. She thought there were multiple sides to this story.

"What are the police saying about his shooting?" asked one newscaster in the studio. Angela nodded and tilted her chin down.

"They're playing this one close to the vest. As Detective Court is an employee of the St. Augustine County Sheriff's Department, they've turned the investigation over to the Highway Patrol. Interestingly, though, Detective Court's supervisory officer is one of the detectives who first investigated Christopher Hughes for sexual assault twelve years ago. The other detective on that twelve-year-old case is now Detective Court's adoptive mother. There are a lot of story lines here, and it's a little hard to keep things straight."

"That's a complicated case," said a newscaster.

"It is, and it's about to get more complicated," said Angela. "In a stunning revelation, I've discovered that the psychologist hired to screen applicants for the state police academy recommended that Detective Court's application be placed on hold pending further psychological evaluation. This hold was overruled by Sheriff Travis Kosen of the St. Augustine County Sheriff's Department, citing a need in his department for more female hires."

"And Sheriff Kosen was the detective who investigated her sexual assault claims twelve years ago?"

They kept talking, but I couldn't hear them over the sound of blood roaring through me. That was my life they were tearing apart. Those were my secrets they were sharing. It was almost surreal. For a split second, it was like a dream. I closed my eyes, hoping to wake up when they opened.

But that didn't happen. This was real. My fingers trembled. My throat closed. Waves of nausea and revulsion passed over me.

I threw the remote at the TV as hard as I could. It bounced off the screen and hit the ground. The batteries rolled across the hardwood. I may have broken it. I didn't know.

"You witch," I said, my lower lip quivering. "You evil witch."

My phone rang, but I couldn't move. Angela Pritchard had just told the world I was a murderous, unstable rape victim who shouldn't have had a badge. It was a lie, but a ribbon of truth moved through it. People who didn't know me well would believe it. My colleagues might even believe it. Already, I could see cracks growing in my carefully constructed life.

More than anything else, my past had been mine to keep a secret. Christopher Hughes had drugged and raped me. I survived, but I had scars. The world didn't need to see them. I didn't need the world's judgment or pity. Those scars were mine. They made me who I was, and I chose whom to share them with.

I stood and balled my hands into fists. There was no one around to hear, but I screamed anyway. This was my story. Angela Pritchard had just ripped it away from me. She had stolen something sacred from me and paraded it around as something cheap and tawdry. Vile, black hate built inside me. Every part of me felt violated. I wanted to lash out at her, find her, and choke the life out of her. I wanted to beat her. I wanted to run and never stop.

I did none of that, though. I couldn't move. My tears stained my shirt as I fell backwards onto my couch. Alone, I sat in the dark and cried until I couldn't cry anymore.

40

My phone rang and rang. I ignored it. Then my cell phone rang. I ignored that, too. Then my cell beeped as people texted. I ignored those, too, but they kept coming for almost twenty minutes. I got up to find out who wanted to get in touch with me.

I had messages from half a dozen colleagues, including Travis, my boss. Julia had called three times. Dad had called twice from his cell. I disconnected my landline from the wall and called Julia back. She was breathless.

"Sweetheart," she said. "I'm sorry. I saw the news. That reporter had no business digging into your life like that."

"I'll never get rid of him, will I?" I asked, blinking. "He's dead. I shot him, and I can't get away from him."

Julia said nothing. I looked at the TV. The news was off now, and one of the late shows was on. As the camera swept over the audience, people waved and smiled as if they didn't have a care in the world. It seemed unfair, so I stood up and shut it off.

"He's a part of your life," she said. "I wish he

weren't, but he is."

It was an honest answer, at least. I paced the hallway that connected the front and rear of my house.

"Did you know about my psych eval?"

She said nothing at first, so I sighed.

"Did you know I failed the psych evaluation before I became a police officer?"

"It was a long time ago," she said. "You're not that same person."

She might as well have stabbed me in the heart. Cold waves spread from my hips to my chest and down my legs. I plopped onto a chair in the kitchen and thought about the bottle of vodka I had in the freezer. I had nowhere to go and very few reasons not to tear that bottle open and have a drink. For some reason, though, I hesitated, and I didn't know why.

"So you knew," I said.

She started to say something, but then she caught herself.

"Yeah. I knew."

I rubbed my eyes, feeling a weight press down on me.

"You should have told me," I said, my voice low. "For my entire adult life, this was who I was. I was a cop. I didn't have a boyfriend, I didn't have a family, I didn't have many friends, but I was a cop. That was all I wanted to be. I wanted to help people."

"You're an excellent police officer, Joe," she said. "I've been in law enforcement for almost thirty years, and

I've evaluated a lot of detectives. You're one of the best I've ever seen."

"I'm a goddamn fraud, Julia," I said. "They shouldn't have even given me a badge. I'm the youngest detective in my department's history. Did I earn that, or did you and Travis nudge the scales there, too?"

"That was all you," she said.

I shook my head and felt tears come to my eyes anew. "Even if I earned a promotion, it doesn't matter. I shouldn't have been in the building in the first place, and now everybody knows it."

"I'm sorry, Joe."

"Me, too," I said. "I've got to go."

I hung up but didn't move from my chair at the breakfast table. I thought about changing into some sweats and going for a run. Then I thought about going for a drive or sitting and listening to music. I thought about a lot of things, but I didn't come to any conclusion. After a few minutes, I didn't want to think anymore, so I grabbed my vodka from the freezer and poured it into a glass.

I didn't have many certainties in my life, but at least I had booze. Even when nothing else in the world had gone right, it made me feel better. I took three shots and then went to bed with my head swimming. I couldn't believe I had felt good a few hours ago. Just a few hours ago, my future had been certain. I had known where I was going and who I was. Now, I had lost everything. Not even a bottle of vodka could make me feel better about that.

I slept, but it was fitful. I ended up waking up hung over and even more tired than I had been when I went to bed. It didn't matter, though. During the night, my unconscious mind had decided for me. I had no business wearing a badge. That was the final lesson Christopher Hughes had taught me. Even from his grave, that son of a bitch insisted on ruining me.

I hand wrote my resignation letter, showered, dressed, and headed toward the office at seven in the morning. Trisha worked the day shift, so she wasn't in yet. That was why I had gone in so early. I nodded hello to the night shift's dispatcher and walked toward Travis's office on the second floor. The door was open, but he wasn't around.

I waited in the hallway and caught sight of him carrying a mug of steaming coffee a few moments after I arrived. He nodded.

"Morning, Joe," he said. "I thought you'd be by. Come on in."

We walked into the office. Travis's office was cozy and neat. He had filing cabinets against the walls and a big window that overlooked the courthouse lawn. Tucked away from the front lobby, it was quiet. He walked around his desk and gestured toward a seat in front.

"Have a seat. We'll talk. You want coffee?"

I shook my head and put my letter on the desk.

"Thank you, but no. I won't stay long," I said. I nodded toward the letter. "That should be everything you need. I signed it this morning. I'll clean out my desk before the day shift comes on."

Travis didn't pick the letter up, but he nodded.

"I thought you'd try to quit on me," he said. "You can't. It'll leave me short-handed."

"You'll be fine," I said. "The Megan and Emily Young cases will probably close soon now that Christopher Hughes and his lawyer are dead. Harry, Delgado, and Martin are here. If you need another detective, promote Trisha. She won't appreciate the promotion, but she can do the work."

"Is that why you're doing this?" he asked, leaning back and crossing his arms. "You think you've let me down?"

"I think I've opened this town to a major lawsuit just by being here," I said. "Don't argue with me. I won't listen to you try to persuade me to stay. It's done. I don't want this job anymore."

"Whether you believe it or not, you've earned your right to be here," said Travis. "I'm not going to read your resignation letter, but I'll hold on to it. If you still feel the same way in a week, I'll start the paperwork. Until then, you're on vacation."

"I won't change my mind," I said.

"I know," said Travis, nodding. "You're as stubborn as your mother."

"My mother was a junkie who barely knew my name."

Travis leaned forward and raised an eyebrow. His

voice was sharper than I expected.

"Your mother is a captain in the St. Louis County Police Department. She's a friend of mine, and she loves you very much. She's sacrificed a lot for you. Maybe you should talk to her instead of me about this."

Julia loved me. I knew that. The rebuke stung more than it should have, but I didn't know why.

"Is that it, sir?"

"Yeah," he said. "I'll talk to you later, Joe."

I turned to leave, but then I stopped myself near the door.

"Travis, who had access to my personnel file?"

He crossed his arms. "If you're asking whether I know who leaked this information, I don't. I'll look into it, though. If this reporter's source came from this department, there will be repercussions."

"I know you'll look into this," I said, nodding and blinking, "but I'm asking you a simple question. Who had access to my file?"

"Me, the detectives investigating your shooting into Christopher Hughes, your former instructors at the Central Missouri Police Academy. A fair number of people."

I looked down. "Would a union representative have access to it?"

Travis hesitated and then nodded. "Yeah. Your rep would get your file to help facilitate your defense."

My back stiffened as a cold, black feeling washed over me. My entire body trembled with anger.

"A detective from St. Louis filed a complaint against me a couple of days ago," I said. "Delgado told me. That means he had access to my file."

Travis looked down at his desk.

"I know there's bad blood between you and George, but I don't think—"

"Just stop," I said, holding up a hand. "Please don't defend him in front of me. He's a bully, and he has no business being a police officer, let alone a detective. Worse than that, he's my union rep. He's harassed me at every opportunity he's had, and I had no one to complain to but you. And you didn't do shit."

He closed his eyes. "I talked to him."

"Lot of good it did. We're done, Travis. I don't care that you were Julia's partner. I don't care that I've known you for a decade. You screwed up, and I paid the price."

"I'm sorry you feel that way."

"I'm sorry it is that way," I said.

Travis looked away rather than fight, and I went downstairs to clear out my desk. Where many of my colleagues had family pictures and houseplants, I kept my desk neat and businesslike. If a stranger walked past, he'd think it was unassigned. I liked it like that. Maybe a part of me even knew I'd leave like this one day and didn't want to become attached to the space. As I was cleaning out my drawers, I heard someone clear his throat to my right. Even without looking at his face, I recognized the sound.

Detective Delgado.

I glanced at him and then focused on the grocery sack I had borrowed from the front desk.

"What do you want?"

"Saw you on the news last night," he said.

I looked at him and felt some of my composure dissolve. Black, venomous hate bubbled to the surface.

"You disgust me," I said. "I don't care who you are or how much you dislike somebody, you don't release somebody's personal information to the media. Those were my secrets. You had no right to share them."

"I've read your personnel file. You don't you think your colleagues deserved to know they were working beside a ticking time bomb?"

I wanted to scream and throw things at him. I wanted to make him hurt the way I did, but he wanted that. He wanted me to scream and lose control; it would prove everything he thought of me. Instead, I focused the pain inward and felt my gut twist and tighten. Tears sprang to my eyes, but I tried to blink them away before anyone could see them.

"I'm not a time bomb. Somebody hurt me years ago. It took a long time to get over that pain, but I'm stronger for it now. I'm no longer that little girl. I don't care what you think of me, but I deserved privacy. Those were my secrets. They weren't yours to share. If you can't see the wrong in what you did, I pity you."

I turned back to my bag so I wouldn't have to look at Detective Delgado again. Somehow, my back felt stronger, and the pit in my stomach felt looser. I may not have been a cop anymore, but I'd survive. I was stronger than him. I was stronger than Christopher Hughes. A man more animal than human had hurt me years ago, but I had survived and grown. I was so much more than the victim Delgado saw me as. If he couldn't see that, it was his loss.

"You should be careful about where you direct that vitriol, young lady."

It was a new voice, but one I recognized. I glanced to the right to see Detective Jasper Martin walking toward my desk. He was older than Delgado, but he wasn't soft. He had a graying mustache, a thin face, and pitted, craggy skin. His voice reminded me of stones rubbing against one another. I had never worked with him, so I didn't have an opinion of him except that he was a solid detective.

"This is a private conversation, Detective Martin," I said, picking up my bag and starting toward the door. "If you'll excuse me, I'm going home."

"George didn't leak your file," said Martin. "That was me."

I stopped in my tracks a few feet from the older man and turned.

"You?" I asked. He nodded. I opened my mouth to say something but found I didn't have words. Then I shook my head, dumbfounded. "I don't even know you, Detective. In fact, this is the most I've ever spoken to you in one conversation. What reason could you have for trying to hurt me?"

He blinked and shifted his weight forward, adopting an aggressive posture, the way he might have when talking to a hostile suspect. I matched it.

"I've put forty years and two marriages into this department. It was my life's work. I love this department and the people in it. You're unstable, Ms. Court. That's not your fault, but that doesn't change the facts. You have no business being here. You may think you're strong, but you're not. When you break, you'll take out everyone around you. If my last action as a detective is to force you out of a department I love before you hurt my friends, I'd say it was a career well spent."

The resolve I had felt earlier slipped.

"Fuck you," I said. "Just fuck you, old man."

I grabbed my grocery bag and walked again. As I did, I found Trisha and Travis a few feet behind Detective Martin. Trisha walked toward me and tried to put an arm around me, but I shrugged her off and kept walking. As I reached the hallway that led to the front of the station, I heard Travis speak again.

"Detective Martin, you're fired. Pack up your desk. You've got an hour to get out of my station."

It was a symbolic move more than it was an actual punishment. Martin would still leave with full retirement benefits and a pension.

I left the building and drove home. For the first time in a long time, I had nowhere to be. I didn't keep a lot of food in the house, but I had bought ingredients for corn muffins when Dad visited. I cracked two eggs into a skillet and then scrambled them in butter. That was the extent of my cooking knowledge, but the eggs tasted good.

Afterwards, I did the dishes and wondered what the hell I would do with my life now that I was no longer a cop. Then I thought smaller and planned my day. I had projects all over the house and yard, but I didn't want to do any of them. I had one thing alone on my mind. It was just a little after eight in the morning, but I grabbed a beer from my fridge, cracked it open, and sat on the porch to watch the world wake up.

I stayed out there for about an hour before I caught movement to my left. I hid my bottle and sat a little straighter. Susanne smiled and waved from near the road. She wore a sundress and tennis shoes. A wooden clip held her hair back from her weathered face. As she got closer, I could hear her breathing hard.

"Hey, Susanne," I said, standing and reaching out my hand to help her up the stairs. "You should have called. I would have gone to meet you."

"That's all right, dear," she said, taking my hand and squeezing before grabbing the railing. "I needed the walk, and this looks like a fine morning. How's Roger?"

I walked to my seat. Susanne sat in the wooden chair next to mine.

"The vet says he'll be okay," I said. "I visited him yesterday, but he was asleep. He's alive. That's the big thing."

"I'm glad. He's a sweet boy and a hero, from what I

hear. I'm glad you two have each other."

"Me, too," I said. "Would you like coffee? I can make coffee."

"No, I had enough coffee this morning," she said. "I came to chat and make sure my friend was all right."

"Thank you," I said, forcing myself to smile. "I am okay."

"I'm glad to hear you say that, but it's not true, and we both know it. It's a little early for a beer."

I grimaced. "You saw that, huh?"

"That, and I can smell your breath," she said. "So tell me, dear, are you all right?"

I thought for a moment and then nodded. "I will be. I've got to figure out what to do with the rest of my life, but I've got time."

"You have a long time to figure out your life. Work helps, too. I was a teacher, you know. Whenever I felt down, I could always count on my kids to make me feel better."

"That's one thing I need to figure out. Maybe I could become a teacher."

"No," said Susanne. "You're a police officer. You're a good one, too, from what I hear."

"I quit this morning."

Susanne said nothing, but she looked over the yard for a moment and then stood up.

"Everything okay?" I asked.

She nodded. "Everything's fine. I'll make coffee. You need it. Stay on your porch."

"You don't need to make me coffee," I said, following her inside. "It's okay."

We went to the kitchen, where she pulled my coffee maker out from the wall. She was serious about this, so I went to my cabinet with coffee and filters.

"I saw the news report last night," she said. "On channel three. Was it true?"

I put my coffee on the counter beside her and blinked before taking a deep breath.

"It lacked context."

"Did the man that you shot in the woods hurt you when you were a little girl?" she asked. I nodded, and she took a step closer. She put a hand on my elbow. "I'm glad you put the bastard down, then."

I wiped a tear away from the corner of my eye. I didn't even realize it had formed until I rubbed it away.

"I don't think you're supposed to say that."

"I'm too old to care what I'm supposed to say," she said, filling my carafe with water at the sink. "He hurt my friend. I'm glad he can't hurt anyone else."

"Me, too," I said. "Thank you."

She turned to the coffee pot.

"The people who hurt us make us who we are," she said. "They don't realize that when they hurt us, but they do it all the same. We can't change our past, and we can't change the people we once were, but we can change our future and our present."

I handed her the filter and coffee.

"I don't know who I want to be," I said.

"That's a fine answer," she said, stepping away from the machine as it brewed. Then she turned. "A couple of days ago, you were working another case involving two young woman. They were your foster sisters. Did Christopher Hughes hurt them, too?"

I nodded. "Yeah."

"Do you want to be this man's victim, or do you want to be the woman who remade her life after a tragedy?"

I raised my eyebrows and shook my head. "It's not that easy."

"I never said it would be easy," she said. "Every day of your life will be a struggle. Then, one day, it won't be anymore. That's how it is."

"What do you think I should do?"

"You find out who killed your sisters. If it was the man you shot, then he won't hurt anyone again. If it was someone else, you'll put him in prison."

I looked down and smiled as I imagined Megan and Emily's reaction to being told that we were sisters.

"We weren't sisters."

Susanne poured herself a cup of coffee and then sat down at the table near me. "Every woman who has experienced what we have is our sister. Never forget that. You're strong enough to watch out for the others. That's your job. I couldn't do that."

I let that sink in for a moment and then swallowed hard. For a moment, neither of us said anything. Then I leaned forward and crossed my arms.

"Do you believe that?"

"I'm eighty-one years old. I've lived a long time, and I've done a lot of things. My biggest regret has nothing to do with the people I've hurt, although there have been a few of those. I've tried to make amends. My regrets, the things that keep me up at night, are the opportunities I've missed to help those who needed me most. Don't do what I did. Help these girls out."

I couldn't look at her, but I nodded. Susanne was my friend. More than that, she was my sister—and she was right.

"All right," I said. "I'll do it. I'll find out who killed Megan and Emily. And then I'll make him pay."

41

Saying I'd find out who killed Megan and Emily was a lot easier than actually doing it. Susanne and I finished our cups of coffee, and then I walked her back to her house. I had five murders to think about, not just two. Megan and Emily, Christopher Hughes, Sherlock, and Warren—the mechanic whom Christopher had visited.

Emily died first and then Megan. Warren, Sherlock, and Christopher followed. Every law enforcement officer on this case was looking at it as if it had started just a week ago, but this case was far older than that. This case started twelve years ago when Christopher went to prison. I wouldn't find the answers I wanted in the present. I needed to look at the past.

After walking Susanne back to her house, I grabbed my keys, locked my front door, and got in my truck. Julia and Doug Green lived in Kirkwood, an upper-middle-class, inner-ring suburb west of St. Louis. The taxes were a bitch—as Dad complained about often—but it was a good place to raise a family.

I drove for about an hour before hitting the outskirts of the city. Within another half hour, I had parked in front of Dad and Julia's sprawling brick ranch home. Neither Julia's unmarked police cruiser nor my dad's truck were in the driveway. Instead, I found an old Toyota Camry with a sticker from a sorority on the rear window and a giant pile of clothes on the backseat. Audrey, my sister, must have come home from college for the weekend.

I shut my door and walked up the brick walkway to the front. Normally, I would have just used my key to get in, but I didn't want to scare Audrey, so I knocked and waited for her to open it. My sister had long, flowing brown hair, brown eyes, and tanned skin. Audrey had all of her mom's best features and a few from our dad, too. She was smart and gorgeous, and she had a great sense of humor. The first time I met her, she was eight years old and had asked whether I wanted her to braid my hair. I had liked her from the start.

"Hey, Audrey," I said. "I didn't expect to see you."

"Me, either," she said, holding her arms out. I hugged her tight. "I wish you had told me you were coming. I would have waited to have lunch."

She let go of her hug and ushered me into the entryway. The house had changed little from my last visit a year ago. The hardwood floors gleamed, the front room was immaculate, and the pictures all hung perfectly even and level on the walls. Somehow, just stepping foot into that home lifted some weight off my shoulders.

"I'm here for work. Have you talked to your mom and dad today?"

"No. I texted Mom this morning, but you know how she is. She doesn't check her messages."

I nodded. "Have you seen the news lately?"

"Too depressing," she said. "Why?"

So she didn't know about the shooting at my house. I loved Audrey, and I'd sit down and talk to her, but I was tired of people looking at me as if I were some fragile doll that could break at any moment. For now, when she looked at me, she saw her big sister. I needed that.

"I was wondering if you had seen the weather," I said, looking down so I wouldn't have to look in her in the eye as I lied to her. "And sorry Julia doesn't respond to your text messages. That stinks. I can text her on your behalf. She always responds to mine right away. The other day, I sent her a message at three in the morning, and she got back to me before I could even turn off my light. Guess that means I'm the favorite, huh?"

"Favorite butthead, maybe," she said, walking into the kitchen and smiling. I followed a few steps behind. "How's work?"

"Work is work. It's no fun," I said. "You'll find that out in a year when you graduate. I don't want to talk about work. Are you here for the free laundry service, or was this a planned visit?"

"Free laundry," she said, nodding and pouring herself a mug of coffee. "And I planned to steal Dad's booze and get drunk. You want coffee?"

"No, thanks," I said. "I can't stay long. I just need to pick up something from Julia's office."

She nodded and put the coffee pot back on its burner.

"I was thinking about going by St. Augustine this evening. Spring Fair still going on?"

I nodded and grunted. "Tonight's the last night, though. If you go, have a sober driver. There are drunks everywhere. The fireworks display is at nine, and then tomorrow is the big hot-air balloon race. I'll be glad once it's over. It's the most stressful week of the year."

She laughed. "Yeah, right. Like anything happens in St. Augustine."

I forced myself to smile. "It's practically Mayberry."

"What's Mayberry?" she asked, raising an eyebrow.

"It's the small town from *The Andy Griffith Show*. Nothing exciting ever happened there, either," I said, straightening and turning so my hips pointed down the home's main hallway. "Will you be around for a few days, or are you going back to school soon?"

"I'll be here until Monday," she said. "Call me. We'll hang out."

"I will," I said. I squeezed her forearm and then headed down the hall to Julia's home office. Like the rest of the house, everything in the office had a place, including the case file outlining her investigation into my sexual assault twelve years ago. I had never looked through that file before, and I didn't want to see it now, but it was the best record I had access to of Christopher Hughes's life twelve years ago. I hesitated and then opened her filing cabinet. My file was in the back, and for a moment, I couldn't do anything but stare at it.

"He's gone, Joe," I said to myself. "He can't hurt you."

I didn't know whether I believed myself, but I took out the file and carried it to the kitchen table while Audrey did laundry downstairs.

Julia's notes were professional, organized, and thorough. It was surreal to see my assault—and the assaults of other young women—described in such frank, almost clinical prose. Back then, I didn't realize how much work Julia and Travis had put into my case, but they must have put in hundred-hour weeks for at least three weeks. They interviewed well over a hundred people and investigated the accounts of almost a dozen young women. It made my stomach turn.

I read the file from front to back and almost closed it without having found anything until I came across a report Julia had written toward the end of her investigation. She had gone to interview Christopher at his home and found him in some kind of business meeting in his garage with four men and his ex-wife. One of those four men was Warren Nichols. The others were Randy Shepard, Steven Zimmerman, and Neil Wilcox.

Aside from Warren, I didn't recognize the names, but now I knew why Christopher had visited Warren's garage in the middle of the night: They were business partners.

I looked up each man on my phone. Google returned few results for Randy Shepard or Neil Wilcox, but Steven Zimmerman's body had just been found floating in the

The Girl in the Motel

Missouri River near a bicycle trail about forty miles west of here. *The St. Louis Post-Dispatch* had picked up the story, but, in isolation, it looked like a simple murder. The metropolitan area got a couple hundred a year, so a quiet murder west of the city didn't get a lot of attention.

It should have, though. It was part of a pattern.

I called Julia. She picked up on the second ring.

"Hey, it's Joe. I'm at your house. We need to talk. I need help."

"I'm at the office, but I can be there in fifteen minutes. Everything all right?"

"I'm fine," I said. "Stay at work. I've been reading an old file involving Christopher Hughes. On April 19th, 2006, you interviewed Christopher Hughes at his house. When you arrived, he was with four people: Randy Shepard, Neil Wilcox, Steven Zimmerman, and Warren Nichols. Your notes described it as some kind of business meeting. Warren Nichols was the mechanic killed at the garage in north St. Louis."

She paused for a moment as she put that together.

"And now Hughes and Nichols are dead. What's your theory?"

"Zimmerman's dead, too. Someone dumped his body forty miles west of town. These guys were business partners. Not only are they dead, so is their lawyer, James Holmes. Someone's cleaning house and dumping the bodies far enough apart that they're being investigated by different departments. We didn't see the pattern because no one knew to look for it."

She went quiet for a moment. "We need to find Randy Shepard and Neil Wilcox. They might be the next targets."

"Someone needs to check out Diana Hughes, too. If she played a role in the business, she could be a target."

"I'll send somebody by the house, but I don't think she's involved," said Julia. "Thank you for sharing this. Good work."

Julia rarely handed out compliments, so hearing her compliment me now for my police work was a big deal. I smiled without wanting to.

"What should I do?" I asked.

"You're home now?"

"I'm at your house," I said. "I'm in the kitchen. Audrey's doing laundry in the basement."

"Great. I didn't know she was coming in. Your father's got money in a cigar box in the pantry, so take two twenties and take your sister out to lunch. Go to Big Sky Cafe. It's near Webster University in Webster Groves. You'll like it. You guys should catch up while she's in town."

The smile left my face as I shook my head.

"You've got to be kidding. This is my case, and this is my find. You're not kicking me off it."

"You kicked yourself off it, sweetheart. Travis called me this morning. He told me about your change of career. You're not a police officer anymore. Because of that, you will stay home. We can talk about your future later."

"I won't sit around while other people work."

"Yes, you will," said Julia, her voice hard. "You're a civilian now. Get used to sitting around. I'll talk to you tonight. Okay?"

I wasn't about to go along with that, but I nodded anyway as if she were near me.

"Sure. Fine."

I hung up before she could say anything else. For a moment, I didn't move as I considered my options, but then I heard Audrey's phone buzz from the counter nearby. I had no business looking at it, but she had just gotten a text message from Julia.

Take Joe out to lunch. Don't let her out of your sight. We'll talk later.

I swiped my finger across the phone to wake it up. Audrey and I hadn't lived together for years, but I knew my sister. Her passcode wasn't hard to guess.

2014

It was the year she turned eighteen and, in her words, became a real woman. I was glad she hadn't become a pregnant woman, too.

I deleted the message and plugged the phone back in before walking to the top of the basement steps.

"Hey, Audrey, I've got to go. Call me before you leave town."

"Okay," she said. "See you later."

I walked to the front door and knelt down. The Missouri Highway Patrol had confiscated my primary weapon—a Glock 19—after I shot Christopher Hughes, but they hadn't taken my backup piece. I transferred it from the holster on my ankle to my purse for easier access. Julia may not have been concerned about Diana Hughes, but I knew her better than Julia did. Maybe they couldn't prosecute her, but her ex-husband wouldn't have gotten away with half the shit he did without her knowledge.

She wasn't Christopher's victim. She was a co-conspirator.

42

The drive from Kirkwood to Chesterfield took half an hour with traffic, and with each passing moment, the knot in my stomach grew tighter. The file in Julia's office had brought back a lot of memories I wished I could forget, and almost all of them had taken place in Christopher's home. I was glad I had shot him. I should have felt bad, but I didn't. He deserved everything that happened to him.

As I turned onto his street, my entire body trembled, and my throat grew so tight I had to pull off to the side of the road and force myself to breathe. For a split second, I was fifteen years old again. I lived in his house. I could feel his breath on my cheek, and I could taste the tropical drink he had drugged me with before raping me. A shudder passed through me, and I gripped my steering wheel as hard as I could so my hands wouldn't tremble.

"He's dead."

In my mind, I knew it was true. I could close my eyes and see his body on the ground in the woods near my house, and I could smell his fresh blood intermingled with the earthy odor of clean soil. Even knowing that, seeing his street made every awful memory I had of him fresh.

"You killed him, Joe," I told myself. "He can't hurt you anymore."

As I stayed there, my heart slowed, and my breath came easier. I was okay. I could do this. I put my foot on the gas and crept forward until I reached the circular driveway in front of his gaudy mansion. Everything looked just as it had when I lived there, save one detail: There was a white paneled van from a carpet cleaning service out front.

I parked behind the cleaners and walked to the open front door on wobbly legs. The van hummed with some kind of machinery, and a pair of hoses snaked out and into the house. Even though the house's front door was open, I rang the bell.

"Diana Hughes?" I called. Nobody answered, so I walked inside. Diana had changed the dining room furniture, and she had added a table in the front entryway, but it looked just as I remembered it. I walked through the front hallway to the kitchen, calling out again. As before, nobody answered, so I walked back to the entryway and then followed the carpet cleaners' hoses to the master bedroom.

There, I found two men in coveralls. One held a normal vacuum, while the other had a commercial steam wand that left steaming patches on the carpet.

"Whoa, whoa, whoa," I called out, walking toward the man with the steam wand. He was running it over red stains on the carpet. Though I was far from an expert, I had seen a lot of blood spatter over the years, and this was arterial spray. The man with the steam wand pulled a handle on his device to turn it off. Then he raised his eyebrows at me. The man with the vacuum stopped what he was doing.

"Can we help you?" asked the steamer.

"Did Diana hire you for this job?"

"Mrs. Hughes did, yeah," said the steamer. "Can I help you?"

If she called in the cleaning crew, this wasn't her blood. It wasn't Christopher's or Warren Nichols's blood, either, because they had died elsewhere. If I had to guess, that spot on the carpet belonged to James Holmes.

"What did she tell you that you were cleaning?" I asked.

"Cranberry juice," he said. "She tried to bleach it, but she couldn't get the stain out. It's well set now, so we're having a hard time lifting it ourselves."

I looked around the room for anything else out of place. The dresser and chest of drawers looked closed and blood free, the laundry hamper was closed, and there were no coffee cups or paperbacks on the end table beside the bed. It could have been a room from a magazine shoot, save one thing: Someone had taken all the pillows off the bed. I pulled back the floral-print cover to reveal a mattress with a massive blood stain in the center.

The two carpet cleaners froze. One cocked his head

to the other and shrugged, confused.

"Everybody out," I said. "Leave your equipment, but go back to your truck. You weren't cleaning up cranberry juice. That's blood. That's why you were having a hard time removing the stain. This house is a crime scene."

Their dumbfounded stares continued, but I got them out of the room and back to their van, where I took their keys so they couldn't leave with evidence inside their vacuum cleaner. That done, I called Julia.

"Joe, I'm busy. I'll call you back."

"Diana Hughes killed James Holmes in her bedroom. His blood's all over the place."

She paused. "Say what?"

"I'm at Diana Hughes's house. When I arrived, I found two men cleaning the carpet in her bedroom. Diana Hughes hired them to remove what she described as stains from cranberry juice. It's blood spatter. There's more on the bed. She broke her husband out of prison, killed him, and now she's moved on to his business partners."

She paused again. "I asked you not to go to Diana Hughes's house."

"I know. You can arrest me for interfering with a police investigation, but get down here."

"I'll call this in and be there as soon as I can."

"See you—"

She hung up before I could finish. I followed the carpet cleaners' hoses outside and found them smoking cigarettes inside their vans. Both men looked pale, and they moved with the deliberate gestures of actors playing roles they didn't fathom. I doubted either was involved in a murder, but the police would still have to clear them. Hopefully neither had too many skeletons in his closet.

I had nowhere to sit, so I stayed outside and paced up and down the driveway. Every part of my body buzzed with anticipation. We did it. Diana was our shot caller. We didn't have enough evidence to convict her yet, but I was sure we'd find it inside her house. Then, once we had Diana, we'd find her accomplices. She couldn't have done this on her own.

I had just solved the biggest case of my life. It wasn't through genius or special insight. It was hard work. I might even get a letter of commendation out of this.

Within five minutes of my call, I heard the first sirens. A pair of marked police cruisers screeched to a halt behind the carpet cleaners' van, and a uniformed officer jumped out of each. I didn't know what Julia had told the dispatcher, but one officer went to the carpet cleaners, while the second put a hand on my elbow and led me toward his cruiser.

"Ms. Court, I've been instructed to take you into custody for interfering with a police investigation."

I scoffed and rolled my eyes but didn't move. Of course she'd do this.

"What did Captain Green tell you?"

"I'm just following orders, miss," he said.

"Did she tell you I'm a detective with the St. Augustine County Sheriff's Department?"

He stopped and looked at me up and down. "Do you have a badge?"

I closed my eyes. "It's a long story. Did she tell you I'm her daughter?"

He hesitated. "Family life is your own. If you're a detective, your CO will talk to my CO and get this sorted out. In the meantime, I need you to have a seat in the car."

We walked to the car, and he opened the rear door for me.

"There's a gun in my purse."

"Do you have a concealed carry permit?"

I cocked my head to the side. "I have a badge in my boss's desk in St. Augustine."

"So you don't have a permit with you."

I closed my eyes and shook my head. "No, I don't."

He made me sit in the car while he searched my purse. Upon my request, he handed me my phone, which I used to text Julia to let her know the first officers on the scene had placed me under arrest for interfering with a police investigation.

You asked for it. I'll see you soon.

I wanted to text her something mean in response, but that would have just made her drive slower. Within moments, more officers came to the scene, including two plain-clothes detectives. About half an hour after I arrived, Julia pulled to a stop in the driveway. She saw me in the back of the cruiser but only came to talk after first speaking with one of the plain-clothes detectives.

"Am I under arrest?" I asked.

"No," she said, shaking her head. "Travis called the police in Chesterfield to let them know who you are. I would have let you rot in jail."

I swung my legs out of the cruiser. "Thanks. I appreciate that."

"You're a civilian. You quit."

"Then I'm a civilian who found something you missed. Is that what you're mad about?"

She crossed her arms and raised her eyebrow. "Don't go there, sweetheart. I'm angry because we may not have a complete chain of custody on any blood evidence you've found inside the house. You know how defense attorneys work. They will look for any weakness in our case, and you've introduced a weakness. Did you even have cause to enter the house?"

"Someone is killing people connected to Christopher Hughes. Diana Hughes has a connection to Christopher Hughes," I said, drawing the inferences. "The front door was open. There were men inside the house. Fearing for Mrs. Hughes's safety, I entered the premises and conducted a safety sweep. Upon arrival in the master bedroom, I found potential blood evidence in plain sight. It's admissible in court."

"That might be true if you were a police officer. Instead, you're a woman trespassing. Your word won't carry a lot of weight in court. You should have stayed outside and waited."

"Two things. If I hadn't come here when I did, the

carpet cleaners would have destroyed the evidence. You wouldn't have even seen it. Second, I still have a badge. Your concerns are irrelevant," I said, folding my arms and looking toward the house and then to my adoptive mother. Her eyes were wide open, and her gaze was hard. "While I was solving your murder, what have you been doing?"

She stared at me for another moment with those angry eyes of hers and then looked away.

"I was trying to track down Randy Shepard. He lives and works in Illinois, but we've had our eyes on him for a while. He's a pimp with a sizable business that specializes in young women. We think he also owns some strip clubs, but we can't tie him to them. I suspect he hired some of your foster sisters once they aged out from the program."

"And Randy worked with Christopher Hughes?"

"We never knew how, but yeah."

Even hearing that made me feel ill. It also made things click in my mind in a way they never had before.

"That was why Christopher wanted us around," I said. "If he were just after sex, he could have bought it from prostitutes. He brought us in because he was recruiting for his buddy."

"That's one theory we worked on," said Julia. "Christopher was part of the pipeline. He used his position as a foster father to find vulnerable young women, whom he then pushed on his pimp friend for a cut of the profits."

I closed my eyes. "I'm glad he's dead."

"Don't say that aloud," she said. "People are still investigating your shooting."

I nodded and looked around the scene. There were half a dozen police cars in the driveway, and already uniformed officers were knocking on the doors of houses nearby.

"When I lived here, Diana and Christopher had sensors on every window and door. Nobody could walk into this house unnoticed. That means Diana let the victim inside and took him to the bedroom. The victim trusted her, and she killed him."

"You seem sure Diana is the killer."

I nodded, more to myself than to her, as my thoughts coalesced.

"Christopher was a monster, but he couldn't think his way out of a paper bag. The moron showed up at my house in the middle of the night and acted surprised when I pointed a shotgun at him. He didn't build his business on his own. He had help."

Julia crossed her arms. "What are you thinking?"

"Diana was the shot caller—and not just today, but twelve years ago, too. I've read your files. Twelve years ago when Megan went missing, your entire case against Christopher rested on my allegation that he had raped me and that he had raped Megan. You didn't even have enough for an indictment, but then Diana gave you everything you needed. She saw an opportunity to stop your investigation, and she took it. She set her husband up and put him away for life before you could dig into her. Now, she's killing off her husband's business partners."

Julia said nothing for a moment. Then she nodded. When she spoke again, her voice was low and almost sounded defeated.

"Why do you think she'd do that?"

I shrugged. "I don't know. Maybe she thought they would turn on her. Maybe they had evidence against her. Maybe she was tired of sharing the profits. The why doesn't matter. She worked with Sherlock to get Christopher out of prison, and then she killed them both."

Julia swore under her breath and looked down. "It's plausible."

"You going to pick her up?"

Julia raised her eyebrows and looked up. "We need to find her first, but yeah. In the meantime, I need you to write an after-action report of what you did today. Go home. Even if you are a detective, this isn't your case anymore."

My mind was already ahead of her, so I nodded.

"Yeah. I'll head out."

I started to walk toward my truck, but Julia stepped in front of me. She crossed her arms.

"I know you."

"I know you, too, Julia," I said, feigning a smile.

"That's not what I mean, and you know it," she said, shaking her head. "You're planning something. I can see your brain working."

"My brain is always working. It keeps me alive."

"No, no, no," said Julia, shaking her head. "You can't joke your way out of this. You know where Diana is."

I blinked a few times and started to say something, but Julia held up a finger and stopped me.

"Reconsider whatever story you planned to tell me," she said. "I've known you for a long time. Please don't lie."

I considered what to say.

"It's a long shot," I said.

"Okay," said Julia. "Go on."

"Diana used to own a health food store in Ladue. Christopher mentioned it once."

Julia blinked and shook her head. "We looked into Diana's finances. She didn't own anything. It was all in her husband's name."

I raised my eyebrows. "I'd say you missed a few things."

Julia exhaled a slow breath. Then she looked toward the uniformed officers on the scene before turning to me.

"You're right. Get your firearm. We're going for a drive."

43

The drive from Chesterfield took about twenty minutes. Diana Hughes's store occupied the entirety of a two-story Queen Anne Victorian off Clayton Road. The building had a large porch with hanging plants and a lush front lawn. From the street, it looked like a cozy bed-and-breakfast, but it was a business built with blood money. I hoped Diana was inside because I wanted to see her face when we put cuffs on her wrists.

We parked in the lot, and I met Julia behind my truck.

"This looks like an antique store," she said. "You're sure Diana Hughes owns this?"

"She did twelve years ago," I said. "How thoroughly did you investigate her?"

"Are you questioning my police work now?"

"No. I'm wondering how hard you went after her," I said. "Is she going to run if she sees you?"

Julia thought for a moment. "You take point. If she's here, she won't want to see me."

"Okay," I said, checking the weapon in my purse in case I had to use it. "Please watch my back and make sure

I don't get shot."

She nodded, and we walked to the store together. The front porch creaked as I stepped onto it. Dried herbs hung from hooks on the ceiling, while a rocking chair swayed in a breeze. A galvanized steel watering can full of flowers rested by the front door. Everything on the porch had a price tag.

I walked into the building while Julia stayed outside. A door straight ahead was closed, while a velvet rope blocked off the stairs. Herbs in glass jars lined the walls of the parlor to my left, while there were teas and coffees in the room to my right. People were talking somewhere, so I followed the sound of conversation to a small coffee shop in what would have been the home's kitchen. Three older women sat around a cafe table, sipping drinks. Each of them had a paper bag overflowing with flowers and other decorative items.

I walked toward the counter behind which a young woman in an apron stood. She smiled at me.

"Our coffee of the day is a Jamaican Blue Mountain coffee. It's a mild coffee grown almost five thousand feet above sea level. It's rich and smooth. Can I get you a sample cup?"

I looked at the older women. One wore a ring adorned with a diamond the size of an almond, while a second carried a Gucci handbag that cost more than my car. The third woman had a diamond tennis bracelet and earrings that looked as if someone had stolen them from the Crown Jewels in London. I turned back to the barista and leaned forward.

"Just to settle my curiosity, how much does this coffee cost per pound?"

"One-nineteen, but if you're a member of our coffee club, you get a ten percent discount."

I lowered my chin. "I assume by one-nineteen you mean it's a hundred and nineteen dollars per pound."

The barista hesitated and then nodded. "Yes. Is that a problem?"

"No," I said, shaking my head. "But I'll stick to Folgers all the same. I'm looking for Diana Hughes. Is she around?"

She hesitated again. "How do you know Mrs. Hughes?"

"Old friend," I said. "Is she here?"

She blinked but said nothing. I took that as a yes.

"Is she upstairs?"

The girl leaned forward. "Mrs. Hughes enjoys her privacy. She doesn't like being disturbed."

"I'm not a fan of disturbances, either, but if you don't tell me where she is, I'll call the county police and bring in dogs to search for her. How's that sound?"

The girl put her hands flat on the counter and lowered her voice.

"I can't lose this job. I've got tuition to pay."

"At this point, that's the least of your concerns," I said. "Where's Diana?"

The girl closed her eyes and leaned back. Then she pointed toward the ceiling.

"Upstairs?" I asked. She nodded.

"Please don't tell her I told you."

I nodded but didn't break eye contact.

"Clear out the building and go to the parking lot. I'll call for more officers."

The girl furrowed her brow. "What's she done?"

"Don't worry about that. Just clear out the building."

The barista hesitated but then nodded and stepped around the counter to hustle the older women out of their seats and to the front door. She'd lose her job, but if she played her cards right, she could sell her story to the news. It wouldn't be all bad.

I slipped my firearm from my purse and walked to the entryway, where I stepped over the velvet rope blocking the second story. The aging hardwood stairs creaked. The second floor had stained hardwood floors with an oriental rug as a runner. Diana Hughes must have heard my footsteps because she came out of a bedroom when I was halfway up the stairs. Her smile was demure, but it looked genuine.

"You look good, Joe."

"You, too, Diana," I said, raising my weapon. "I was at your house this morning. I saw the mess you left on your bed and in the closet. You're under arrest."

She blinked, and then her posture softened. "Come on up. We should talk. Girl to girl."

"We'll talk, but not here. Put your hands on the wall so I can frisk you. After that, I will put handcuffs on you while I check out the rest of the building to make sure we're alone."

She rubbed her wrists and took a step back before sweeping her hand across the hallway.

"By all means," she said. "Frisk me, secure me, and search. I have nothing to hide."

As I climbed the steps, I held my weapon in front of me. This was too easy. A woman willing to kill her ex-husband and all of his business partners to cover up a prostitution ring wouldn't come in this easily. She had something planned.

"Put your hands on the wall."

She did as I asked and then looked over her shoulder as she bit her lower lip.

"I didn't know you were into this kind of thing."

"Shut up," I said, running a hand down her back, sides, hips, and arms. She wore a pink pencil skirt that hugged her body and a white, sleeveless button-down shirt. Her clothes didn't leave a lot of room to hide a weapon. After searching her, I put my pistol in my purse and took out a pair of handcuffs.

"Lower your right hand to your waist," I said. "Keep your palms towards me at all times."

"Kinky," she said. As I hooked up her right wrist, I felt a little better.

"Left hand, please," I said. She lowered her left hand, and I hooked that up. I put the cuffs on tight, but not so tight that they'd cut off her circulation. Once I had the cuffs on, I wriggled them to make sure they were secure. "Stay here. I want to make sure we're alone up here."

"Make sure you check the closets," she said. "They're

fabulous. I had them all redone."

"Good tip," I said, walking toward a bedroom at the end of the hall. Diana Hughes married a moron, but she wasn't one herself. I didn't know what she was up to, but she wasn't the first intelligent suspect I had ever dealt with. The key, I'd found, was to let them think they were in charge. If you give an arrogant asshole enough rope, he's bound to hang himself.

I checked the rooms one by one and found that we were alone on the second floor. Then I walked out to find Diana leaning against the wall in the hallway as if she didn't have a care in the world. Despite having cuffs on her, an uneasy pit grew in my stomach.

"Diana Hughes, you're under arrest for the murder of a still unknown person inside your home. You have the right to remain silent, but if you choose to talk, I can use whatever you say against you in court. You have the right to an attorney and to have an attorney present during any interrogation. If you want a lawyer and can't afford one, the court will provide one at the government's expense before we question you. Do you understand your rights as I've described them?"

She smiled and nodded. "I do."

"Bearing your rights in mind, would you like to talk and clarify a few things?"

"Sure," she said, standing straighter. "Why don't we go in my office, though? It's much more comfortable."

"If that's how you want to do this. I'll record the conversation with my cell phone."

"I thought you might," said Diana, sauntering toward her office door. She spoke over her shoulder as we walked. "I'm glad to see that you're doing so well. I worried about you. Megan and Emily had business sense, but I could see you going either way. Police work suits you."

"Your thoughtfulness is touching."

"Haven't lost your caustic sense of humor, either," she said, stepping into her office. It was a big room with dark woodwork and a heavy desk near the far window. There were bookshelves along the wall and a chaise lounge in a corner. Diana walked to the desk and rested on an edge. I sat in a chair nearby and took my cell phone from my purse. "For what it's worth, I'm sorry."

I leaned back but kept the barrel of my firearm pointed at her as I turned on an app to record everything we said. "What are you sorry for?"

"Everything that happened to you," she said. "I didn't know my ex-husband was such a monster."

"Please don't lie to me," I said. "Your husband was a buffoon. We both know who the real brains behind his organization was."

She smiled but didn't acknowledge my point.

"As sorry as I am for what he did to you, I'm glad you could stop him from hurting anyone else. It felt nice to shoot him, I'm sure."

I locked my gaze on Diana.

"I'm not here to talk about that," I said. "Did you send Christopher to my house?"

"No," she said. Her smile held just a hint of melancholy. "That was James. I haven't spoken to my ex-husband in over a decade."

"And by James, you mean James Holmes. Sherlock," I said. "Christopher's lawyer."

"Yeah," she said, nodding. "James was special. Christopher became convinced that someone was trying to kill him. He asked James for help. James sent him to your house, knowing your dog would see him. James wanted Christopher dead and thought you would be glad to help."

"Did James arrange anyone else's deaths?"

"Emily and Megan Young. He had Emily tortured into revealing her sister's whereabouts. Megan had gone to St. Augustine to find you. She thought you could protect her."

"He told you this?" I asked. She nodded.

"Some men like to talk when you're giving them a blow job."

"Did he kill Warren Nichols, too?"

She nodded. "Yes. James wanted Christopher's business, so he was trying to isolate him and take over. He also killed Steven Zimmerman and a handful of other people. He tried to kill me, too. You found his blood in my bedroom. It was self-defense."

And there it was. Her defense. She'd paint Sherlock as a dangerous psychopath willing to kill anyone who crossed him. She would claim she was just another innocent victim caught in a treacherous web.

"I'm glad to hear you survived his vicious attack," I

said, nodding. "Did you call the police?"

She shook her head and then looked down. "I was scared. I called Alonzo Morrison and Scott Gibson. They worked for James, but I thought I could trust them. They took his body, and I took a shower. I don't know what happened after they disappeared."

The lies rolled off her tongue. I didn't envy the prosecutor who got assigned to this case. Diana was gorgeous, articulate, and intelligent. The men and women on the jury would love her—even as she lied right to their faces.

"Did they call the carpet cleaning service, too?"

She shifted her weight and sighed.

"You shouldn't have seen them," she said. "I booked them to come at six in the morning. I paid double their rates for emergency work. They should have been gone before the rest of the world woke up. Nobody would have been the wiser."

"It was a reasonable plan," I said, standing. "And who knows? You're rich. Maybe your lawyer will sell it to a jury still."

"Oh, honey," she said, tilting her head to the side. "People like me don't go to jail. Can you do us both a favor and take these handcuffs off me? They were fun at first, but they're getting a little old now."

"I can't see that happening."

She nodded and slid toward me. "I tried to keep you safe, you know. You were always one of my favorites. That's why Christopher wanted you. Then, after he had you, he didn't care. You were damaged goods."

I felt the bile rise in my throat.

"You're quite the humanitarian. I'll tell the prosecutor how kind you were when I was under your care."

Her eyes left mine, and she focused on the carpet for a few seconds before she looked at me again.

"I always wanted a daughter. You know, when you first moved in, I thought it might have been you. You were special."

"This is getting creepy. Maybe we could move the conversation along?"

She smiled. "I always liked your sense of humor, too. I was glad to hear Captain Green adopted you. You love her, don't you?"

"That's none of your business," I said. "My backup should be here any moment, though, and I'm sure they'd be more than interested in hearing about your mother-daughter fantasies."

She gave me a patronizing, almost wistful smile. "Honey, if you had backup coming, don't you think they'd be here by now?"

The unease I had felt earlier spread through my body.

"Don't move," I said, walking to a window overlooking the parking lot. She was right. The county had almost a thousand police officers on patrol, and the city of Ladue would have thirty or forty. Diana and I had been talking long enough that someone should have come by now.

I took my cell phone from my purse and found that I had a new text message from Julia. It was a picture taken from the parking lot. Julia was in the trunk of a maroon vehicle, unmoving. My stomach plunged into my shoes, and my breath caught in my throat. Then I looked at Diana.

"Something wrong?" she asked.

Seeing the smug smile on her face made something inside me break. I jammed my weapon against her temple.

"Call your friends, and tell them to back off."

"You hurt me, Captain Green dies," said Diana. "If you listen, there's no reason we can't all walk away. It's your choice."

My finger slipped from the trigger guard to my firearm's trigger. My breath was shallow. I wanted to kill her even more than I had wanted to shoot her ex-husband. Then I pictured Julia in the trunk.

"If Julia's dead, I'll kill you and hunt down everyone you've ever worked with."

"She's not dead, sweetheart," said Diana. "My men won't hurt her without my say-so. Can you take off my cuffs, now?"

I took the pressure off her head.

"Thank you for listening to reason," she said, glancing at me again. "Now unload your weapon—including the round from the chamber—place it on my desk, and then remove these handcuffs."

"I don't think so," I said.

"If we don't leave soon, Scott and Alonzo will kill

Julia. Afterwards, they will come here. You might kill me, but Scott and Alonzo are very dangerous men. You won't take them both out. Instead, they'll take you to a cabin in the woods and use you in ways Christopher never dreamed of. Then, when they're done with you, they'll kill you."

"They'll kill me anyway," I said. "If I've got a gun, I've at least got a chance."

"Julia doesn't, though," said Diana. "And they won't touch you without my say-so. They're loyal, and I won't let them hurt you as long as you cooperate. Consider it an apology for everything that happened to you under my roof."

I looked to the picture on my cell phone again.

"How do I know she's still alive?"

"If I wanted her dead, you'd see holes in her chest," she said. "Believe me, I know the consequences of murdering a police officer. Your colleagues would hunt me to the end of my days. I'm not interested in killing either of you if I don't have to, so please don't make me."

It went against every bit of training I had, but she was right. Julia and I were both dead unless I cooperated. I slid the magazine out of my firearm and then removed the round from the chamber before putting everything on her desk. As I pulled my hand back, I palmed a paper clip from the desktop and slipped it into my jeans pocket, hoping I wouldn't have to use it.

"And now my handcuffs," said Diana, standing. I nodded and unhooked her. She turned around and picked up my weapon. I drew in a deep breath as she pointed it at my face and pulled the trigger. Even knowing the chamber was empty, I flinched as the weapon dry fired.

"It's a nice piece," she said, sliding the magazine into the grip. She chambered a round and looked down the sights but didn't point it at me. "It's light and comfortable to hold. It's a lady's gun. I think I'll keep this. Thank you."

"I hope you shoot yourself."

She smiled but didn't take the bait.

"I'm glad you came to your senses. Now let's go find your partner, sweetheart. We need not draw this out any longer than necessary."

44

Diana led me outside. The barista had abandoned her post at the coffee shop, and the elderly women who had been drinking the overpriced brew were gone. Diana and I weren't alone, though. There were three men behind the building. Two were large and rough looking, while the third was older and thin. A duffel bag over his shoulder threw his balance off so that he walked with an odd tilt.

"I'm here, and I'm cooperating," I said, glancing at Diana. "What happens now?"

"Alonzo will cuff you, and then you will climb into the rear seat of the Oldsmobile. He will sit beside you. I will be in the passenger seat. Scott will be our driver. Once we reach a safe destination, we will allow you and Captain Green out of the car. You'll be able to walk to safety, and you'll never see me again."

I looked to the third man, the one who hadn't spoken.

"What's his role?"

"Mr. Mendoza is none of your concern," she said. "You won't see him again after today, either."

"Let me see Julia."

Diana shook her head. "If I wanted Julia dead, she'd be dead. You would be dead, too. You're still breathing. That should tell you something."

I held my breath, hoping to hear a siren in the distance. Nothing. Diana's crew must have gotten to Julia before she could make the call. This was bad. Diana may have promised to let us go, but more than likely, she planned to drive us to the middle of nowhere and kill us outside the prying eyes of any neighbors. Still, the longer we were alive, the better our chances were of escaping.

"Did you hurt her?"

"I used chloroform," said Alonzo. "She'll wake up with a headache, but she'll be fine."

I nodded and looked to Diana.

"You tried to keep me safe," I said. "You tried to keep Christopher away from me."

"I did," she said, nodding, her eyes closed. "I'm ashamed of what happened to you beneath my roof. That shouldn't have happened."

"Were there others you didn't keep safe?"

She blinked a few times and considered before speaking.

"Christopher had a list of girls I thought were special. He wasn't allowed to touch them."

"What happened to girls who weren't on that list?"

"I never asked," she said.

I nodded and felt my face grow hot.

"So they were fair game."

She walked toward me and tilted her head to the side.

"You may not approve of the things I've done, but I was a businesswoman. I was saving you so that you could go into business with me. You could have lived like a princess. I would have given you a wonderful life."

"And what would I have had to do?"

She looked at me up and down. "You would have used what God gave you to make men happy. In return, they would have paid us as if they had been fucked by a queen. Now get in the car. I'm tired of talking."

It was about what I had expected to hear. Everyone here had blood on his or her hands. I couldn't let any of them get away, but I couldn't let them hurt Julia, either. Unfortunately, that didn't leave me with many options. I walked toward the Oldsmobile and then felt a strong hand grab my elbow. It was one of Diana's thugs.

"Hands behind your back."

I did as he asked and then felt a pair of metal handcuffs dig into my wrists. They were secure but not so tight that they'd cut off circulation. I could move my hands a little. The thug opened the door, and we piled into the vehicle. The creepy guy with the duffel bag, Mr. Mendoza, disappeared.

I didn't have a plan, but any first step required me to take off the cuffs. Police-issue handcuffs had a ratcheting lock with teeth held in by a locking bar. If I could get something between those teeth and the locking bar, the lock would disengage and the cuffs would slide wide open. I had done it before with a special tool, but if I were to have any chance of getting out of this alive, I'd have to make do with the paper clip I had taken from her desk.

"You're quiet," said Diana, turning and looking over her shoulder as I straightened my paper clip into a wire.

"I don't have much to say," I said.

"You know, we could have been friends," said Diana. "You and I are a lot alike."

"Oh," I said, nodding. "Did you once live with a psychopath who wanted to turn you out as a high-end prostitute, too?"

Her smile slipped from her lips.

"I never knew my parents."

"Well," I said, slipping the tip of the paper clip into the handcuffs. It wouldn't go in very far, but I had expected that. "Aside from the psychopath thing, I guess we do have a lot in common, then."

"Your attempt to deflect uncomfortable conversations with snide remarks doesn't reflect well on you."

"It's a character flaw I've been working on," I said, pulling my wrists together so I could squeeze the rings. The ratchet clicked as the cuffs tightened, drawing the paper clip inside a little more.

We drove for about half an hour before pulling off the interstate. I didn't know where we were, but we couldn't have been too far outside St. Louis County. About ten minutes after we turned off the interstate, we crossed the Meramac River at a bridge I didn't recognize. After that, we turned onto a side road that led to a wooded area.

"Are we going camping?" I asked.

Diana smiled and shook her head but said nothing before her phone buzzed. She didn't take her eyes from mine, but she answered the phone and spoke quickly. I couldn't hear what the other party said, but she said she understood. She was getting orders, probably from Mr. Mendoza. I didn't know Diana's end game, but we had to be getting close to it. There was nothing out here.

As the road grew rougher, I heard something banging inside the trunk.

"Sounds like Julia woke up," said Diana, turning to glance over her shoulder. I squeezed the handcuff tighter and felt it click once more. My locksmith training had included little work with handcuffs. I hoped my paper clip trick was working because I couldn't keep squeezing much longer.

"The moment she gets out, she'll try to kill you," I said, squeezing again. The locking bar clicked once more, biting into my wrist. I could feel the bone compress. The paper clip was stuck. It had to be almost there. "Please don't hurt her."

Diana looked over her shoulder again and held up my pistol. "No guarantees, but you'll be there to calm her down. She'll listen when she sees a gun pointed at your head."

For emphasis, she pointed the weapon in my direction before turning around again. I drew in a deep breath, straightened my back, and then coughed. The noise covered up the sound of my handcuffs ratcheting once more. The metal bit into my flesh, but then the ring went slack as the paper clip blocked the ratcheting lock.

My hand was free, but that didn't improve the situation much. Even if I could get the gun away from Diana, I'd only have one or two shots before the other guys around me reacted and pulled their own weapons. I had to make this count.

"What did Mr. Mendoza want?" I asked.

"He wanted to hear how we were doing."

"It sounded like he was giving you orders," I said, eyeing the man beside me. He winked and then pursed his lips as if he were giving me a kiss. I slid on my seat to the left as if he scared me. He snickered and looked out the window. Diana rolled her eyes.

"You don't need to worry about Mr. Mendoza. I have you now."

"You won't let him hurt me, will you?" I asked, allowing a tremble into my voice.

"Not if you're a good girl," she said, still pointing that weapon at me. She turned and looked at the road ahead of her.

I pulled my hand out of the cuff but kept both hands behind my back. Diana's grip looked tight, but she kept her finger outside the weapon's trigger guard. It would take about half a second for her brain to respond to a threat and a split second longer to move her finger to the trigger. That didn't give me much time.

But I didn't need much time.

I waited for the man on my right to look out the window. That was my moment.

God, please let this work.

I whipped my hands from around my back and lunged forward. Diana must have sensed something because she whirled her gaze toward me at the same instant my fingers touched the frame of her weapon. I twisted the barrel as hard as I could, but she fired before I could wrench the weapon from her hand. It didn't matter who held the gun, though. I just needed to bend her wrist enough to move the barrel and point it at the driver.

The gunshot was deafening. A curtain of blood coated the driver's side window the instant after the round pierced his skull. One down.

Before the man to my right could react, I yanked hard on the weapon again. Diana fired once more, and this time, the round shattered the window to my left. The now deceased driver slumped to the right, dragging the steering wheel with him.

The Oldsmobile's tires crunched as they left the gravel, but then the heavy car hit the uneven grass beside the road. I bounced out of my seat and then slammed forward and back as the sedan careened into a tree. The airbags popped open, slapping Diana in the face. She slumped forward and dropped her firearm. My head hit the back of the driver's seat with a dull thud, and my vision washed white.

The world spun, but I forced myself to focus. My life depended on it. I looked at the guy beside me.

He dove for the gun Diana had dropped, but his seat belt held him in place. I hadn't worn one, though, so I bent down and snapped the gun up before he could touch it. Diana had fired two shots, which meant I had plenty left. My hand wrapped around the firearm's grip just as a fist slammed into the back of the head. My vision blurred once more, and I felt my hands go weak, but I didn't drop the gun.

I couldn't. If I did, I'd die.

I sat up and raised the weapon to fire, but the thug reached for my arms and pushed the barrel toward the ceiling just as I pulled the trigger. The sound was deafening, but I couldn't focus on it. I had to get away. I brought my legs up and kicked him in the face while trying to get some distance between us. He didn't even flinch. His eyes looked crazed and angry. Blood dribbled from his nostrils.

With his left hand forcing my weapon toward the ceiling, he reached for my neck with his right. He had long arms, and my legs weren't strong enough to push him away. His body crashed against me. I gasped but didn't let go of my firearm. With his heavy body pressed against mine, I couldn't move.

Then, my door popped open, and a guttural, animalistic scream filled the car. It was Julia, and she had a tire iron. She whacked the thug on the back of his skull once and then again and again. Every time she hit him, he grunted, but he didn't move.

Tears filled my eyes as I pushed with my legs. He was

so heavy and so strong. With every passing moment, I felt his fingers overpower mine as he tried to pry the weapon from my grip. He was stronger than me, but if I let go of that gun, I was dead. So was Julia. She had risked her life to save me; I couldn't let that happen.

Digging into some reserve I didn't know I had, I flexed the muscles of my legs hard, forcing him back. Julia must have seen what I was doing because she hooked the tire iron around his neck and jerked hard. His head lifted, and then I grunted and pushed again, forcing him out of the car.

The thug fell onto the ground outside and eyed me and then my foster mother. I could see the mental calculations in his eyes. He could overpower me, but I had a gun and some space now. He wasn't going anywhere, so he put up his hands. Julia kicked him as I slid out of the car.

"That's enough," I said, looking at them. "Roll onto your belly and put your hands above your head."

As I said that, the front passenger door slid open, and Diana tumbled out. She looked at me and then rolled onto her belly and ran. I didn't hesitate before raising my weapon and firing wide to her right.

"I swear to God and all that is holy that I will shoot you in the back just like I did to your husband, Diana!" I screamed. "Put your hands up and lie on the ground."

I needed to sound angry and unhinged. I needed her to believe that I'd shoot her. By her tense shoulders and the way she stopped moving, I'd say I had succeeded.

"Back up until you hit the vehicle. Then turn around and put your hands on the hood."

I shifted to my right, creating space between me and the still living thug while keeping Diana in my line of fire.

"Julia, there are handcuffs in the car," I said. "Find them and lock this asshole up."

She did as I asked and then handcuffed my assailant. I felt better with him restrained.

"What do you want to do about Diana?"

I glanced at Julia and then walked toward the vehicle, still giving the thug a wide berth.

"Diana Hughes," I said. She looked at me but kept her hands on the hood. "You're under arrest for the murder of James Holmes and a bunch of other bad shit. You know the drill. I'll use what you tell me against you in court, the court can appoint a lawyer if you can't afford one, and you don't have to tell me anything."

She looked straight in my eyes.

"I'll give you five million dollars cash if you shoot Captain Green in the head and let me go."

Without thinking, I balled my right hand into a fist and punched her in the jaw. It had been a lot of years since I had last punched someone, and pain lanced down my knuckles and into my wrist. I gasped, but Diana fell back.

"No thanks, bitch."

45

I wish life returned to normal after that, but it didn't. Travis had given me a week off to think about my job before he accepted my resignation, and I planned to use every moment. As soon as I could, I picked up Roger from the animal hospital. He moved slower than before, and he had to wear a cone for a while so he wouldn't pull out his stitches, but I had my buddy back.

Susanne came over every morning that week for coffee. We'd talk for an hour, and then she'd go home to work in her garden or to clean her house. She was lonely. I hadn't seen that before, but I did now. Maybe I was lonely, too.

To keep myself busy in the day, I planted a garden. I doubted my tomatoes would produce anything, but it was nice. I also tried to stay abreast of the investigation into Christopher Hughes and his former associates.

We charged Alonzo with the murders of Emily and Megan Young, Warren Nichols, and Steve Zimmerman. To avoid the death penalty, he pled guilty to every charge. He also filled in a lot of gaps in our understanding of what happened. Diana Hughes had nothing to do with most of the murders, but she had killed James Holmes, and she had abducted Julia and me. Even if she had killed Sherlock in self-defense, she couldn't say the same about a kidnapping. She'd die in prison.

Agents from the Treasury Department arrested Randy Shepard and Neil Wilcox—Christopher Hughes's only surviving business partners—for money laundering. They'd go to prison but not for long on those charges.

Everything came down to money. Sherlock had a scheme to make himself rich, but it blew up in his face and got people killed. Only Mr. Mendoza did well for himself. Diana said she gave him ten million dollars. I suspected we'd never see him again.

Several days after we arrested Diana Hughes, a woman I went to the police academy with, Gwenn Collins, called me out of the blue as I sat on the front porch with Roger. Since Gwenn and I had been the same size and age, she had been my partner during the self-defense portions of our training, making her one of only two people I had ever punched in the face. Thankfully, she didn't hold that against me.

"Gwenn, hi," I said. "It's been a while. How are you?"

"I'm good," she said, her voice soft. Gwenn had a lilting southern accent that a lot of men found beguiling and the tender heart of a kind woman. From almost the first day I met her, I worried about her, not because she was weak or fragile, but because she was good. Before joining the academy, I had lived with a police officer. I understood how it could drain a person, and I hated the idea of watching the world extinguish Gwenn's light. "You're famous now. I don't know many famous people."

"I am famous now," I said, smiling to myself. "Just this morning, I got a call from my high school asking whether I'd give the commencement speech at next year's graduation."

"Really?" she asked.

"No," I said, smiling. "I made that up. You're the only person in the world who thinks I'm famous, so I wanted to revel in it a little longer. What can I do for you?"

"I work in the crime lab in Clayton, and I'm calling because I've got a box with your name on it. It's evidence from a case twelve years ago."

"Oh," I said, feeling my shoulders drop some.

"I've read the reports about what you've gone through," she said. "Your case is closed for good now. I thought you might like to see the evidence before it's destroyed. It might help you get closure. I hope I didn't overstep."

"You didn't," I said. "Some bad things happened back then."

"I get it. I'll box this up and have it sent off. If you're ever in the area, call me. There's a great wine bar by my apartment. We should catch up."

I almost told her that sounded great, but I caught myself before I did.

"I would like to catch up sometime. We'll do that,

but don't send the box out yet," I said. "I'm in St. Augustine, but I'd like to see it. This is part of my life. I can't run from it forever."

"Are you sure?"

"Yeah," I said, nodding, my voice stronger. "I'll be up as soon as I can."

I thanked her and then hung up. Before leaving, I filled the dog's water bowl, and then I drove. Traffic wasn't bad, so I made good time to Clayton. Gwenn met me in the county police headquarters's lobby and escorted me to her office in the basement.

I didn't know what to feel as I saw the white file box on her desk. Though Julia had kept her own interview notes and paperwork, that box held the physical evidence used to put Christopher Hughes in prison twelve years ago. I pulled the top off to uncover dozens of clear plastic evidence bags, each of which had Julia's or Travis's signature on the chain of custody form.

"Do you need a minute?" asked Gwenn.

I looked at her and nodded. "Please."

She nodded. "I'll get coffee, then. I'll be back in a few."

She stepped out of the office, and I reached into the box for an evidence bag holding a navy blue scrunchy that had belonged to a girl named Sarah. I never knew her, but I was her sister. Christopher had done the same to her that he had done to me. I reached into the box again and pulled out bags holding hair ties, necklaces, and panties. All of them came from young women

Christopher had raped.

Then, I pulled out a bag with a young woman's white cotton underwear. It was my bag. I couldn't look at it, so I put it away. Near the bottom of the box, I found the ring that had sealed Christopher's fate. It had belonged to Megan Young.

And my heart jumped because it was all wrong.

I boxed up most of the evidence but took the ring bag to the floor's break room. Gwenn was cleaning out the coffee maker as I entered.

"Can I take this upstairs?" I asked, holding up the evidence bag. "I need to show it to somebody. It won't leave the building."

She paused for a moment. "I'm not supposed to let it out of my sight."

"It's important," I said. "I'll take it up to Captain Julia Green, and then I'll take it right back. It was her case twelve years ago."

She blinked and then sighed before nodding. "If it's not going to leave the building, go ahead."

"Thanks," I said, already rushing out of the room. My heart was pounding, and my stomach churned a mile a minute. I didn't want to wait for the elevator, so I sprinted up the stairs to Julia's floor. Her office door was open, so I didn't knock before sticking my head inside. She was on the phone, but when she saw me, she told her caller that she'd call him back. Then she smiled.

"Hey, hon," she said. "Something wrong?"

I walked inside and shut the door behind me. As a

captain, Julia had a corner office with windows on two sides. It was bright and clean. I crossed the room and put the evidence bag on her desk beside a half-full coffee mug.

"You bagged this twelve years ago," I said.

Julia looked at it and then looked at me with her eyebrows raised.

"Refresh my memory. I've bagged a lot of evidence over the years."

"This is Megan Young's ring. Diana Hughes found it in a box in her garage. Christopher supposedly took it from Megan's body after he killed her."

"Okay," said Julia, leaning back and crossing her legs and arms. "I remember now. That box did him in. Before Diana found it, he claimed he was innocent. Afterwards, he confessed to murdering Megan. In retrospect, Diana must have been collecting things for a while to set her husband up. It was a tough case."

"I want to believe that."

Julia said nothing at first. Then she laced her fingers together and leaned forward.

"Why don't you believe that?"

"Megan Young's case was originally given to two detectives in homicide. When I came forward and claimed Christopher Hughes had raped me, you and Travis opened a parallel investigation into those claims."

"That's right," she said, nodding.

"You investigated me. You talked to people I knew at school, you talked to my teachers, and you talked to my old boss at the movie theater. You talked to Megan's teachers, friends, and sister, too. By the time you finished your investigation, you knew more about me than anyone alive. You knew more about Megan than anyone else knew, too."

"That was my job."

"And you did it well," I said, nodding and sliding the evidence bag toward her. "So when Diana Hughes showed you this box, you recognized this ring as belonging to Megan."

She took a sip of coffee and then drew in a breath. Her eyes widened and then closed as she realized what I had found.

"I did."

"You showed it to Christopher Hughes. He included it in his written confession. He said he took it from Megan's body and then hid it in the box as a souvenir of what he had done, but you knew that was a lie."

She said nothing for at least twenty seconds, but then she nodded.

"I lived with Megan. I didn't get along with Emily, but Megan and I talked some. This was a promise ring. Megan's boyfriend gave it to her and promised to exchange it for an engagement ring one day. She wore that ring for six weeks before her boyfriend broke up with her, and then she never wore it again. She kept it because it was gold and she planned to sell it when she aged out of the foster care system.

"You were a sex crimes detective. You knew

everything there was to know about Megan Young's sex life. You knew she and that boy had broken up, you knew she didn't wear this ring, and you knew Christopher Hughes didn't take it from her dead finger. You knew Christopher Hughes's confession was bullshit, and yet you and Travis let him make it."

She drew in a slow breath. Her entire body seemed deflated.

"All true," she said, her voice a whisper. "The moment Diana showed us that box, we knew she was setting her husband up. I persuaded Travis not to say anything. It was my fault. Don't blame him."

"Is that why he moved to St. Augustine? He didn't want to work with you anymore?"

Her eyelids fluttered, but then she shrugged.

"You'd have to ask him."

"I will," I said, "but he'll tell me it was his fault and that you had nothing to do with it."

"That sounds like him," she said. She paused and then looked down. "Christopher hurt you and a lot of other girls. He would have hurt a lot more people if we didn't stop him. We didn't have the evidence to put him away, so when Diana showed us that box, it felt like an answer to our prayers. Travis and I just had to keep quiet about what we knew."

I nodded. "Did you tell Christopher what to say?"

She shook her head. "We showed him the evidence we had against him, and he wove his own story. In exchange for his confession, the prosecutor dropped the rape charges against him and agreed to a sentence of life without parole."

"Thank you for the truth."

Neither of us said anything for another minute, but then Julia cleared her throat.

"So what happens now?"

I looked at the table, unable to look her in the eye.

"Almost everyone connected to this case is dead or in prison," I said, swallowing hard. "Nobody wins if I turn this over to your internal affairs division."

"You should, though. It's the right thing to do."

"Forget the right thing," I said. "I'm tired of doing the right thing if it only hurts the people I care about. Christopher Hughes deserved everything he got."

Julia locked her gaze on mine and then looked down as she reached to her waist. A moment later, she put her gold captain's badge on the desk and slid it toward me.

"If my decision twelve years ago costs my daughter her integrity today, I'm done. I don't deserve to wear the same badge she does. Travis doesn't, either."

Julia loved being a cop. It was part of her identity. I shook my head.

"Don't do that," I said. "You did it to protect me."

"That doesn't make it right. I've been at this job long enough to know what happens when you stop playing by the rules."

I looked at the table.

"I'm sorry I put you in this position, Mom."

She stayed silent long enough that I looked up at her

to make sure she was okay. She smiled and reached toward me. I let her hold my hand.

"You've never called me Mom before," she whispered. "Thank you."

I swallowed a lump in my throat.

"I never called you Mom before because I thought I hated my mom. I thought my mom abandoned me when I needed her most. Erin Court wasn't my mom, though. You've been my mom since the day I met you. I'm sorry it's taken me this long to figure that out."

She squeezed my hand.

"I love you."

"I love you, too."

I stayed in the office for another few minutes but then stood when Gwenn knocked on the door and poked her head inside.

"Just checking to make sure that thing we talked about is still okay," she said, looking at me. Then she looked at Julia. "I'm sorry if I'm interrupting anything, Captain Green."

"It's just Julia now," she said. "And it's good you're here. My daughter needs to get going. I've got a letter to write."

I looked to my mom. "You going to be okay?"

"I'll be fine," she said. She looked at Gwenn. "Can you give me one more minute, Officer Collins? I'll send Joe right down."

"Yes, ma'am," said Gwenn, stepping outside. Mom looked at me.

"Are you sure you're okay?" she asked.

I nodded. "I will be."

"Good," she said, standing. "The last time I talked to Travis, you had given him a letter of resignation. You still going to quit?"

I shook my head.

"No. They need me. There are two missing kids we're worried about, and there's always Spring Fair next year. Without me, they'll fall apart. I'm the linchpin that holds the entire department together."

"I'm glad you've kept your sense of humility over the years."

I smiled at her and started for the door but stopped when I touched the handle.

"Do you and Dad still make a big lunch on Sunday after church?

"Every week," she said. "Assuming we can rouse him from bed, your brother will be there. You want us to set you a plate?"

It had been almost four years since I last sat down with the family on Sunday afternoon. Dad had never stopped asking, but I kept turning him down every time. If these past few weeks had shown me anything, though, it was that I needed my family. Julia and Doug weren't my birth parents, but they were the mom and dad I'd chosen. What's more, they had chosen me. It was time I stopped pushing away the people I loved most.

I nodded.

"Yeah. Set me a plate. I'll see you on Sunday."

Enjoy this book? You can make a big difference in my career

Reviews are the lifeblood of an author's career. I'm not exaggerating when I say they're the single best way I can get attention for my books. I'm not famous, I don't have the money for extravagant advertising campaigns, and I no longer have a major publisher behind me.

I do have something major publishers don't have, something they would kill to get:

Committed, loyal readers.

With millions of books in the world, your honest reviews and recommendations help other readers find me.

If you enjoyed the book you just read, I would be extraordinarily grateful if you could spend five minutes to leave a review on Amazon, Barnes and Noble, Goodreads, or anywhere else you review books. A review can be as long or as short as you'd like it to be, so please don't feel that you have to write something long.

Thank you so much!

Did you like The Girl in the Motel? Then you're going to love The Girl in the Woods!

Detective Mary Joe Court returns in the second novel in *New York Times* bestselling author Chris Culver's gripping Joe Court series.

A volunteer found the body while searching the Missouri backwoods for a pair of missing teenagers. Somebody shot her in the chest and dumped her at a campsite deep in the woods.

It's tornado season in central Missouri. The air is still. The sky is dark green. There's a wall cloud to the west.

A nasty storm is coming…

Detective Joe Court knows her team shouldn't be out there, but they need to collect as much evidence as they can before it's destroyed.

Little does Joe know, that storm should be the least of her concerns…

Available January 15, 2019!

Stay in touch with Chris

As much as I enjoy writing, I like hearing from readers even more. If you want to keep up with my world, there are a couple of ways you can do that.

First and easiest, I've got a mailing list. If you join, you'll receive an email whenever I have a new novel out or when I run sales. You can join that by going to this address:

http://www.indiecrime.com/mailinglist.html

If my mailing list doesn't appeal to you, you can also connect with me on Facebook here:

http://www.facebook.com/ChrisCulverbooks

And you can always email me at chris@indiecrime.com. I love receiving email!

About the Author

Chris Culver is the *New York Times* bestselling author of the Ash Rashid series and other novels. After graduate school, Chris taught courses in ethics and comparative religion at a small liberal arts university in southern Arkansas. While there and when he really should have been grading exams, he wrote *The Abbey*, which spent sixteen weeks on the *New York Times* bestsellers list and introduced the world to Detective Ash Rashid.

Chris has been a storyteller since he was a kid, but he decided to write crime fiction after picking up a dog-eared, coffee-stained paperback copy of Mickey Spillane's *I, the Jury* in a library book sale. Many years later, his wife, despite considerable effort, still can't stop him from bringing more orphan books home. He lives with his family near St. Louis.

Printed in Great Britain
by Amazon